"THERE ARE CONSEQUENCES TO OUR MAKING LOVE...."

Grant's words felt warm on Terra's flushed cheek.

"I know," she replied softly.

"Do you? Do you really?" She could hear the catch in his voice as he fought to hold back the passion that glazed his eyes.

For a moment she closed her eyes in response to the wave of feeling that washed over her. Every time he made the slightest move, her body tingled with new excitement. His skin against her own was fire.

"I want you," he breathed. "I want you so much...."

"Grant," she sighed. How she longed to love this man, to let him make love to her. It was a gift she had never given before—the gift of herself. Love made her unafraid.

"Please," she whispered. "Grant, please...."

WELCOME TO ...

SUPERROMANCES

A sensational series of modern love stories
from Worldwide Library.

Written by masters of the genre, these longer,
sensual and dramatic novels are truly in keeping
with today's changing life-styles. Full of intriguing
conflicts, the heartaches and delights of true love,
SUPERROMANCES are absorbing stories —
satisfying and sophisticated reading that lovers
of romance fiction have long been waiting for.

SUPERROMANCES

Contemporary love stories for the woman of today!

JOANNA JORDAN

NEVER SAY FAREWELL

A SUPERROMANCE FROM
WORLDWIDE

TORONTO · NEW YORK · LOS ANGELES · LONDON

Published July 1983

First printing May 1983

ISBN 0-373-70072-5

Printed in Canada

TO THE READER

All of the events, incidents and characters in this story exist only in my imagination. Both the lost edition and the facsimile edition are fictional and bear no intentional resemblance to any edition of Elizabeth Barrett Browning's works or those of any other author. The story of the Brownings at the breakfast table, however, has been cited by several sources. I would like to thank rare-book librarian Peter Hanff, of the Bancroft Library at the University of California, Berkeley, for his assistance with this manuscript.

CHAPTER ONE

PAUL FOSTER'S FINGERS drummed an impatient rhythm on his desk as he waited for Terra Scott to close the office door and take a seat in front of him. "When are you going to finish writing our publicity brochure for the rare-book fair?" he demanded before she had a chance to settle herself into the overstuffed chair. Then, without waiting for an answer, he continued, "You've been working on it for more than a month already. What's the holdup?"

Paul was smiling, but Terra could see the faint lines of annoyance at the corners of his mouth and could hear the thin trace of anger in his tone.

She tried to keep her voice calm. "I know this brochure is taking longer than expected, Paul, but I'm having trouble finding all the information I need. Before we advertise that we have copies of a lost edition of Elizabeth Barrett Browning's sonnets for sale, we have to be sure they're genuine."

"Of course they're genuine," Paul snapped. "The rare-book experts have swarmed all over them. You've read the reports." He tilted back in his swivel chair, raked his short, curly blond hair with his fingers, then sat upright abruptly, startling Terra. His wide blue eyes narrowed and his usually pleasant expression hardened.

"If you haven't been able to come up with sufficient information to prove they're the real thing it's because you're handling the investigation all wrong. I never did understand why dad put you in charge of research, and now I'm beginning to see it was a bigger mistake than I realized. How old are you?" he asked.

"My age has nothing to do with this, Paul," Terra replied patiently, "but if you must know, I'm twenty-four."

"Well, as far as I'm concerned you're still wet behind the ears. A job of this kind should be done by an expert. I'll give you one more chance, but I expect results—and soon."

He leaned toward her, his pale blue eyes boring into her serious face. "You've got all the proof you need. Those pamphlets are part of the first edition of one of the most famous little books of poetry in the world. Before I found those copies, everyone thought all the originals of the first edition had disappeared. Then I discovered ten copies in the personal library of the printer's granddaughter."

Paul got up and strode to the window. His light tan suit seemed a tiny bit loose on his wiry frame. At one time Terra had found him quite attractive, but he had been so much less tense then. Now the pressure of running Fosters' seemed to be getting to him. Not only was he difficult to deal with, but he even looked different. His once smooth complexion was beginning to show signs of premature aging; he was only thirty-one or so, but he appeared older. Terra felt sympathy for him—which was good. His treatment of her tried her patience severely, and without that little edge of pity she felt for him she would have been compelled to storm out of the bookshop long before the present meeting.

He paused for a moment, gazing out at the tree-lined alley behind the shop, then turned to Terra.

"Each of these copies is worth at least $200,000, but I can't sell a single one until I have a brochure vouching for their authenticity. People aren't going to pay that kind of money without some written guarantee. Quit stalling and start writing, Terra. I can't wait any longer, do you understand?"

"Yes, Paul," was all she said, though she might once again have pointed out to him that she, too, wanted to be absolutely certain the pamphlets were genuine before she included them in the sales brochure of Foster and Son, Rare-Book Dealers. The firm had a fifty-year history of producing careful, scholarly brochures and catalogs, and Terra felt she couldn't compromise that tradition, despite pressure from Paul. She would have reminded him of this, but the obstinate set of his jaw told her he would be no more receptive to her reasoning now than he had been in the past. She kept silent.

Paul remained at the window. Glancing past him, Terra could see the trees and flower-filled tubs that made the alley an attractive shortcut through the fashionable San Francisco business district in which the shop was located. She waited for Paul to say something more, and her eyes wandered around his newly redecorated office. She didn't exactly resent the luxurious furnishings of his executive suite or the large amount of space it consumed, but she could not forget that the rest of the bookshop was desperately overcrowded and in need of basic repairs.

Paul's office had been the best in the building before the remodeling, and now it clearly outclassed its surroundings. The oaken bookshelves had been torn out to make way for decorator wallpaper, the hardwood floors had been covered by wall-to-wall carpeting and Paul's father's marvelous old oak desk had been replaced with a sleek executive unit. With its new look the office might well have belonged to a Montgomery Street financier instead of to the head of the world-famous rare-book firm of Foster and Son.

Evidently realizing she was not going to speak further, Paul turned toward her and began again, this time with exaggerated patience.

"Look, Terra, business has slipped a lot since

dad died. I'm not blaming the staff," he continued hurriedly, noticing her frown, "but what we need now is a big break—something that will draw the old-guard collectors back to Fosters' and convince them nothing has changed. These pamphlets are our big chance."

He walked over to the front of his desk and perched on the corner, his arms folded and a smug smile on his face.

"Sometimes I don't believe I actually pulled it off. From the moment I discovered those pamphlets in Miss Waltham's library I tried to persuade her to sell them to me, but because they were part of her father's personal papers she refused to part with them. Then she died, and I found she had left them to me in her will. Apparently my interest, combined with the firm's reputation, had impressed her. Now the pamphlets are mine, and when I sell them next month at the fair, our financial picture is going to look good—very good, indeed." He grinned in obvious satisfaction, but with the lightning quickness that characterized his moods lately he sobered suddenly. "But I can't sell anything without that brochure, so get with it."

He stood, indicating the interview was over. As Terra herself got up, he put his hand casually on her shoulder. The heavy pressure of his touch, however, contradicted the friendliness of the gesture.

"I can count on you, can't I, Terra?"

She nodded and silently left the room. Climbing the stairs that led to her office on the third floor, she let out a deep breath and shook her long brown hair in an effort to dispel the melancholy feeling that had settled over her. Interviews with Paul were becoming more and more distasteful. When he had first taken over the firm a year ago his habit had been to drop into her office whenever he had something to talk about. They had discussed things then in a casual and relaxed manner. Since he had remodeled his office suite, though, he insisted on formal meetings downstairs, and the pretentious surroundings only seemed to encourage his increasingly autocratic manner.

But Terra felt the new office alone could not explain the changes in Paul or the increasing difficulty she was having in working for him. They had got along so well, had even dated three years earlier, when Terra had first joined the firm as a secretary in the research department. She had been fresh from university then and eager to start on a career. Paul's father had still been alive and had put Paul in charge of the firm's London office. But Paul had returned often to San Francisco and on one of those trips had asked Terra to dinner.

His knowledge of business and the warm friendly manner he had had in those days had impressed Terra considerably. For a while she had fancied herself ready to fall in love with him. But when his interests shifted she felt no real regret—and concluded she had nearly fallen in love with love, not Paul. They had remained casual friends, with no hard feelings on either side, and until today she had thought Paul had approved of her steady rise under his father's tutelage.

A year ago, Paul's father had died, leaving the bookstore to his son. Looking back over the past year, Terra could see that gradual changes in Paul had begun almost immediately. His manner had become more authoritarian, and he had increasingly neglected to consult Terra before making major decisions that affected the research department. When he had left for England to pick up the copies of the lost edition, Terra had hoped his good luck would have a mellowing effect on him.

During the week he was away things were very quiet. On his return the excitement over the lost edition had driven worry about Paul from Terra's mind. She had been ecstatic when Paul had assigned her total responsibility for proving the authenticity of what the book world was calling the "discovery of the century." Together she and Paul had shown one copy of the pamphlet to hordes of experts, none of whom had expressed the least doubt concerning it. The research into the printing of the edition had absorbed her attention so thoroughly it was a few weeks before she realized that all the commotion and publicity was affecting Paul, making him more unreasonable than ever. Confrontations with Terra, such as this one over the brochure, occurred more often and were more intense.

Other people on the staff were also suffering from his dictatorial manner and swift changes in mood, and several long-term employees had recently quit, increasing the work load and the tension in the office.

Terra was not yet ready to look for another job, but she did wish Paul would show more understanding of the problems involved in proving the genuineness of a first edition. She was working as hard as she could, but she still had not found conclusive evidence that these pamphlets were indeed part of the coveted lost edition. Terra didn't actually doubt they were genuine, but believing it and proving it were two different things. William Foster, Paul's father, had built an impeccable reputation by his adherence to the very principles Terra was applying to her research. She had no intention of deviating from the methods William had taught her, no matter how impatient Paul was becoming.

Back in her office on the top floor of the brick building that had always been the home of the firm, Terra relaxed. Until recently the top floor had been used only for storage space, but when Paul had redesigned the ground floor to make room for a larger administrative area, Terra had volunteered to move her office to what she now called the garret. When Paul's father had been alive, Terra had enjoyed working downstairs amid the bustle and activity. William Foster had been a true bibliophile. Despite his expertise and his keen business sense he had never lost his love of books, his joy at being among rare and wonderful things. Unlike Paul he had never been impatient. He had been eager to teach any interested employee, eager to share his inexhaustible knowledge. Working with him had been almost an adventure, and being in the thick of things had excited Terra. But now she was relieved to be away from the turmoil and conflict that seemed to have become an inseparable part of office life. The third floor, although crowded with cartons, books and objects that were no longer needed, was at least quiet.

Terra had not been able to convince Paul that even a storage area should have some semblance of order, so much of the chaos had remained untouched. But by enlisting the help of some of the clerks, she had cleared a small space in front of the row of windows to serve as an office. With a strategic placement of bookshelves she had walled off her sanctuary, creating a cozy little corner, flanked on two sides by bookshelves and on the third side by windows overlooking the alley. Paul had been reluctant to involve the decorator in the furnishing of an attic office, but to Terra's delight had given her permission to spend a modest amount on a few new things.

Mr. Foster's wooden desk dominated the office. It was such a treasure that Terra sometimes put up with Paul just so she could keep on using that desk—or so she laughingly told herself. She made the piece the center of her decorating scheme, and she chose an area rug and curtains in shades of brown and gold, thinking those colors would set off the deepened patina of the desk, which shone with years of respectful use and meticulous care.

The row of windows that formed one wall of her office added a feeling of openness to the small space. As a final touch she had brought in half a dozen plants from her home across the bay in Berkeley. The light from the windows provided ideal growing conditions, and some members of the staff laughingly referred to the alcove as "Terra's jungle."

Terra slipped out of her suit jacket and hung it on one of the curling arms of the Victorian hat rack that served as her coat closet. Along with the full-length oval mirror that was now mounted on the end of a tall bookshelf, the rack had been discovered during lunchtime visits to antique shops. By shopping carefully, she had been able to give her little office a warmth and intimacy, which contrasted sharply with the modern slickness of Paul's domain. All that remained for her to buy was another chair so that anyone visiting the tiny office would have a place to sit.

She stopped in front of the mirror and straightened the lace collar of her high-necked blouse. Eyeing the effect created by the sky-blue tailored skirt and the white Edwardian blouse, Terra decided the outfit achieved that blend of

businesslike appearance and feminine style she
favored in her working clothes. Leaning a bit
closer to the mirror, she casually inspected her
face. She was a bit flushed from her run-in with
Paul, and she noticed the faint tinge of red
along her softly rounded cheeks. What she did
not notice was a flawless and youthfully pale
complexion and a gently pouting mouth that
charmingly revealed the little streak of stub-
bornness that ran through her personality. It
was an arresting face, pretty, innocent, but
aware. She didn't stop to wonder whether that
face was capable of attracting the sort of man
she sometimes hoped she'd find. She always
seemed to have other things on her mind. She
had other things on her mind now.

On her way to her desk she paused, still feeling too restless to settle down to work right
away. She turned toward the windows and
gazed at the buildings clustered around the alley
below. The entire neighborhood had undergone
considerable refurbishing in the past few years,
and the alley, once a rather shabby back street
filled with disposal bins and loading bays, was
now a chic pedestrian thoroughfare. Garbage
cans had been replaced by laurel trees in large
redwood planters, and motor vehicles were dis-
couraged by signs limiting through traffic and
prohibiting parking.

As Terra looked down through the thin mist
that was beginning to settle over the city, a silver
Mercedes sports coupe turned the corner and,

without the usual hesitancy of cars entering the narrow alley, advanced confidently at a rapid pace. Just before passing Fosters', the car slowed unexpectedly and swung between two potted trees that flanked the back entrance to the bookshop.

Terra watched in mild interest. Paul was a zealous defender of the no-parking area by the store and would often rush out and confront anyone he saw violating the parking regulations. Although the no-parking sign was clearly visible in front of the car, the driver appeared totally unconcerned. Unaware he was being observed, he slid out from under the wheel and leaned back into the car to reach for his jacket. Even at a distance Terra could see that his dress shirt barely disguised the tensile strength of his broad shoulders and tapering back. Watching the white expanse disappear from view under a perfectly tailored gray suit coat, she sensed this was a man who willingly donned the trappings of conservative urbanity without being subdued by them.

As he settled his jacket over his shoulders and locked his car, there was a confident grace about his movements that Terra found vaguely disturbing. His face was still turned away from her, and she leaned closer to the window in an attempt to get a clearer view. She didn't recognize him from the back, and yet there was something undeniably familiar about the thick dark hair and sculptured shape of his long frame. He turned toward the store and paused. Then, as if directed by a sixth sense, he glanced up at Terra's third-floor window.

Terra gasped and shook her head slightly as though trying to clear her vision. Grant Ingraham! She stepped back quickly from the window, her heart pounding and her throat suddenly dry. She must be mistaken. After all, she hadn't seen him since she had been a teenager. Yet somehow she knew that ten years were not time enough to erase those sharply defined features, that easy languid grace of movement from her memory. What was Grant Ingraham doing here after all this time?

The flurry of activity on the floors below told her others had also recognized the impending visitor. She could hear Margaret White, the sales manager, calling excitedly to Paul, and soon effusive greetings floated up the stairs.

Grant Ingraham would have been a welcome visitor to any store, for his wealth was reputed to be extensive. In fact, he was generally considered one of the most successful men in his field. But no doubt it was not this alone that accounted for Paul's enthusiastic greeting. Grant had been a valued customer of William Foster, a knowledgeable book collector who had traveled widely in order to add to his personal collection. Rumor had it he had given up collecting, though, and that seemed to be true. When Terra had first started working for William Foster, she had worried that her new job might mean inevitable meetings with Grant. Yet she had soon realized that Grant was not interested in browsing in Fosters'. She had heard he occasionally had done business with William Foster at his home in the Pacific Heights district of the city, but he had never come to the shop in all the time Terra had worked there. She had forgotten about the possibility of running into him. She had nearly forgotten about *him*. But not quite.

Of course it was inevitable that Grant should know Paul. Even if Grant had not been a friend of Paul's father, Paul would have made an effort to know a book collector who had so much money to spend.

Seeing Grant after so many years brought back all Terra's anxieties about a reunion with him. She considered the possibility of sneaking out of the shop but quickly rejected the plan as foolish. The only way down to both the front and back doors was through the main foyer, which would mean being in full view of the rest of the staff. Uncomfortable as it would be to meet Grant again, explaining her flight to Margaret would be even worse. And unless she told Paul why she was leaving, he would assume she was trying to get out of doing her work.

After a little thought Terra calmed down. Escape was both cowardly and unnecessary. No doubt she was safe on the third floor amid the flotsam and jetsam of the bookshop. Paul himself rarely came up there, and it was inconceivable he would bring an impressive visitor up to an area of the store of which he was a little ashamed.

Besides, Terra chided herself, even if Grant were to see her, he might not recognize her now that she had grown up. She had been only nine when her father had first brought him home for dinner after a meeting of the San Francisco Bookman's Club. Grant had been a graduate student in business at the University of California and had had a passion for collecting nineteenth-century first editions. It was this interest that had brought him into contact with Terra's father, for he, too, had been a specialist in that area of collecting. The two men had become fast friends despite the difference in their ages, and Grant had been a constant visitor at the Scotts' Berkeley home.

Looking back on those years had often caused Terra to blush. She had adored Grant with all the ardor of a first crush and had not been at all shy about declaring that when she grew up she would marry him. Grant had behaved toward her in the manner of a fond older brother, taking her to the zoo, playing hide-and-seek in the front yard and listening solemnly to her forays into the world of adult conversation. Her relationship with him had been easy and casual in those days, as if being with Grant were the most natural thing in the world.

But as she had got older her shyness in Grant's presence had increased. For a while she had tried to impress him by her knowledge of

her father's hobby, and she *had* impressed him
in the way of a precocious child. Intuitively she
began to realize that his kindness was patroniz-
ing, that he was humoring her almost as though
he knew her interest in him was no longer childlike—almost as though he pitied her because of
that fact. Eventually she became so unsure of
herself when he was around that she arranged to
be out with her friends when he came. Or she
would even hide in her room, hearing his strong
voice float up to her and wishing she had the
courage to go down and face him.

A few years after Grant completed his studies
and received his master's degree he left San
Francisco and moved to the East Coast to manage the New York office of his family's publishing firm. Surely he had made many trips back
since then, but Terra had never seen him
again—not until the moment he pulled up beneath her garret window.

When he had first left she had been heart-
broken. It seemed as though something had
gone out of her life that could never be replaced.
As time passed, her despair had given way to a
lingering embarrassment tinged with disappointment that he had never come back to visit
her family. She knew that after he had managed
things in New York for five years the death of
his father had made him head of the firm—
which meant he was technically in charge of the
home office in San Francisco. But he had preferred to remain in New York, and from there

skillfully led the business into the multiple-interest, international corporation it was at present.

Even without having seen him, Terra knew much about him. Her father had kept track of him, and there were newspaper stories. The consolidation and growth of his company had received a great deal of publicity—not at all favorable. Terra's father had maintained that any change on the scale Grant was attempting was bound to be controversial, and those left out of the action usually didn't hesitate to spread rumors. Despite her father's opinion that Grant had done nothing but grow older and more successful, Terra was afraid success had corrupted him, and after a while that feeling had become a conviction.

In addition to reports of the Ingranam Corporation's meteoric rise to conglomerate status, the newspapers frequently featured more personal information about Grant, both in the society pages and gossip columns. It had been a while before Terra had realized Grant was considered socially as a sort of "local-boy-makes-good" success story. The image the press presented was that of a capricious and most definitely confirmed bachelor. The gossip columnists prided themselves on keeping up with his latest love interest and often repeated the observation that to appear in public twice with Grant was to have made a real conquest. His women were all glamorous, whether they were socialites, actresses or models. Apart from their beauty, their only common denominator seemed to be the short duration of their relationship with Grant.

Terra might have dismissed these accounts as exaggerations aimed at ensuring readership of the columns if she had not received more direct confirmation of Grant's ways from Margaret, the sales manager at Fosters'. An attractive divorcée, Margaret had befriended Terra from her first day on the job, and the younger woman had discovered that Margaret not only followed the gossip columns avidly but had many friends who moved in Grant's various circles. Margaret swore that his rakish reputation had been well earned and delighted in keeping Terra up to date on his latest exploits. Terra didn't believe everything Margaret told her, but she felt that enough was true to make her disapprove of the new person Grant had become. For years she had dreamed of seeing him again, but lately she had been content to remember him as he had been, rather than risk a meeting. She wasn't sure how she would behave faced with a man who was now a stranger but had not always been so. It was a relief that their paths hadn't crossed until that moment, and she couldn't imagine why he would suddenly pay a visit to the store. His business was undoubtedly with Paul, and Terra hoped that although he was in the shop she would be able to avoid him.

The sound of rapid footsteps on the stairs interrupted her thoughts. Margaret popped into view, talking as she approached Terra.

"I've only got a minute, but I had to tell you the big news. Grant Ingraham is here!" The stress she placed on the last four words told Terra that Margaret considered the visit to be a very important event. "He's with Paul right now, but if you'll come down with me, we can pretend to be working at that little table outside Paul's office, and when they come out they won't be able to avoid us."

While she was talking, Margaret darted over to the mirror and began patting her blond hair into place and inspecting her face critically. "I should have brought my makeup pouch with me," she complained, "but I forgot you had this lovely mirror." She tilted her chin upward to catch the light from the window. "Do you have any eye shadow up here?"

Before Terra could reply, Margaret answered her own question. "Of course you don't. You never use the stuff. Those brown eyes of yours are gorgeous enough without assistance. And no crow's feet. Oh, to be young!"

Terra laughed in spite of herself. Margaret could be quite dramatic. "I use eye shadow in the evenings," she said, "but I don't have any here at work. You look fine the way you are, Margaret."

"Oh, well—" Margaret sighed elaborately "—those of us who carry our faces in bottles just have to learn to bring the bottles with us wherever we go." She made a face at herself in the mirror.

Terra chuckled. "You can get away with saying things like that because you look as if you stepped out of the pages of *Vogue*."

"Oh, I suppose I'll do." Margaret took a step backward, cocked her head and appraised the total effect she made. "But I'd trade it all in a minute for that peaches-and-cream complexion of yours. You always manage to look beautiful without any effort at all. It just isn't fair."

Terra blushed. "Stop kidding me, Margaret."

"I mean every word of it. Just give Grant one look at you, and I don't think you'll be spending the next couple of weeks by yourself. Of course, he'll move on to someone else after a while, but a night or two with Grant would be better than nothing at all."

"That's a pleasure I think I'll have to pass up, thanks." Terra had learned not to take Margaret's outrageous remarks too seriously, and she was amused rather than piqued at the comments her friend tossed off. "You go down now," she told the older woman. "I have a lot of work to do up here."

Pleased she had so skillfully evaded that attempt to coerce her into meeting Grant, Terra decided to get to work. She began flipping through page after page of notes, hoping to find a clue that might lead to more information. She ignored Margaret's dramatic accents and the sounds of other voices that drifted up from the floor below. Becoming engrossed in her labors, she jumped when she heard Paul's voice near at hand.

"Terra, may we interrupt you for a moment?" he said, entering the attic. Behind him, nonchalantly glancing at the surroundings from the top of the stairwell, was Grant Ingraham.

Even from where she sat she could see the ten years had had their effect. Her gaze fell on a confident, virile, fully mature man. He seemed to have grown much taller, though that had to be Terra's imagination. His broad shoulders filled his impeccably tailored jacket, and the fine fabric of his slacks emphasized the strength of his leg, bent at the knee as he stood poised on the top step. His hands and face were lightly tanned, as though he had not just stepped off a plane from the East but had spent some time in California. Terra had but an instant in which to observe the sculpted planes of his face, the thick black hair. Seeing him from the window had been startling, but seeing him at closer range was even more devastating. Time seemed to stand still as she waited for him to join Paul, who was advancing toward her. She stood, but in her nervousness knocked her chair backward and sent it crashing into the bookcase behind her.

Now that the meeting she had been dreading was imminent her mind began to whirl. She wanted to appear cool and unconcerned, in no way agitated over seeing Grant again. She hoped her clumsy movement with the chair had gone unnoticed by the visitor. Moving toward Paul, she caught a surreptitious glance at herself in the mirror and was relieved to see that none of the confusion she felt was reflected there.

"This way, Grant," Paul called out, motioning with his hand, and Grant stepped away from the relative darkness at the top of the stairs into the full light of Terra's space.

Seeing him so close, Terra felt a wave of memories wash suddenly over her. For one impossible instant she was again a teenager wanting to run from the power of his presence—and wanting at the same time never to let him out of her sight. Much about him appeared to have remained the same, and yet she sensed immediately that a change had occurred, a change difficult to pin down. Even though he didn't know who she was, she expected a warm greeting from him. Business etiquette alone demanded as much. Yet his expression was remarkably impersonal as his eyes met hers. If Paul had mentioned her name, it seemed impossible he would not remember it, even if he did not recognize her face, but she could read in his impassive features no sign he knew who she was.

"This is Grant Ingraham, an old customer of dad's." Paul's voice was pleasantly friendly, in marked contrast to his tone earlier in the day. "I've just shown him the lost edition, and since he's an expert in nineteenth-century printing,

I've asked him to take a look at your notes. Maybe he can help you get over the rough spots in your draft for the brochure."

Turning to Grant, Paul continued. "All the information needed to write the brochure is here, but our Terra is a perfectionist and can't resist the temptation to dig out more material, even though it's not really necessary in this case. We're getting down to the wire on the deadline for printing the brochure, so maybe you can convince her she's got all she needs." Paul's tone was one of lightly teasing affection, and it infuriated Terra. He had no right to comment on her work in front of an outsider. But then the finer points of good employee relations were lost on Paul.

"I'd be happy to read the notes and discuss the problems," Grant said, and Terra was startled. His voice hadn't changed one bit. It was still the smooth, sonorous, deep sound she had listened to from her adolescent hiding place so many years earlier. She wanted to tell him his assistance was unnecessary, no matter what Paul might think. She wanted to explain to Grant that she was a competent professional well able to handle her responsibilities without the aid of any passerby who might wander into the shop. But she said nothing, and Grant, apparently not finding her silence unusual or impolite, continued. "Let's take a look at what Miss Scott is doing." He directed a small efficient smile toward Terra, then dismissed Paul summarily by declaring, "I'll come back down to your office when we're through."

Paul appeared less than pleased with Grant's suggestion. "You don't have to stay here in this mess," he said awkwardly. "We can take the papers downstairs, where you can look them over in comfort."

"I'll read the notes here, if you don't mind," Grant said with compelling assertiveness. "The clutter doesn't bother me at all. In fact, this little alcove is quite inviting." He made a sweeping gesture that took in all of Terra's office, his polite words only partially masking the finality of his tone.

Paul started to protest and then stopped, giving in to the inevitable. "Whatever you prefer," he said, and with a warning look at Terra he retreated downstairs.

"Shall we begin?" Grant asked. There was faint amusement in the question.

Terra stepped back toward her desk and in the process bumped into a carton of books that sat on the floor. As she recovered her balance she tried to decide whether she should acknowledge that she knew him. He moved toward the desk with an easy stride, and his expression was pleasant enough at the moment, but it still didn't reflect any recognition. His eyes seemed shrouded by a dark curtain, and she could discern in them no flicker of friendship or interest beyond mere politeness. Not quite willing to be the first to mention their previous acquaintance and yet distinctly uncomfortable about ignoring it, Terra took refuge in formalities.

"It really is most generous of you to offer advice about the lost edition," she began, "but I can handle matters myself. However, if you insist on seeing the notes, I suggest you take them downstairs. I'm afraid facilities are somewhat limited up here. This desk chair is the only place to sit. If you do want to stay up here, why don't you sit at the desk—I'll finish some work I have to do downstairs. You can call me after you've gone through the notes. We'll talk then."

Grant had deftly threaded a path around bulging boxes toward her cozily decorated corner. He smiled slightly but otherwise gave no indication he recognized her attempt to get away from him as anything other than polite conversation.

"We'll manage all right up here," he said dryly. "I'd like to hear your account of the investigation before I read your notes, so please, sit down." He gestured toward the chair.

When she had designed her office, Terra had deliberately positioned the bookshelves to enclose a very small corner of the attic in an effort to make her part of the big room seem more private. Grant seemed to make the space even smaller than it really was, and Terra had to squeeze by him to get to her chair. As she slipped past him her arm brushed his, and the fleeting contact sent a shiver through her body. She sat down quickly and waited for him to speak.

He glanced around the minuscule office with its bookshelf walls and forest of potted plants and then seated himself on a corner of her desk. The space was so cramped that in his present position he was much closer to Terra than she thought she could stand. She tried to roll her chair back a bit but was stopped by a bookcase. All she could do was sit far back in her chair and act as if his closeness had no effect on her at all.

"Very pleasant," Grant said, "but not set up for company. You really need another chair if you want to entertain."

Disliking the feeling he was passing judgment on her efforts, Terra chose not to explain that she hoped to find a suitable chair very soon. Instead of defending herself, she considered once again whether she should somehow let Grant know who she was. Continuing to pretend he was a stranger was difficult, but his guarded manner didn't encourage an admission of friendship. Unless he was putting on a marvelous act, he genuinely didn't know they had met previously. In that case, Terra decided, it would be best to let him take the lead. If she revealed nothing, perhaps she could get through the encounter without his discovering her identity.

"I understand you're in charge of proving that the Browning pamphlets Paul has discovered are part of the lost edition. That's quite a responsibility...."

"If you mean to imply I'm too inexperienced to handle this investigation, I can assure you I have gone over and over all the possibilities and have done everything imaginable to verify their authenticity." Terra was startled by the sharpness in her own voice. She would actually have welcomed real help, from Grant or anyone else. There were answers that still needed finding. But she didn't relish the thought that Grant, like Paul, doubted her ability as a researcher.

Grant's eyes narrowed slightly at her prickly response. "I'm sure you've left no stone unturned," he commented without sarcasm. "Paul says the evidence proves conclusively that the pamphlets are genuine copies." His voice had changed from its previous neutral tone. Terra thought she detected a faint challenge beneath the cool words, as though he were testing her.

"The evidence seems to point that way," she began cautiously. "The lost edition was supposed to have been printed in 1848. I've had the ink and the paper analyzed, and both appear to have come from approximately that period."

"How about the typeface? Did you check to see that face was in use in the late 1840s?"

"Of course," Terra snapped, again angered by the implied criticism of her working methods. "It was introduced by the Waltham Press in 1842 and used continuously by them until World War I."

Grant shifted his weight and crossed his legs. Underneath the smooth fabric of his suit his well-muscled thigh tensed. Terra glanced at it, then caught herself and quickly looked away.

"You've also documented the printing history of the edition, I'm sure." His voice was now velvety smooth, in obvious mockery of her defensiveness.

"Yes, it's all very straightforward. Paul brought me the work log of the Waltham Press, and it clearly shows that twenty copies were ordered by a close friend of the Brownings. The booklets were to be printed in England and then, presumably, shipped to Robert and Elizabeth in Italy."

Terra paused, reluctant to say anything about the romantic story connected with the writing and printing of Elizabeth Browning's sonnets. From what she knew about Grant's reputation she assumed he would be cynical about love, and she had no desire to listen to skeptical comments about one of her favorite stories.

"That's right. The Brownings were living in Italy then, weren't they," he mused. "They eloped because her father was opposed to their marriage. As I recall, Elizabeth was very reluctant to have the love sonnets she wrote to her husband printed. In fact, she was even shy about showing the poems to him, if we can believe that famous story. You've heard it, I'm sure. Browning is sitting at the breakfast table several months after their elopement, when his wife rushes in, stuffs the manuscript of the poems in his pocket and flees. Quite touching— if it's true." Mocking glints danced in Grant's dark eyes.

"Of course it's true," Terra shot back indignantly. "It's been proven without doubt. Just because some people aren't capable of feeling that kind of love doesn't mean it doesn't exist for others. I think it's a beautiful story."

There suddenly seemed something vaguely ridiculous about arguing over the devotion of the Brownings. Grant laughed in a way that was at least a little teasing. Nettled, Terra hastened to resume the account of her research.

"After the printing of the pamphlets the trail gets harder to follow. No one knows exactly who received them, and although one or two did show up through the years, they've all disappeared now. That's why they've been called the 'lost edition' and there have always been those who felt its existence was mere myth. A very small, privately commissioned edition of very personal poems is, of course, of great interest to scholars and collectors alike. So few copies were printed it does not seem unusual that none survived—or at least it was assumed that none survived, until Paul's discovery.

"If one accepts the validity of Paul's find, the most logical assumption is that Joseph Waltham, the printer, must have sent only ten copies to the Brownings. He must have kept the other ten for himself, eventually passing them on to his descendants until Jessica Waltham broke the chain by willing them to Paul. In a way it's a shame they should leave the family, but like other families, the Walthams have died out over time. At any rate, all of this is conjecture. The work log states only that twenty copies were printed. It doesn't specify how many of those went to the Brownings.''

Grant leaned forward, his dark eyes and sensuous mouth dangerously close. Terra looked into his face unflinchingly, determined to remain professional and calm. ''That explanation may be only conjecture,'' Grant stated, ''but you must admit it sounds logical. What further proof are you looking for?''

Terra let her breath out slowly. ''I'm not really sure. It would be ideal, of course, to compare our copies to ones that are known to be genuine. But as far as we know, that's impossible. It would be helpful to compare them even to descriptions of the genuine edition, but I haven't been able to find the pamphlet described anywhere. I think it might be possible to find specific mention of how many copies were actually sent to the Brownings. That would at least add weight to the argument that the Walthams' ten copies are part of the same edition.''

''Under the circumstances I would think you've done all you can. Yet you seem to be looking for something beyond what the existing evidence can prove. Why?''

For a brief moment Terra considered confiding her uneasiness about the pamphlets to Grant. She had no concrete reasons for thinking they might be forgeries. The fact that they had definitely come directly from the printer's family was very compelling evidence of their authenticity, and yet the circumstances surrounding their appearance somehow seemed strange. Paul had accepted the story of their passage down through the family completely, but he had strong financial reasons for wanting to believe they were genuine. Grant was an acknowledged expert in this field. Perhaps if she told him her concerns he might be able to advise her as to whether she had real grounds for suspicion.

"Does your silence imply you believe the pamphlets are forgeries?"

Hearing the word *forgery* spoken out loud startled Terra. In her business that word was as reprehensible as the word *fake* was to a reputable jeweler. Perhaps she should be more cautious about admitting to anyone, and certainly to a virtual stranger, that she was worried that Paul's monumental discovery might not be what it appeared. If any whisper of her doubt reached Paul, the consequences would be chilling.

"No," she replied coolly with all the confidence she could muster. "In fact, all the experts I've consulted are quite convinced we are dealing with the real thing. My job as researcher, however, puts me in the position of devil's advocate. I'm obliged to prove our claims beyond any doubt. That type of assurance of authenticity has been a Foster trademark. William Foster, according to my father...."

Terra stopped, conscious she might be introducing a topic of conversation she wished to avoid. But Grant did not seem to notice the breach. He rose and stepped over toward the window, staring thoughtfully at the alley below. When he spoke it was to ask her for her notes.

She handed them to him, and once again he settled onto a corner of the desk, then began reading. He turned the pages of the notebook almost soundlessly, but for some reason Terra's eyes were drawn toward his hands. His fingers were long and tapered, his palms broad; he had the large hands one might expect in a man of his size. And yet she could see just by the way he touched the papers that those hands possessed a remarkable gentleness. They were hands one could trust to handle the sometimes fragile pages of rare books. Perhaps one might even trust such hands to touch oneself.

Terra shifted restlessly in her chair, then looked out the window, trying to concentrate on something other than the man seated so close to her. Outside the sky was a leaden gray and the mist had thickened. In the distance the tall buildings of Montgomery Street loomed like giants in the fog. Terra knew the San Francisco office of the Ingraham Corporation was located in that financial district. She had thought about it before but had never made any effort to find out its address.

After a minute or two her glance drifted back toward Grant. His chiseled features were more mature than in her memory, but they still showed the calm strength she remembered from her childhood. Feeling that so much about Grant was still the same, Terra tried to analyze what had changed. His eyes seemed older, harder. She sensed a wariness, a reserve she did not recall having been aware of in earlier years. In her memory his eyes had danced with lively emotion, and now she searched his face intently for some of the relaxed warmth that used to soften his features.

He looked up unexpectedly, his eyes meeting and holding her probing gaze. "Still planning to marry me, Terra Scott?" he asked softly.

Her breath stopped; her head reeled. The years sped away, and she was once again an awkward teenager consumed by impossible love. Wordlessly she stared into the gently mocking eyes that captured her own and would not release her.

It took only a moment for her to remember who she was now—not a girl, but a woman. Anger filled her. He had known all along. What a cheap manipulative trick to pretend otherwise! His impersonal behavior had been a game he had chosen to play with her. If she needed any further proof that time had destroyed the sensitive young man she used to know, his present charade showed clearly how little he now regarded the feelings of others.

"Why didn't you tell me you remembered?" she demanded indignantly. "How dare you come in here pretending to be a stranger?"

Grant regarded her outburst with amusement.

"Your own greeting wasn't overly friendly, as I recall," he commented. "But now that we've finally admitted we know each other—" his ironic tone softened and became personal "—it's nice to see you again, Terra."

He eyed her appreciatively, his glance lingering on the rising folds of her silk blouse. "Time has treated you well. You're a beautiful woman."

His sudden shift from distance to familiarity did nothing to assuage her anger. The ease with which he evidently felt he could move from indifference to intimacy was insulting. He might be accustomed to immediate adoration from other women, but he would quickly find out it took more than an insolent glance to sway Terra.

Unable to handle the personal implications of this absurd scene, she made a valiant attempt to recapture the businesslike spirit that had prevailed until so short a time ago. "About the notes?" she remarked steadily.

For a full minute his eyes imprisoned hers, refusing to let them turn away. There was emotion there, but naming it was beyond Terra. The dark eyes danced teasingly. They were full of mockery or amusement or even of expectation, but then they became sober, and when he finally spoke his voice was businesslike.

"You say you've gone over the work log of the Waltham Press, but you don't mention the other papers of the firm—delivery records or receipts. Those might shed more light on the circumstances of the printing.''

Again Terra was annoyed at the implication her work had not been as complete as it should have been. She pointed to the notebook. "I've tried to locate the rest of the business papers of the press, naturally, and you can see for yourself I haven't got very far. Paul originally purchased the log from Miss Waltham. I asked him about the other records, and he said that if Miss Waltham had had any other relevant papers he would have purchased them at the same time. I took that to mean nothing else of importance was available."

"What did you find at the Blansford Library?" Grant asked.

"I haven't been there," Terra responded, and then hurried on when she saw his frown. "It's not that I haven't tried. I know as well as you do that the Blansford is *the* library for research into nineteenth-century printing, but it's a private library, and they restrict use to only a few scholars each year. It's very difficult to get a pass for the kind of research I need to do and virtually impossible within my time limits."

"Can't Paul pull any strings for you?" Grant asked.

"He has in a way," Terra explained. "The work log now belongs to the Blansford, and because Paul sold it to them, they allowed him to bring it here for me to examine. He also checked their card catalog for me and said he didn't think they had anything else that would help."

"You never know for sure until you look yourself," Grant commented dryly.

"Of course I'm aware of that." Terra gave an irritated sigh. "But I'm stymied. I've called the Blansford several times, but I can't get past the secretary." Sensing he didn't accept her excuse, she snapped, "I suppose you think you can do better."

"Why, yes," he replied slowly, "I think I can." Then, without further comment, he changed the subject. "What does your father say about the problem? This is his special field."

Terra knew there was no logical reason why Grant should have known about her father's death. Her dad had been inactive in the Bookman's Club for years, and only by chance would Grant have run across the news. Nevertheless she wished he had known.

"Dad died of cancer three years ago," she said quickly.

Grant leaned over and took her hand in both of his. "I'm sorry, Terra. I've been out of touch with the Bookman's Club until recently so I hadn't heard."

Determined not to let herself be overwhelmed by the emotions rising within her, Terra smiled, and after several seconds pulled her hand away.

Grant straightened. "Do you still live in the same place?"

She nodded. "I thought about moving but finally decided to stay. No other place in Berkeley would feel like home, and I've known some of the neighbors for so long they seem like family to me.''

Grant looked at his watch. ''It's almost five. Have dinner with me tonight, Terra. I want to get to know you again.''

Terra realized with a slight shock that he had invited her out. It must be typical of the new Grant that an invitation sounded like a command. Her feelings were mixed. Years ago she would have jumped at the chance to see Grant again—but the Grant she remembered, not this imposing stranger. This new person, who could go from the personal to the businesslike so swiftly, who seemed to assume she would rush off to dinner with him at a moment's notice, disturbed her intensely.

Then, too, she was not at all sure she wanted to rake up old memories. Grant's present friendly interest was likely to last for a much shorter period of time than it had ten years earlier. And although she did not think she was as vulnerable to him now as she had been then, she didn't want to go through the pain of disappointment again. Far from being eager to get to know him again, she felt it was much better to end this meeting quickly and forget she had even seen him.

''I really wish I could,'' she began her polite rejection, ''but I have other plans. You probably remember Jeff Baxter, the proverbial boy-next-door?''

"Is he your boyfriend?" Grant came right to the point.

Terra hesitated. Much as she wanted to claim a serious relationship with Jeff in order to discourage Grant, she couldn't bring herself to lie outright. The truth was that Jeff was causing her quite a bit of anxiety at the moment. For years they had been close friends, had spent a lot of time together. As far as Terra was concerned, they could go on like that forever. But lately Jeff seemed to be changing his attitude. Terra suspected he was in love with her, and it was not an emotion she could return. His friendly kisses were becoming demanding, though his chances of having his demands met were growing slimmer by the day. She simply could not think of him in any way other than the way in which she had thought about him all these years. He was a good neighbor, and that was that.

"We're very close," she compromised, hoping Grant would infer what she didn't feel like saying.

"But friends, not lovers." Grant drew the correct conclusion instantly. "In that case he certainly wouldn't object to your having dinner with another old friend, especially if you explain the circumstances. Call him."

Terra hesitated again, not knowing how to refuse but unwilling to give in.

"Terra," Grant said, moving closer, "we haven't seen each other in ten years...." He took her hand, and his thumb lazily inscribed a little circle on her skin. The apparently absent-minded gesture made Terra acutely uncomfortable. "Dinner will be an opportunity to renew an old acquaintance," he continued. "I'm sure Jeff will understand." He released her hand and stood up. "I'll meet you in about fifteen minutes in Paul's office."

Terra stared helplessly at his retreating back. It made her angry to think she had not been allowed to refuse his invitation. She thought she had made it quite clear she didn't want to go to dinner with him. Yet Grant had ignored her wishes. He had enforced his will on her without being sensitive to what she wanted. That iron will was the dimension that years of success had added to his personality. The hard glint she had noticed in his eyes was, she concluded, a refusal to brook any opposition to his will, a refusal to compromise. Well, she herself was not so blatantly stubborn. She would give in—but just this once.

With reluctance she picked up the telephone to call Jeff.

CHAPTER TWO

TERRA HUNG UP the phone and stared at the receiver glumly. Now that Grant had gone downstairs and she was temporarily away from the force of his personality, she knew that going out with him would be a mistake. Jeff's reaction to her call had strengthened her reluctance.

"I'm not so sure that's a wise idea, Terra," he had warned. "You know Ingraham's reputation as well as I do. Don't expect him to act like your older brother, now that you've grown up."

"You sound as though you think he's going to seduce me." Terra had laughed at the seriousness of his tone.

"Just watch your step" were his parting words, not denying her teasing conclusion.

Terra didn't share Jeff's specific concern. She was capable of handling unwanted advances in the unlikely event they did occur. Though she could never claim to have been in love, she had dated as much as might be expected in an attractive woman of her age. She considered herself quite skilled at keeping things on an even keel. But she did agree with Jeff it would be best to avoid further acquaintance with Grant. That chapter in her life had been firmly closed, and she could see no reason for opening it again. If only she had been more firm in her refusal earlier!

Unhappily she glanced down at the papers strewn over her desk. Fifteen minutes was not nearly enough time to do all the work that should be finished before she left for the weekend. Not only did she want to organize materials to work on at home, but she had a small pile of notes from other members of the research department to look through. The Browning brochure was just one of several projects that had to be completed before the bookfair, and although the work in the other areas was going well, Terra wanted to respond to the questions of her colleagues as quickly as she could in order not to cause even the slightest delay. Her unfinished work was just one more good reason why going out with Grant would be foolish.

Wishing she had thought of that excuse while she had been talking to him, Terra decided it was a strong argument. If she told Grant in Paul's presence, she was sure Paul would back her up, since he always encouraged her habit of staying late at work.

On her way down to the first floor she met the other two researchers and chatted briefly with them. They were through for the day, so the three of them walked downstairs together. Margaret was hovering near the foot of the stairs, and her eyes, full of curiosity, sought Terra's. Ignoring Margaret's silent questions, Terra continued her conversation with the others. Finally they piled out the door, calling cheerful goodbyes, and Terra turned back to Margaret's inquisitive face.

"What happened?" Margaret whispered urgently. "I simply couldn't believe it when Paul came back down the stairs alone. He usually doesn't let important customers out of his sight. What kind of a bribe did you offer him?"

"Don't be absurd," Terra responded. "Paul simply wanted Mr. Ingraham to comment on the progress of the research on the lost edition. He's an expert in that field, you know."

"I know very well what he's an expert in." Margaret's eyes were dancing. "And you don't fool me for one minute with that 'Mr. Ingraham' stuff. I bet he asked you out."

"Well, sort of," Terra admitted grudgingly. "But not in the way you're thinking. He just suggested we have dinner and talk about old times. He was a friend of my father's, remember?" She didn't add that his suggestion had been more in the nature of a command, but she did want to be sure Margaret understood she didn't plan to go. "I really don't think I can spare the time from all the work I still have to do, so I'll probably beg off."

Margaret's face was incredulous. "Are you saying you're turning down a date with Grant Ingraham?" With a melodramatic gesture she reached over and felt Terra's forehead. "You must be ill."

"It's not a date," Terra explained patiently, "just a chat between people who haven't seen each other in ten years. I'm sure he only asked me out of politeness. He'll be relieved to be off the hook." *And so will I,* she added silently to herself.

"I wouldn't count on it, honey," the older woman said, but before she could say more the door to Paul's office opened and the two men started down the hall, still in conversation. Although they were about the same age, Grant seemed older. He overshadowed Paul completely, not just because of his height but because of the absolute assurance of his bearing. Beside him Paul looked like an insecure schoolboy trying to impress the principal. Terra's confidence began to slip just a little, but she knew that unless she said something at the moment, she would be on her way to dinner with Grant very soon.

With a show of self-assurance well beyond what she was really feeling she walked forward to meet the two men. As she approached, Grant's eyes traveled over her blouse and down to her empty hands. He frowned slightly, making Terra momentarily falter in her resolve, but she joined them and waited for Grant to finish what he was saying to Paul.

"The lost edition doesn't fit into my own collecting plans right now, but I know a few people who will be very interested. Dan Forbush, president of the Bookman's Club, will be particularly anxious to add to his collection of Browning first editions.''

Paul looked a little uneasy. "Mr. Forbush has been here several times looking at the pamphlets, but he didn't seem very enthusiastic.''

"No?'' Grant raised his eyebrows. "They are exactly what he collects. He probably didn't want to seem overly eager. When I see him I'll be glad to talk to him about it.''

Paul looked very pleased and launched into profuse thanks. When he had finished Grant turned his attention to Terra, and the congenial look he had worn during his conversation with Paul hardened slightly.

"Are you ready?'' he asked. "Terra and I are on our way out to dinner,'' he added for Paul's benefit.

Terra had carefully rehearsed a tactful little speech, but it seemed more difficult to say it out loud than it had been to say it in her head, and she had to abandon her prepared line of attack.

"I don't think I'd better go,'' she began, sounding awkward and childlike as if the next thing to say would be, "My mother won't let me.'' But she collected herself and continued. "I have a lot of work left to do, and I'm sure Paul would rather I stay here and finish it.'' She had hoped to handle the whole thing with more grace than she had managed, but at least it was out.

One look at Paul's face, however, told her she had made a mistake in expecting him to support her against Grant. His whole bearing, from his expression to his gestures, announced his eagerness to please Grant, and he contradicted her immediately.

"No need to stay," he said jovially. "You've worked hard all week, and I'm sure you intend to work on the brochure over the weekend, so I wouldn't think of having you here any longer, especially on a Friday night."

"Go and get your things, Terra," Grant said quietly. "I'll wait for you here."

Once again she was at a loss. Grant seemed to take control of every situation he encountered, and she felt powerless against his subtle force. Other than stamping her foot and refusing to go, she could see no way out.

Trying to keep her resentment under control, she slowly climbed the stairs back to the third floor. Perhaps they could go somewhere for a quick dinner, and then he could put her on a bus to Berkeley.

She sorted through her notes, singling out those she would need over the weekend and placing them in a side compartment of the leather handbag that doubled as a briefcase. Then she slipped on her jacket, tucked the purse under her arm and appraised her reflection in the mirror. Her classically cut suit presented a look that was pleasing and neat for the office and also stylish enough for most weekday evening occasions. She whisked a comb through her hair, thankful it behaved well regardless of the weather.

As she once again descended to the ground floor, Terra saw that Grant was now standing close to the door. A little group had formed around him, laughing and talking like old friends. A stranger viewing the scene would have assumed Grant was a frequent and well-liked visitor to the shop. He was perfectly capable of being quite charming when it suited him, Terra observed. It was probably very fortunate that in her encounter with him after all this time he had first shown her the impersonal and manipulative side of his character, rather than the charmingly smooth facade she was seeing now.

Her pace had slowed to a stop during her reflections. Grant glanced up suddenly, and seeing her standing motionless on the stairs, his laughter subsided. Again that look of expectation shone in his eyes. As she walked over to join him his gaze moved slowly over her. Terra was uncomfortably aware that the lightweight suit molded itself to her figure, emphasizing its softly curving lines. Slightly jangled by such scrutiny, she tilted her head upward and met his eyes defiantly. Embarrassed that the others were aware of Grant's meticulous inspection, Terra was especially irritated by the smug smile on Margaret's face.

They were ushered to the back door with such

a clamor of exhortations to have a good time
that Terra felt very much like a teenager on
her first date. As soon as she glimpsed the
Mercedes she remembered that Grant had
parked in the no-stopping zone. She looked
back at Paul, expecting some sort of protest, but he seemed totally oblivious to Grant's
infringement, and after Grant had unlocked
her door, Paul held it open for her, smiling
broadly. Grant walked around to the other side,
and as he slid behind the wheel and out of
Paul's view, Paul leaned close to Terra and
whispered, "This is a big one, Terra. Play it
cool."

As the Mercedes purred smoothly down one
hill and up another, Terra sat silently, watching
San Francisco slide by. She felt she had been
rushed into things with no opportunity to gather
her thoughts. She despaired of finding a way to
open conversation with Grant. Perhaps if the
whole evening promised to go by in such silence,
he would realize their going out together was a
mistake and would not keep her too long.

"I assume you managed to get in touch with
Jeff," Grant's emotionless voice broke the
silence.

"Yes," Terra answered succinctly. She didn't
want to discuss Jeff's reaction to the news that
she was having dinner with Grant. She let the
subject drop and silence descended again. Traffic was thick at this time of the evening, and the
car had to stop and start repeatedly. Grant paid

close attention to his driving, but eventually he spoke.

"I'm afraid I've already made several commitments for this evening, so I can't offer you a completely free choice of entertainment. We'll meet a friend of mine for a drink first and then have a leisurely dinner. I'm obligated to drop by the home of some old friends afterward, but we don't have to stay long." He paused, allowing her time to comment if she chose. Taking her lack of response for consent, he continued. "I think you'll like Elaine and Ray. Elaine was a childhood friend of my mother's, and our families have always been close."

The idea of spending a long meal with Grant, followed by a visit with his close friends, alarmed Terra. It all seemed so intimate. "I really don't want to intrude on plans you've already made," she replied. "Perhaps we could have a quick dinner someplace near here, and then you can drop me off at the bus station. I take the bus home every night, so don't feel you have to escort me to my door."

The corner of Grant's mouth tensed a bit. "I've asked you to come with me. I can hardly consider your presence an intrusion." Stopping the car at a red light, he turned to face her.

"Look, Terra, if you really don't want to have dinner with me, stop playing games and say so. I have to meet someone at six o'clock, but I can take you home right afterward, if that's what you want." His tone was cold,

almost a little defensive, which surprised Terra.
She opened her mouth to speak, but he hadn't
finished.

"I want to get to know you again. You were a
cute kid, a real smart little girl. It doesn't seem
too much to ask to want to see what kind of
woman you've become. I thought a little pleasant conversation might let us both catch up on
what's been happening during the past ten
years. But unless you relax a little it isn't worth
it for either of us. Maybe you haven't grown up
at all. I've got better things to do with my time
than to spend it with a bad-tempered child."

Terra was so infuriated she hardly noticed he
had resumed driving and had swung the car into
a curved driveway in front of the imposing entrance of one of San Francisco's most elegant
hotels. A doorman in a purple frock coat
trimmed with gold braid stepped out instantly to
open her door, and a valet appeared to park the
car.

"Let's call a truce while we have a drink,"
Grant suggested. "Then you can decide whether
you want me to take you home without any supper."

Terra was becoming angrier by the moment.
Who did he think he was, speaking to her as
though she were a ten-year-old. Even when she
had been a ten-year-old he hadn't spoken to her
like that. Suddenly she was taken by a strong
wave of nostalgia, a remembrance of the Grant
of her youth. An inexplicable sadness filled her

and momentarily blotted out her anger. She had
wanted to shout at him in defense; now she
wanted to cry. Wordlessly she followed him into
the lobby of the hotel. Despite her state of mind
her attention was drawn to the high ceiling and
its great chandelier.

The present hotel was the epitome of Victorian elegance and the successor of a grand hotel
that had become a symbol of luxury for the
whole world. Destroyed by fire after the earthquake of 1906, the magnificent old hotel was a
living memory of some San Franciscans, and
Terra noted with interest the beautifully framed
photographs of its courtyards and gardens.

As they walked through the spacious lobby
toward the bar, she peeked through a stately
arch at the hotel's well-known restaurant.
Starched white tablecloths and elegant place set-
tings beckoned through the curtain of greenery
that gave the restaurant an air of seclusion and
quiet.

They reached the bar, and as Grant held the
door for her, she preceded him into the darkened lounge. Inside Terra hesitated before going
farther, waiting for her eyes to adjust to the dim
light. Grant put his hand lightly on her elbow.
She felt like shaking it off, but of course she
couldn't be so impolite. He guided her toward a
booth at the far corner of the room. His hand
lingered, and through the fabric of her jacket
she could feel the strength of his fingers exerting
gentle pressure to steer her around chairs she

could not yet clearly see. As soon as they reached the booth she gave her arm the tiniest of jerks, and his hand fell away. Even in the dim light she detected the sidewise quirk of his lips. Apparently he found her anger quite amusing indeed! They slid into the booth, and Terra sat as close to the edge as possible, leaving plenty of space between them.

The waitress approached, and as Grant finished ordering their drinks he spotted a balding, middle-aged man standing at the entrance to the bar and peering in uncertainly. After telling the waitress they were being joined by a third person, he hurried over to greet the newcomer. The two men shook hands warmly and then spent several minutes in earnest conversation. Recognizing the other man as Mr. Forbush, president of the Bookman's Club, and remembering Grant's promise to recommend the lost edition to him, Terra thought Paul would be pleased if he had known Grant would be talking to Forbush so soon.

When they returned to the table Grant made the introductions. As Dan Forbush shook her hand he commented, "I usually don't remember faces, but it would be difficult to forget yours. We've met before, though I regret to say I don't recall your name."

Terra explained that she worked at Fosters' and that although they hadn't been introduced, she had seen him at the shop several times.

"You may also recognize Terra's name in

another regard, Dan,'' Grant interjected. ''She's Alexander Scott's daughter.''

Dan Forbush slid into the booth beside her and began to talk warmly about her father. The waitress returned for Forbush's order and brought their drinks. Conversation centered on the Bookman's Club. Terra gathered that Grant had reactivated his membership only a few weeks earlier, though she wondered what had motivated him to reestablish this old connection. Forbush was eager to fill Grant in on all the activities he had missed. Many of the names he mentioned were familiar to Terra, and the stories reminded her of those her father used to tell during his days as president. It was reassuring to know that some things, such as the club, didn't change.

Wedged in between the two men, Terra was extremely conscious of Grant's nearness. Although she wasn't actually touching him, an electric current seemed to leap between them, sensitizing her skin and making her quiver. She shifted her legs slightly, and as if responding to a magnet, his leg shifted, too, to rest solidly against hers. As he was talking, Grant changed position, so that his arm lay casually along the back of the leather booth, above Terra's head. This new position aligned his whole body closer to hers, almost cradling her in the curve of his uplifted arm.

Unwilling to move any closer to Dan Forbush, she found herself within a few inches of

Grant's solid chest. Grant leaned forward slightly to emphasize a point he was making to Dan, and Terra was afraid to budge lest her cheek touched his. She could almost feel his heart pounding and hoped he couldn't detect hers responding to his nearness in an erratic rhythm. All her attention was absorbed by the pressure of his body against her own, and she lost track of what was being said at the table.

With a metallic snap, a flicker of light broke in on Terra's hypnotic trance. "I should have asked if you'd like a cigarette," Forbush said, pausing in the middle of lighting his own with a silver lighter.

"No, thanks," Terra replied, forcing her mind to attend to the conversation. She realized Grant was talking about his visit to Fosters'.

"Paul showed me one of the pamphlets from the lost edition you're considering buying." Grant took a sip of his drink, using his free hand. The other one still rested lightly above Terra's head. "It's in mint condition, no sign of wear and tear."

"Ordinarily I'd be suspicious of 134-year-old pamphlets that showed no signs of use," Forbush remarked, "but since they belonged to the family of the printer, I imagine they were extra copies that were kept packed away all this time." Forbush took a short nervous drag on his cigarette, as though he were not as confident about matters as he pretended.

"Terra's in charge of the research on the

pamphlets," Grant commented. "Perhaps she can shed some light on why they're in such good shape."

For a second Terra thought she had stumbled onto the real reason Grant had insisted on her company. It seemed too coincidental that Forbush was one of the most interested prospective buyers of the lost edition. But then, she reflected, Grant had been planning to meet Forbush before he had seen her, so the whole thing couldn't have been engineered just to give Forbush the opportunity to question her.

"You've hit on the explanation, Mr. Forbush," Terra replied. "According to Paul, Miss Waltham kept her family's books and papers around her for sentimental reasons, but she rarely looked at them. Paul said that when he found the pamphlets the box looked as though it hadn't been opened in years."

Forbush gazed at her thoughtfully. "Paul showed me the lab reports verifying the possibility of the 1848 date. You agree with the verification, don't you, Miss Scott?"

Terra felt as though she were being drilled, but if Mr. Forbush was contemplating paying a huge price for one of the pamphlets, it was only natural for him to question Fosters' chief researcher. She avoided a direct reply. "The experts we've consulted are at the top of their field." She turned to Grant. "You looked at all my notes today," she challenged, "what's your opinion?"

"As you've said before, Terra, all those experts can't be wrong," he replied smoothly. The glint in his eyes told her he was very much aware she had intended to put him on the spot. Without changing the position of his upper body, he moved his thigh squarely against hers, and Terra knew he was enjoying her discomfort.

She wished she had the nerve to reach under the table and give him a good pinch. Instead she discreetly pulled away, even though that meant holding her breath so she didn't touch Mr. Forbush. *Really,* she thought, *this is too ridiculous.* Feeling her move, Grant shifted, too. One more move and Forbush was going to pop out of the booth and onto the floor. The thought somewhat lessened Terra's anger at Grant. He was obviously playing a game, so she gave up fighting and pretended to ignore the contact under the table.

"I must admit I'm seriously considering buying one of the booklets." Forbush drained the last of his Scotch. "The price is steep, though," he said thoughtfully. "I'll be looking forward to seeing your brochure when it's finished, Terra."

Terra nodded wordlessly.

They talked a little longer, then left the bar. In the lobby Forbush shook hands with both of them, told Grant he would be in touch and said goodbye. When he had gone Grant looked at Terra quizzically.

"Do we have dinner at the Gardens, or shall I take you home?"

Terra was stunned. The Gardens was an institution in the city. Its clientele could be divided into two categories: those who came for the elegant atmosphere and superb cuisine and those who were willing to pay the high prices in order to be able to watch the Gardens' regular diners. In the last group belonged the newspaper reporters, whose gossip columns often included the phrase "seen at the Gardens last night...." Terra's desire to take a closer look at the restaurant into which she had peeked earlier was intense. It seemed a shame to pass up the opportunity to have dinner there when she was so close, but a twinge of hesitation held her back.

The Gardens was not a place to go for a quick meal; nor was it the place to go when one wished to be unnoticed. If Grant had wanted to advertise he was in pursuit of someone new, he couldn't have chosen a better spot. See and be seen.

He was waiting for her decision. On an impulse Terra let the excitement of being in such famous surroundings carry her along. She nodded her consent.

They walked through the archway and into the crowded waiting area. As soon as they entered the maître d' spotted them and beckoned them forward.

"Right this way, Mr. Ingraham."

Terra wondered briefly whether Grant had called ahead. Surely he wouldn't get this kind of service if he had just dropped in.

As they made their way through the dining room, Terra noticed that many of the other diners, particularly the women, were staring at them intently. Were they feeling sorry for her, thinking that Grant had made yet another conquest?

Too proud to let them pity her, she met their gazes straight on. And then she realized they were neither censuring nor disdainful—they were blatantly envious.

The waiter led them to a side table that was partially shielded from the rest of the dining room by a beautiful fig tree. The brilliant green of its delicate leaves was intensified by a well-placed spotlight. Half hidden by plants, the table had a deceptive air of privacy.

After they were seated, Terra understood why the numerous plants were all growing so well. Above them the roof of the restaurant was glass. Outside Terra could see the sky darkening into night and could begin to distinguish the image of the diners reflected off the panes. One by one the candles on the table were being lighted as the waiters made their rounds. And as each tiny flame sprang into life on the table, its counterpart on the ceiling flickered in harmony.

The maître d' approached again and, with a ceremonial flourish, whisked Terra's napkin from the table and placed it on her lap.

As he did the same for Grant, he kept up a steady stream of friendly chatter and then handed them a bulky leather-bound menu printed in

French. Terra had studied French in high school; however, she owed her ability to understand the menu not to her schooling but to her love of gourmet cooking.

Reading through the pages of selections, she could not restrain her delight at the number of unusual dishes. The explanations included a detailed description of the sauces, spices and wines. "Just glancing over the menu is an education," she exclaimed to Grant. "I can't wait to try out some of these ideas in my own dishes."

"You must like to cook. Seems to me I remember batches of fudge and brownies in the old days." Grant winced dramatically as though he still had the taste of some of those efforts in his mouth. But as he put down the menu he smiled at her, and in spite of herself Terra smiled back.

"Times change," she said, unable to suppress a hint of sadness. "But what could you expect from a ten-year-old who was just learning? It was nice of you to suffer so in the cause of encouraging a budding cook, but I don't think you'd find my cooking as difficult to take these days. I grow and dry my own herbs. And I've just learned to mix a curry powder that doesn't knock your head off. I think I've come a long way from brownies and fudge."

Grant's eyes drifted lazily down from hers in a blatant gaze that acknowledged and obviously admired her change from girl to woman. "Yes,

I'd say you have come a long way," he drawled, and the mood that had been nostalgic suddenly became electric.

Terra turned her head abruptly and stared out into the dining room. Grant's habit of interjecting sexual overtones at the most unexpected moments unnerved her. She was quite experienced at discouraging unwanted familiarity with impersonal banter, but she couldn't call Grant's behavior flirting, at least not of the kind she knew about. He wasn't teasing or baiting. His frank appraising looks seemed to come from a natural and genuine sexuality, part of the same alive awareness that was evident in all his actions. He was a very vital man, and that vitality was hard to resist. Well, she had every intention of resisting him, no matter how attractive he was.

"Terra?"

She turned toward him.

"Terra...." He reached out and took her hand. "You're a beautiful young woman with a beautiful body. You don't need to be embarrassed by my appreciation of you."

"I'm not embarrassed, just bored," she lied. She pulled her hand away. "I don't see why two people can't have dinner together without sex becoming involved."

Grant's eyes narrowed. "Whenever two people include one man and one woman, sex is involved," he said.

Before Terra could offer a retort the waiter

appeared, and Grant gave him their orders. Terra tried to shake off her annoyance. Grant was certainly living up to everything she had heard about him, and she just wanted to get through dinner and get home.

Their drinks arrived, and Grant raised his in a toast. "To a continuation of our truce?" He raised his eyebrows.

Terra reluctantly smiled and raised her glass. "All right," she said, "to our truce."

"And to our renewed friendship?" he added.

She nodded, though she wondered what sort of future their so-called friendship could possibly have.

"How long have you worked at Fosters'?" Grant asked. It was a deliberate shift into neutral territory, and Terra appreciated the change of topic.

"I've been there about three and a half years," she said. "When dad got sick I had just finished university. I had hoped to do some graduate work, but the way things turned out I was lucky to find a way to support myself."

"You must have worked for Paul's father, William, before he died," Grant commented.

"He's the reason I applied for the researcher's job. He and dad had been friends for years, and dad thought that working for William would be an opportunity to learn about books— and about the business—from an expert. We had talked about it for quite some time, even before I was ready to take a job."

"And did you learn from William?"

"Oh, yes. The two years I spent with William Foster were probably the best training I could have got. He was so thorough and so meticulous about verifying everything."

"And how about working under Paul?"

"Well, it's different." Terra paused.

"In what way?" Grant looked at her questioningly.

As Terra was struggling to put her feelings about Paul into words, the waiter appeared to ask if they wanted another drink. Grant said no without consulting Terra, then narrowed his attention on her again. "In what way?" he repeated.

The insistent note in his voice made her hesitate. His questions seemed to go a little beyond normal conversational interest. Perhaps she should be a bit more cautious in her replies. She had no idea how well he knew Paul, and she certainly didn't want him repeating anything that might sound disloyal.

"For one thing he's younger," Terra joked flirtatiously. She was surprised to see a flicker of displeasure cross Grant's face.

"Surely you don't have hopes in that direction," he remarked with evident disapproval.

"If I did it wouldn't do any good." Terra laughed. "Paul's taken. He and Stephanie Duke are considered inseparable."

"Are you a friend of Stephanie's?" Grant asked.

Terra smiled. "She's a little out of my league. She isn't even aware I exist. But I know who she is because she comes to the shop to pick up Paul. She doesn't seem much interested in books, though. She seldom comes in."

Grant looked thoughtful all of a sudden, and there was a strained silence at the table. Terra searched for a question to fill the void. "You must know Stephanie, then?" she asked.

Grant shook off his introspection and chuckled. "Yes, I think you could say that. Her parents are giving the party we're going to tonight."

Again Terra felt faintly uncomfortable. She really didn't want to go with Grant to this party, where she was sure to be out of place, but she was reluctant to protest again.

"You've risen to a very responsible position pretty rapidly," Grant observed. "You must enjoy working in the rare-book field."

"It's fascinating," Terra replied enthusiastically, momentarily forgetting all else. "The value of a book depends on so many different things—its age, the reputation of its author, how many other copies are still in existence and all the details of its printing history. It's like a gigantic jigsaw puzzle that has to be fitted together. Sometimes when you've fitted together those pieces you end up with nothing very special at all. Yet the challenge is that sometimes you come up with a real gem."

Grant smiled at the eagerness with which she

spoke. "Ever think you might like to open your own bookshop?" he queried.

"Perhaps I might consider the idea in the future, but for now I'm happy to let someone else handle the business end of it. I like researching a book's history, distinguishing a first edition from later editions and writing up all the information for brochures, lists and catalogs."

"The book trade certainly needs knowledgeable researchers, whether they work in libraries or bookshops. Collectors sometimes get carried away in their enthusiasm to own something rare, and they aren't always as skeptical as they should be."

"Well," Terra said thoughtfully, "a book is an object as well as an investment. Sometimes it's an irresistibly beautiful object. I think collectors can be forgiven if their sense of beauty occasionally interferes with their sense of the financial value of things—or even with the historical value of things."

"Nicely put," Grant said with admiration. "But if collectors were more cautious, forgers would have a tougher time. With tests for dating papers and inks and sophisticated ways of comparing typefaces, it's almost impossible to pass off a work printed in modern times as an old book." He paused for a moment. "I would think these scientific methods almost guarantee that Paul's edition is genuine."

"They should." Terra sighed. "That's what has me going round and round. Technically there's almost no way they can be forgeries, and yet...."

Grant took a sip of his Scotch and waited. When she didn't continue he prodded softly. "And yet...?"

Terra hesitated. The sky was completely dark now, and the interior of the restaurant was reflected on the glass roof with startling clarity. The pinpoints of candlelight seemed like so many brilliant stars interspersed among the diners in the sky.

On their table the candle cast a glowing arc of light that encompassed them both. Opposite her, Grant appeared so solid, so trustworthy, she could not imagine any harm coming from asking his advice.

"I have only intuition to go on," she began, "but it just doesn't make sense to me that Robert Waltham would keep copies of those sonnets all wrapped up and never try to sell them. They were worth a lot, even when he was alive, and although he wasn't poor, I'm sure he could have used the money."

"I see your point, Terra, but that certainly doesn't constitute proof you're dealing with the work of a forger."

"I know that!" Terra had expected a more sensitive response to her suspicions. After all, he had pried them out of her. "But I still feel that if I just keep digging, I'll turn up something more. Only I'm running out of time," she admitted ruefully.

The waiter returned and placed a beautifully decorated plate before her. She looked at the perfectly browned lamb chops as though she had forgotten ever having ordered them, so intent had she been on her conversation with Grant. But she was hungry, and the appetizing aroma wafting up from the dish made her mouth water. Grant smiled at her. "Dig in," he said, and the pleasantly casual comment brought back memories of him seated at her father's table.

A steward appeared with wine and poured a small portion into Grant's glass. Without pretention he swirled the liquid, sniffed it and took a sip. "Excellent as usual, Gaston," he said to the man, who smiled appreciatively and then proceeded to fill Terra's glass.

For a while they ate in silence, but Terra, unable to forget the problem plaguing her, returned to the subject of the pamphlets.

"I still feel I need more facts," she said. "I wish I had been able to get into the Blansford. You were right this afternoon," she acknowledged apologetically. "I do need to check that collection. I guess I was touchy about it because I'm having trouble getting in."

"And Paul hasn't been able to arrange an appointment for you?"

Terra answered with hesitation. She had tried to convince Paul of the necessity of her visiting the Blansford in person, but he simply would not listen. Not wanting to reveal any more about Paul than she had to, she stated simply, "As I told you, he's done quite a bit by bringing in the work log and checking the collection for me."

When Grant said nothing she added, "I don't think he can do any more. That library is just very fussy about how its material is used and by whom."

Grant refilled her glass, looking at her reflectively. "You'll have to finish the catalog soon, or Paul will assign it to someone under you."

"I know that, and believe me, I plan to spend all weekend on it. It's difficult to work with full confidence when I have reservations about what I have to say, but I'm determined to come up with something Paul can use, no matter how many hours it takes."

She meant what she said. If she had followed her original plan, she'd be at home at that very moment doing the work, though she couldn't really be sorry she had ended up going out with Grant.

In a momentary lull in the conversation the strains from a harp drifted to her ears. The music mingled with the delicate tinkle of fine crystal glasses and elegant china plates. The barely audible steps of the waiters as they crossed the thick carpet was so relaxing a sound that Terra was, for an instant, tempted to forget all about work—and all about her determination to keep Grant at a distance. The good food, the wine, the lush and comforting ambience of the restaurant all conspired to transport her into another world.

"Are you enjoying the wine?" Grant asked, looking at her with a slight smile of amusement.

"Very much," she replied. "I'm not a connoisseur, but it's lovely."

Grant nodded. "I like to experiment with wines—the way, I imagine, you must do with cooking. But I keep coming back to this one because it's hard to ignore such a fine old friend."

On the word *friend* he reached across the table and gently took her hand. Somehow Terra could not find the energy to pull away this time.

"And speaking of old friends, Terra," he said softly, "now that I've found you again I don't think I'm going to lose track of you...."

He stroked the back of her hand with a sensuous motion that was not deliberately provocative, though Terra thought she could feel it right down to the soles of her feet. The candlelight played softly over his face, emphasizing the depth of his dark eyes and causing her to wonder how she could ever have considered them remote.

"Grant Ingraham!" A high voice shattered the intimacy of the moment, and Terra pulled her hand away quickly. "I had no idea you'd be here. How lucky to run into you!"

Terra looked up to see a tall, elegantly slim woman approach. Her striking red hair was pulled into a tight knot on one side and the sweep of its strands across her forehead played up the porcelain perfection of her skin. She had startling green eyes...eyes now trained directly on Grant.

"Hello, Stephanie," Grant said evenly as he rose and bent his cheek to receive the kiss she was so obviously eager to give. "Paul," he reached behind Stephanie to shake Paul's hand. "Seems as though we just left you. Terra, this is Stephanie Duke. Perhaps you've met?"

Terra put out her hand in response to Grant's introduction, but the redhead seemed not to notice. She merely nodded at Grant's words without taking her eyes off him.

"Please, sit down," Paul urged. "We can only stay for a minute."

It occurred to Terra that Paul might have seen Grant's hand covering her own, and she was momentarily embarrassed. He was not above mentioning such a thing at the office on Monday. Grant caught the worried look she had directed toward Paul, and again that flicker of disapproval marred his expression. Without speaking to Terra he turned to Stephanie. "I'm surprised to see you here," he said. "Shouldn't you be at home helping your mother prepare for this evening?"

"Too much hustle and bustle for me," Stephanie replied airily. She smoothed her already flawless hair as though pushing it back into place. Her perfectly manicured hands sported dark nail polish that made her fingers look slender and white. "We plan to show up after the party gets going, when the work's all done. You're coming, aren't you, Grant?" She smiled appealingly at him, still ignoring Terra.

"Don't worry," he answered. "We'll be there."

From the other woman's half-concealed pout Terra was certain this was not the response Stephanie wanted.

"Mother will be furious if she doesn't get to have a nice long talk with you. She was saying just yesterday that it seems like an awfully long time since we saw you last. Why don't you spend next weekend with us? Mother would be thrilled."

Terra glanced toward Paul to see his reaction to the warmth Stephanie was demonstrating toward Grant, but Paul revealed no emotion. He seemed content to stand in the background, waiting for Stephanie to finish what she had to say.

"Thanks for the invitation," Grant replied. "Unfortunately my plans are pretty well set now. I'll call your mother if they change."

Stephanie frowned, but before she could reply Grant continued. "I'm collecting books again, and that's taking most of my free time."

This announcement brought Paul to life, and he hastily assured Grant that Terra—and everyone else at Fosters'—would be at his disposal to help him expand his collection.

At this little speech Stephanie snapped her

fingers in sudden recognition. "Now I remember you," she said to Terra. "You're a clerk in Paul's shop, aren't you?"

Terra flushed at the condescension in the other woman's voice, but rather than argue with her about titles she simply stated, "I work for Paul, yes."

"Well, darling—" Stephanie turned to Grant "—if it's advice about rare books you want, you're always welcome at my grandfather's. If it's something else you're looking for—" her glance swept over Terra haughtily "—you know where you can get the best of that, too."

Terra was appalled at the vulgarity of the statement, but Grant appeared completely unmoved by Stephanie's coarse remark. He calmly replied, "Thank you, Stephanie, I'll be sure to remember."

Paul, however, seemed at last to realize the awkwardness of the situation. He put his hand on Stephanie's arm. "I think we'd better be going, love. The party's just starting, so we're going to be nearly an hour late as it is."

Stephanie threw an annoyed glance at Paul and then quickly gave Grant a teasing kiss. "See you later," she whispered, and without a glance at Terra turned and left.

"Now you've met the closest thing I have to a sister," Grant commented with a little smile. "Stephanie and I practically grew up together, and she still feels she should look out for me."

Sister, my foot! Terra thought with

annoyance. An old friendship might pass for an excuse for Stephanie's predatory behavior toward Grant, but Terra wasn't that easy to fool. She couldn't understand how Stephanie could have the nerve to pursue him so openly in the presence of Paul, when it was obvious Stephanie wanted Grant to herself—at least for tonight. She had made it abundantly clear she resented Terra's presence—all the more reason why Terra didn't belong at the Dukes' party. For one brief moment she had allowed herself to be swept into Grant's glittering world, but Stephanie's treatment of her reminded her she would always be a stranger there. Grant's domain was not her own. Times change. The truth of the matter was sure to be evident to him very quickly—if it wasn't evident already.

CHAPTER THREE

TERRA LEANED BACK against the cool leather upholstery. As the car left the downtown area and hurtled around the concrete skyway that led to the Bay Bridge, she realized they were leaving the city and heading for Berkeley.

She smiled to herself. The encounter with Stephanie had been uncomfortable, but at least it had shown Grant he should go to the party alone. She was sorry he had to drive all the way across the bay to chauffeur her home and then drive back to San Francisco for the party, but she had offered to take the bus. If he preferred an hour and a half's drive to accepting one of her suggestions, she was quite content to ride home in comfort. But she couldn't resist commenting on his change of heart.

"I see you're taking me home before the party. I'm glad Stephanie could persuade you to listen to reason, even if I couldn't."

"Jealous of Stephanie?" The corners of Grant's mouth turned up in a quick wry smile.

Terra was indignant, but she kept her tone very cool. "I see no reason why I should be jealous of Stephanie. I find her flirtatious behavior surprising in a person of such obvious breeding, but it's none of my concern. I'm just grateful to her for showing you I don't belong at that party.''

"What makes you think I've changed my mind about taking you with me? We're both going, although we won't stay long.''

"But we're on our way to my house in Berkeley,'' Terra protested. "Don't the Dukes live in San Francisco or somewhere in Marin County?''

"Jumping to conclusions is a bad habit, Terra,'' Grant teased. "It could get you into a lot of trouble. The Dukes live in the Berkeley Hills, only about ten minutes' drive from you.''

They were now crossing the suspension bridge that extended its long graceful arc from San Francisco to Yerba Buena Island. Traffic bound for Berkeley used the lower deck, so Terra could see very little of the lights across the bay or of the massive system of cables and girders that supported the bridge.

"Most people take the Bay Bridge for granted,'' Grant commented, "but when it was first proposed in the early thirties it was extremely controversial. Lots of experts said the swift tides and the soft bottom made any bridge an impossibility.''

"I'm glad there was someone who didn't believe them.'' Terra laughed. "I can't imagine not being able to zip back and forth between Berkeley and San Francisco whenever I want.''

They passed through the tunnel on Yerba
Buena Island and continued onto the eastern section of the bridge. Although the Mercedes was
quite roomy, Grant's size made the car seem
tiny. Terra's shoulder was separated from his by
only an inch or two, and when he swung the car
into another lane or around a curve, their shoulders brushed. She found herself abnormally sensitive to his every move. He reminded her of a
sleek graceful animal, confident and powerful.

Again she went over in her mind the things
she knew about what he had become in the years
since she had seen him last. Not only had he
taken over his father's business and catapulted
it to international success, but he had other interests, as well. According to rumor, he had a
hideaway up north, in Washington State or
Oregon. A little love nest secluded in the woods,
Margaret guessed. But Terra had heard from
another source that the "hideaway" was actually a fully operational lumber ranch that he ran
"as a hobby." He was also on the boards of
several charitable organizations—Terra had
seen his name on the letterheads of circulars that
had come for her father. And then, of course,
there was his reputation as a playboy to consider. Quite the full life. *The man must be a
machine,* Terra speculated. Machine? Animal?
She was mixing her metaphors. She laughed
softly to herself.

"Want to share the joke with me?" Grant
queried.

Blushing, she tried to hide her confusion at being caught out in her private ruminations. "It wasn't a joke, really," she said.

"Share it with me anyway," Grant insisted.

Terra had composed her thoughts somewhat, and she replied glibly, "I was just wondering whether people are animals or machines, and I was laughing at the absurdity of the idea of being both."

"People," Grant questioned, "or me?"

She wanted to groan. How was it he seemed so able to read her mind?

"Not you in particular," she fibbed, "just people in general."

"And what's your conclusion about me?" he asked, ignoring her denial that she had been thinking of him. "Am I a machine or an animal?"

Realizing she was in too deeply to back out now, Terra decided to take the offensive.

"Which do you consider yourself?"

"If you're limiting me to just those choices, I'd say a little of each."

"No, you can't have it both ways." Terra laughed. "Either you're a machine that gets things done efficiently, doesn't make mistakes and doesn't get tangled up in emotion, or...." She paused for breath, really enjoying herself now. "Or," she continued, "you're an animal that acts by instinct alone."

As soon as the words were out of her mouth she regretted them. She hoped he wouldn't read a sexual implication into that last remark, but his mocking smile assured her that indeed he had not missed the connection.

"Why don't we save that question for later on tonight? Then you can tell me whether I act by instinct alone."

Terra let out a sigh. She didn't want to give him the satisfaction of knowing he had aroused her pique once again.

"Actually, your question touches on an interesting problem." His voice had resumed an emotionless timbre. "Some people believe man can be a totally rational being all the time. They deny his instincts completely—a mistake that often has disastrous consequences."

Terra listened without comment.

"It makes much more sense to acknowledge both aspects of the nature of man and work toward keeping each in its proper place. I don't want a lawyer giving me an opinion based on instinct, and I certainly don't want a love affair founded only on logic."

"But isn't there more involved than just reason and instinct?" Terra protested. "What about emotion and love?"

For a moment Grant was silent, as though he were carefully thinking about what to say next. His expression was serious and thoughtful. But then the mocking smile returned to light his face, and he quipped, "*Love* and *emotion* are nothing but fancy words for animal instinct, don't you think?"

His grin made Terra wonder whether he were joking, but knowing his reputation, she concluded he believed what he said.

"No," she replied earnestly, "love is something completely different from sex. Love involves commitment, sharing, passion. It's more than just coupling."

"If you don't think that animal instinct, or sex as you call it, involves passion, then I'd say your education has been sadly neglected."

Ignoring the fact that her education—whatever that meant—was none of his business, Terra continued seriously, "There's passion and there's passion. I'm talking about the kind that comes with caring, with committed binding love."

Grant's face was grave. "Love doesn't bind," was all he commented, and Terra wasn't sure she knew what he had in mind. She thought he would explain, but instead the corners of his eyes crinkled in amusement and he teasingly said, "Well, Terra, we can always do a little research. You know how you love research. We can put your theories to a scientific test."

"Oh, come on," Terra groaned, "I thought we were having a serious conversation."

"I am serious," he protested. "Your theories sound like fine intellectual ideas that haven't been tested by experience. I think I can offer plenty of evidence that sincere passion between a man and a woman doesn't need chains like the sanction of a marriage license or even a lasting friendship to be satisfying and valuable.''

"I don't need your kind of evidence," she flashed indignantly. "The kind of passion you're talking about isn't love or anything like it. You're talking about hedonism, pleasure for the moment for the pure sake of pleasure. It sounds as if you're the one who's lacking in experience—the experience of love that's worth hanging on to, that makes passion more than mere pleasure."

"Maybe you're right. Maybe I do lack that experience," Grant said, a note of anger in his voice. He fell silent, and Terra was sure the conversation was at an end. She hadn't intended to become so personal in her argument, but he had started it.

They came to the end of the bridge, and Grant guided the car deftly through the complex interchange before heading down the freeway to the University Avenue exit.

"Pleasure isn't a crime, Terra." His voice was barely audible in the darkness. "If two people are attracted to each other and both agree, pleasure can be an all-consuming experience, and no one gets hurt."

"Consenting adults, isn't that what it's called?" Terra shivered slightly and pulled her jacket tighter around her. "Well, pardon me if I pass that one up. For what it's worth, I'm the old-fashioned type. I still believe in commitment, in love for life. Sounds corny, I know," she said with false flippancy, "quite out of style in your crowd."

When he didn't respond, she continued. "Anyway, what happens when one of the consenting adults wants a commitment and the other doesn't? Then someone does get hurt."

"If the conditions are clear from the beginning, then each person should know what to expect. You can't blame one partner if the other one decides to change the rules and then calls foul."

"I most certainly can—if the rules include no falling in love. That's something that can't be controlled."

"Another theory?" Grant asked skeptically.

"One that's been very well tested throughout history, I'd say." Terra looked at him, an intense frown wrinkling her forehead.

Grant's sudden laughter broke the tension. "We'll need to get you a soapbox," he teased. "But before you go nationwide with your campaign I'd suggest you get some real-life experience to back up your theories."

They had left the flat land and were now winding into the hills of one of Berkeley's oldest and most fashionable neighborhoods. They pulled into a narrow lane, and Terra was surprised at the number of cars that lined the street in both directions. When Grant maneuvered the car into a parking space between a blue Mercedes and a deep black Rolls-Royce, she realized they had reached their destination.

"Quite a crowd," Grant commented.

"You mean all these cars are because of the party?" she exclaimed. She looked down the street and saw several couples walking toward a large wooden house she assumed must belong to the Dukes. The house could only be described as imposing, and to Terra's dismay, the approaching women were wearing long gowns and elegant evening wraps.

"Grant, I still don't think it's wise for me to come to this party. After all, I wasn't actually invited...."

"Of course you should come. I was invited and I invited you." He got out of the car, held the door for her and then steered her down the street.

Terra kept quiet for a while, but as they neared the Dukes' driveway she tried again. "I had the impression from what you said that this was a casual get-together. I don't think I'm appropriately dressed for a formal party." She glanced down involuntarily at her sky-blue suit. It was attractive, but it was quite clearly not designed for an occasion such as this.

"Of course you're appropriately dressed," Grant answered patiently. "You couldn't look more lovely." He gave her a quizzical look. "Somehow I didn't think you were the type to be easily intimidated."

"Nothing you or your friends could do would intimidate me," she flared, angry he had mistaken reluctance to go where she was not welcome for feelings of inferiority.

"I was just trying to save you some possible embarrassment," she went on, ignoring his amused smile.

"Nothing you or your friends could do would embarrass me," he mocked.

"That's not what I meant at all," she retorted, thoroughly exasperated at his failure to see the awkwardness of her position. This party was clearly a formal affair, the host and hostess had no idea she was coming, her business suit was chic but could not qualify as a party dress and the hostess's daughter didn't want her there. *Adds up to a real fun evening,* she thought. It was difficult to see how this could be anything but a complete disaster.

But she offered no further protest as they arrived at the massive front door. Grant rang the bell, and his summons was answered by a dignified butler in stately black livery. Glancing past him, Terra could see an elegant vestibule with gilt-framed mirrors and a crystal chandelier. Beyond that she caught a glimpse of the glittering guests. The attendant offered a very small smile to Grant, as though he knew him and, bowing almost imperceptibly, motioned them toward the main room.

Standing at the edge of the crowd, Grant gave Terra's hand a squeeze and whispered, "Stick with me, kid, and you'll be fine." She would have been angry had she not been grateful, for the sight of the crowd scared her in spite of herself.

A slim, gray-haired woman in an evening gown of pale blue silk noticed them and came toward Grant, extending her diamond-bedecked hand in greeting. "Grant," she exclaimed as she took his hand enthusiastically, "Stephanie told us she was with you and Paul at the Gardens. If it had been anyone else, I would have scolded her for breezing in forty-five minutes after the party started."

"You'll have to give Paul credit for taking Stephanie out to dinner, Elaine." Grant smiled as he hugged his mother's friend. "Stephanie caught sight of us just as she was leaving, and we chatted for a few minutes. I'd like you to meet Terra Scott."

Elaine Duke looked slightly confused, as though the two accounts she had heard of the meeting did not completely agree, but she recovered quickly and greeted Terra warmly.

After a few moments of polite conversation Mrs. Duke said, "I hope we'll have a chance to really talk later on tonight, Grant, but if we don't, Stephanie mentioned you would be spending next weekend with us."

Grant took her hand affectionately. "I told Stephanie I had already made other plans but that I'd call you if they changed. And I promise we'll get together sometime soon."

Once again Terra had the uneasy feeling Elaine Duke had expected a different reply.

By this time others had noticed Grant, and he was besieged with greetings. He moved among these sophisticated people with ease and comfortable familiarity—as if he were quite at home. He had never been awkward as far as Terra could recall, so she shouldn't have been surprised at his social grace. *Perhaps,* she thought, *surprised is the wrong word. Impressed would be more like it.* Yet she didn't see why she should let herself be impressed by anything so superficial as mere good manners. Grant was polished, urbane—he was a man of the world. And Terra knew it was only natural for a person in his position to be skilled in social relations. She wondered whether he was nearly so adept at personal relations. Judging from their conversation, she decided he probably was—in the same slick manner, of course.

True to his word, Grant tried to put her at ease by introducing her to stranger after stranger, but Terra could see these old friends—most of whom seemed to be women—were totally uninterested in his present companion.

At first she made a conscientious effort to associate names with faces and to follow the conversation, but she soon realized the effort was wasted. After perfunctorily acknowledging Grant's introduction, each person resumed talking to him. Almost no one spoke to Terra, so she just stood silently at his side, moving when he moved and flashing an automatic smile whenever she heard her name.

"Terra, this is Dr. Duke, Stephanie's father." An affable-looking older gentleman standing next to Grant reached across and shook Terra's hand cordially. She would never have been able to guess that Stephanie was his daughter. His easygoing smile was as warm as her disdainful expression had been cold.

Grant moved on to talk to another group of people, and Dr. Duke stepped closer to Terra. His worn tweed jacket, conspicuous among the dark suits of the other men, smelled of tobacco. It was a warm night for such a jacket, but Terra thought that perhaps it served Dr. Duke as some sort of uniform, without which he could not feel comfortable. Puffing occasionally at his brier pipe, he didn't seem to fit among the elegant guests milling about restlessly in his home.

"I understand you're in rare books," he commented in a friendly tone.

Thankful to have someone to talk to, Terra told him where she worked and what her job was.

"So you're the one who's been doing all the detective work on the Browning booklet," he beamed. "Paul has given us a blow-by-blow account of how you actually proved the pamphlets were genuine. It sounds like an excellent piece of scholarship."

Slightly uncomfortable at what she considered premature praise, Terra murmured a noncommittal response.

"I don't mind telling you it was a great relief

to me to hear you had conclusive proof of their authenticity," he continued. "Those pamphlets have become extremely important to our family, what with Stephanie's connection with Paul. Naturally we wanted to be as certain as possible they are genuine."

Terra wasn't at all sure what he meant, and her puzzlement must have been clearly written on her face. Dr. Duke elucidated. "Our family, or more correctly my wife's father, has a fine collection specializing in nineteenth-century works. I just assumed that working for Paul you knew about us. You might say we'll be sponsoring the pamphlet—exhibiting it, including it in our own catalog and so forth. Stephanie's influence with her grandfather is rather strong, and she's very supportive of Paul...." He paused. "Since the discovery of so many copies of such a rare work is unusual, to say the least, I am very relieved to hear they're genuine."

Terra was becoming more and more uneasy. She seemed to be meeting an extraordinary number of people who had a stake in the lost edition and were convinced she endorsed it. Again she wondered whether Grant's attentiveness to her was motivated by his interest—and the interest of his close friends—in the work she was doing. When that thought had occurred to her earlier in the evening she had scotched it quickly, but now it was not so easily dismissed. She wondered why she cared.

Eager to move the discussion away from the

lost edition, Terra fished for something else to talk about. "What is your special area of collecting?" she asked Dr. Duke.

"My own poor efforts have yielded nothing as magnificent as the collection of Stephanie's grandfather, you can be sure. My teaching responsibilities at the medical school keep me too busy to leave much time for systematic book collecting." Dr. Duke knocked his pipe against the side of a glass ashtray. "Since knowing Paul, I've bought the occasional facsimile edition."

Terra was not surprised; Paul spent quite a bit of effort cultivating an interest in the collection of facsimiles, and it was only logical he should have tried to convert Dr. Duke.

Facsimiles—exact copies of rare editions—often appealed to busy people who did not want the involvement of an expensive authenticated collection but who loved beautiful books. Since these editions imitated the originals right down to style of type, they were quite satisfying to collectors whose major concern was beauty and not genuine rarity. The facsimile edition of the Gutenberg Bible was one of Fosters' best sellers.

"Ray." Mrs. Duke appeared at her husband's elbow. "I'm sorry to interrupt you, dear, but I need your help."

Nodding cordially to Terra, Dr. Duke followed his wife out of the room. Alone once more, Terra looked for Grant and discovered him immediately at the center of a circle of women. Amid the sea of faces that swirled around him she saw only one familiar person. Stephanie was clinging to Grant's arm, and the two of them seemed to form a constant center in a shifting vortex of people. While Terra watched, Stephanie offered Grant a glass of wine and softly caressed his hand as he took it from her. Terra wondered where Paul was. Surely he could not ignore this obvious display of Stephanie's interest in Grant.

Searching the room, she finally located Paul. He was talking and gesturing in an animated fashion, surrounded by a group of affluent-looking men.

How typical of Paul to use a social occasion to cultivate prospective customers, Terra thought, *but this time his behavior is likely to cost him his girl friend.* She had no doubt that if Grant gave Stephanie the least bit of encouragement, Paul's cause was lost. Not that it mattered to her. She shrugged. Being involved with Grant was a dangerous business, and she felt she would actually be relieved if Stephanie triumphed tonight, even though any such conquest of Grant was bound to be temporary.

She was suddenly aware of the stifling atmosphere in the room. Smoke hung hazily around people's heads, and the air didn't seem to be moving at all. Several flashbulbs went off nearby and when she blinked to clear the afterimages from her eyes she felt dizzy. She elbowed her way to Grant's side and, leaning toward him, whispered in a soft voice, "I need some fresh air." From the way he inclined his head she felt sure he had heard her, although he did not respond to her remark. She spotted a refreshment table by the double doors at the far end of the room and threaded her way toward it.

As she stood sipping her grapefruit juice in the welcome breeze, Paul came up to the table for a refill of his wineglass. Spotting Terra, he paused on his way back to his companions.

"I see you're getting along pretty well with Grant," he commented. Terra thought his smile was almost a leer, and she shifted uncomforably beneath his gaze. "I hope he convinced you you've got enough material to write the brochure."

Earlier in the day Terra would have answered with an honest negative, explaining that her position had not changed. But now she felt so confused by the events of the afternoon and evening she wanted time to think things out before she made any more statements about the lost edition to anyone.

"He was very helpful in sorting out the issues, Paul. I'm certain I'll have something for you by next week," she responded.

"You damn well better have," he muttered, and rested his hand heavily on her shoulder. "Any later than that and the printer won't be able to guarantee delivery in time for the book-fair." His fingers were now digging into her shoulder. As she tried to ease out from under his grasp Terra realized he had had too much to drink.

Paul let his hand fall, but he leaned closer to her. "Be nice to Grant," he whispered. "He's got a lot of contacts. Don't mess this one up for me, Terra, I'm warning you." He swung into an upright position with a lurch and moved on. Terra looked after him in disgust. It was becoming increasingly evident to her that Paul was a very mercenary man. All he seemed to care about was getting money; the ethics of matters didn't appear to interest him at all.

A gust of wind swept invitingly through the open door, and she stepped onto the patio for a stroll, wanting to clear her head. Outside she took a breath of the invigorating night air. As she glanced back through the doors to the living room, she could see Grant and a coterie of beautiful women framed in the brightly lit interior. Remembering that Grant admitted he saw nothing wrong with casual affairs, Terra wondered how many of these women had been intimately acquainted with him. Several of them were behaving in a very provocative way, but whether they were deliberately trying to attract his attention or whether they were responding instinctively to his own sexuality she couldn't tell. Nor was she interested, she reminded herself.

She couldn't deny that Grant had a galvanizing effect on her, too. The difference between her and those other women was that she understood his charm for what it was—pure animal magnetism. She didn't assign any significance to it whatsoever, and she realized that allowing herself to respond to it would be to court disaster. For a moment she stopped to lean against an ivy-covered pillar, her hands behind her and her eyes directed toward the starry sky.

"Lost in your dreams?"

The unfamiliar male voice close to her ear caused her to start and stand upright away from the pillar.

"I'm sorry. I didn't mean to frighten you, but you looked so ethereal I had to find out if you were real. I'm Ross Morton."

Terra introduced herself in return, glad for the chance to talk to someone who wasn't part of Grant's following. Ross was an architect, he said, and the conversation flowed from comments on the unusual design of the Dukes' house to a discussion of Berkeley architecture in general. After mentioning that some of the most outstanding examples of early contemporary homes were within blocks of this more traditional neighborhood, Ross paused. "I could take you home and we could drive past them on our way," he offered.

"That's awfully kind of you," Terra replied, "but I'm here with Grant Ingraham." She wondered if she had imagined the shadow of disappointment that had seemed to flash across the man's face. "We're just business acquaintances," she clarified with a slight smile. "He's a customer of the firm I work for."

Ross's face brightened considerably. "I've enjoyed this little chat," he said. "Maybe we could get together for a drink sometime?"

Terra nodded; she didn't see any reason to refuse.

"Let me just get your number, then," Ross said, taking a small book from his jacket pocket and balancing it on his knee while Terra wrote. Leaning over him, she was aware of the lemony scent of his after-shave, but his closeness sparked none of the electricity she felt at the mere knowledge that Grant was in the same room as she. In fact, she almost felt as though he were near at that moment, and just as she was smiling her assurance that she would remember who Ross was if he called, she straightened to see Grant framed in the patio doorway.

Ross noticed at the same time and, with a hurried goodbye to Terra and a nod to Grant, disappeared into the house.

Grant looked at her for a long moment before he spoke.

"Are you ready to go?" His clipped syllables seemed to signal displeasure. Not wanting to ask why, Terra nodded and silently preceded him into the house.

They had already said goodbye to the Dukes and were almost out the door when Stephanie assailed them. "Grant," she called in a voice that stopped conversation around her, "you're not leaving already?"

"I'm afraid we have to," he replied as Stephanie sidled up to him. "I promised Terra I'd get her home early."

Stephanie turned a saccharine smile toward Terra. "I'm so sorry you're getting away before we had a chance to talk. I looked around for you earlier, but you seemed so occupied with Ross Morton I didn't have the heart to break in."

Terra saw a muscle tighten in Grant's face, but otherwise his reaction to Stephanie's remark was in keeping with his smooth manner.

"I'm sure you'll have plenty of other chances to talk to Terra," he replied. "Thanks again, Stephanie," he said, and without waiting for a response practically shoved Terra out the door.

He kept his hand under her arm, forcing her to walk at his own brisk pace down the driveway. Annoyed at his overbearing behavior, Terra tried to tug her arm free, but he tightened his hold, and they walked on to the car without speaking.

Once inside, Terra asked Grant if he knew the way to her house from there, and he nodded curtly. He was clearly very familiar with the area; he chose the back-door route through hillside lanes. After a long silence he spoke.

"You seemed to have a good time in spite of your apprehensions."

Not quite liking his tone, Terra answered

noncommittally, "It was a pleasant enough party."

"I didn't see you slip away. The first thing I knew you were alone in the moonlight with Ross Morton." Grant's voice was accusing, and Terra couldn't imagine why he was speaking in such a tone.

"I didn't slip away," she said. "I told you quite distinctly where I was going, but you were so absorbed with Stephanie and the rest of your admirers you obviously didn't even notice I wasn't there until you were ready to leave. Since Ross was one of the few people at the party who bothered to say more than two words to me, I should think you would be grateful to him rather than angry."

"Yes, Ross can always be depended on to entertain unattached females," Grant commented sardonically. "And your part of the conversation necessarily included giving him your phone number?"

Outrage welled up in her at Grant's insultingly possessive attitude. He felt perfectly free to encourage Stephanie and every other woman at the party, yet he was furious at her for one conversation with another man. Who did he think he was anyway?

"Terra, when I take a woman to a party, I will not be embarrassed by having her flirt with other men. My women stay with me."

"Is that so?" Terra replied angrily. A small voice warned her not to tackle this subject head on, but she was too incensed to follow her own better judgment.

"The way I hear it nobody stays with you. I am not your woman. Nor is there any possibility I ever will be. So just mind your own business, okay?"

There was a moment's dead silence, in which Terra wished she could just disappear. She was sure he was going to retaliate for her vicious comments, and she just didn't know how she was going to handle the anger she herself had stirred. After a while she cast a furtive glance toward him, expecting his face to be livid; instead she saw a thoughtful sadness there, as though she had hurt his feelings. This so surprised her and made her feel so guilty she lowered her eyes without answering.

"You were my guest, Terra," Grant said softly. "You should have stayed with me."

Something broke in Terra, and she lost her composure entirely. "Why should I have stayed with you when you didn't pay any attention to me at all?" Now the words flowed freely, and she didn't even bother to try to stop them. "I can see there's a little footnote to your theory of male-female relationships. A man can do what he likes, but a woman sticks close to a man."

Grant pulled the car over to the side of the road and turned off the motor. There were few houses in this heavily wooded section of the Berkeley Hills, and through the window Terra could see the dark shadows of trees.

"I'm surrised to hear you complain," he said. There was anger in his voice now, as though he'd totally lost patience with her. "You're the one with the fancy ideas about a woman sticking with a man year after year ad infinitum. You're the one who thinks love is some kind of glue. I'm tired of your theories, Terra. Either a woman is supposed to stick to a man or she isn't. Make up your mind!"

"You're missing the whole point," Terra ground out in frustration. "I was talking about a mutual commitment of love—something you can't understand. You act as though you want a harem. Well, don't hold your breath, because I'm not going to stand in line waiting for my turn."

"Nobody asked you to get in line," Grant nearly shouted.

"Good, because I won't."

"Fine."

There was nothing more either of them could think of to say, and they sat, both staring straight ahead. Finally Grant's voice, barely above a whisper, reached Terra's waiting ear.

"Be careful, little girl," he warned. "It takes more than scrappiness to scare away a man. If you want to play with the big boys, you better be sure you want to stay in the game."

Terra's breath was uneven. She turned to him, seeing his eyes full of an emotion she didn't understand. Studying the set planes of his face, she wondered what would happen next.

She felt powerless to alter the hostility her remarks had brought about. She sat perfectly still, a slight frown marring the composure of her face.

In a motion so slow it seemed to take hours Grant raised his hand. Gently he lay a finger across her lips. "Stop," he said. And as though it were the most natural thing in the world, as though he were comforting her, he drew her into his arms. For a moment he held her there, and she felt the steady beat of his heart. Without even thinking, she raised her own hand and placed it on his chest. She lifted her eyes to his, and she could see a smile there before it even reached his lips. "Terra...." His mouth descended on hers, sweetly caressing her closed lips.

Involuntarily she yielded to the pressure of his kiss, a wild fire beginning to burn away her anger. She forgot why she had been arguing with him. She forgot he was a playboy, a slick manipulator. She forgot everything but the thrust of his tongue as it explored her open mouth, the heat of his large hands as they held her face. Her own hands tentatively reached for the dark strands of his hair, and she let her fingers graze the locks at the nape of his neck. She could feel the vulnerable softness of his skin where the thick springiness of his hair ended just above his collar. She leaned even closer to him, not realizing, not caring, that she was acting more boldly than she had ever intended.

The intensity of his kiss subsided, and she felt the pressure of his lips lighten. His mouth left hers, but his face remained so close the warmth of his breath tickled her skin.

"You seem to have grown up, Terra," he said without mockery. "But I don't know about those theories of yours. I'm interested in women, not in children who are playing with love...."

He released her, turned on the engine and silently guided the Mercedes through the twisting maze of North Berkeley streets, stopping at last at the foot of the stairs leading to Monterey Walk.

Early Berkeley architects had built clusters of homes around beautifully landscaped paths, so that with no roads the neighborhood had the feel of a private park. Ordinarily Terra loved the five-minute stroll from the street to her front door, but tonight she wanted to get inside, to get away from Grant as quickly as possible. Her feelings were in turmoil, and she didn't need any witnesses to her distress, especially a witness who had caused that distress in the first place!

"Thank you for dinner," she said mechanically, opening the door almost before the car had come to a complete stop. "You don't need to see me to the door."

Grant got out of the car and, without bothering to respond, started climbing the steps. Terra had no choice but to follow.

When they reached her front door he held out

his hand, demanding the key by his gesture. He unlocked the door and held it open for her.

In spite of her agitated feelings Terra couldn't suppress her curiosity. She wondered what it would feel like to be with him again in this house after so many years. The house had changed very little since he had left; even the furniture was still arranged in much the same way.

As she turned on the lights, Grant walked into the living room and stood gazing at the walls lined with bookshelves and the comfortable overstuffed furniture. "It's as if I never left," he said softly.

Terra stood uncertainly in the hall. She was still shaken by his unexpected kiss and not at all sure what it had meant. She was also wary of sparring with him again. She was ashamed of her behavior, but she was too upset to apologize, and he didn't seem about to apologize, either. It was all so confusing she just wished he would leave.

Grant turned and, seeing her hovering in the entry obviously waiting for him to go, smiled reassuringly.

"I'm not going to bite you." His voice was pleasantly neutral. "I'd like a cup of coffee before I drive back across the bridge, if you wouldn't mind." He reached out his hand to Terra. "Friends again?"

Reluctantly she stepped toward him and took his hand. "You mean you want to resume our truce?" she queried.

Still holding her hand, he regarded her seriously. "I have no intention of fighting with you again."

"What a relief!" She forced a cheerful laugh and stepped back, extracting her hand. "I'll go and fix the coffee."

While she was measuring the water for the coffee maker, she heard him moving around in the living room. She would have preferred him to leave quickly, but she also wanted him to feel welcome for the sake of her father's memory. It would be unthinkable to make him uncomfortable in a home in which he had spent so many happy hours.

With that thought in mind she brought out her handmade earthenware coffee set and arranged it on a tray of rich burnished walnut. The nubby linen napkins she pulled from the drawer picked up the beige flecks in the pottery, and her wooden-handled cutlery completed a picture that could have been taken from a magazine ad. Terra loved to entertain, and she chose the service she used as carefully as she chose her recipes.

She poured the coffee into the pot, added several slices of her homemade pumpkin bread to the tray and carried it into the living room.

With the familiarity of a frequent visitor Grant had dimmed the lights and put a string quartet by Mozart on the stereo. He was now lighting a fire in the fireplace. As she walked in he spoke. "Some people can't believe we have fireplaces here in northern California, but sometimes I find it a necessity. I have one in New York, too, and up north.''

"Up north?" Terra asked.

"Surely you've heard about my northern love nest?" Grant questioned teasingly. "I have the whole bachelor package deal—comfortable but seldom used apartment in San Francisco, a convenient and well-used apartment in downtown Manhattan and a hideaway for my helpless victims somewhere in the wilderness. I can't tell you where, of course—we playboys have to have some secrets. Never know when I'm going to have to spirit someone off without letting her know where she's headed!''

"You really know how to do things right, don't you," Terra said, only half teasing. She sat on the couch and watched as his strong hands piled small sticks on top of crumpled paper to start the fire. She reflected that the fireplace hadn't been used since her father had died. Before that a fire had been a regular part of a family evening.

When the fire was blazing, Grant settled himself on the sofa next to Terra and she handed him some coffee and pumpkin bread. As they sat in the flickering light, music playing softly in the background, she began to relax. Her anger and confusion melted away. It no longer seemed important that Grant had kissed her and then dismissed her as though she were a child. Well, it seemed important that he had kissed her but.... She would have plenty of time to think things over later. For now it felt right just to relax with him for a few minutes, just to let the evening end on this friendly note.

"I can't believe it's been so many years since I sat in front of this fire the night before I left for the East Coast. It was June," he continued, "almost ten years exactly."

Terra was startled and pleased at the preciseness of his memory. Every detail of that last night stood out clearly in her mind. It was nice to think the evening had been important enough for him that he still remembered it.

"Do you like New York?"

"I do now—love it in fact—but I can't remember how I felt then. I suppose that sounds odd, but I was so busy getting our East Coast operation together I hardly did anything else."

"Didn't you have people to help you?"

"The staff was large enough, but most of what I had to do couldn't be delegated. I went out there to establish some new programs for the company, to lead it in some new directions. It took a while to convince everyone I was on the right track."

"Is that why you stayed out there—to keep an eye on things to make sure the old ways weren't reverted to when you left?"

"To a small extent, but there were other reasons." He paused. "You never met my father, did you?"

"No, I never had the pleasure of meeting your father."

"He was a tremendous guy—and an excellent businessman for his times. But he just couldn't see that the days of the small private publishing company were over."

Grant got up and placed another log on the fire. "I tried to convince him the only way we could keep a little publishing firm viable was to expand and make it part of a larger group of companies involved with printing and communications in addition to publishing."

A thin smile curved his lips. "It was never my idea to give up the publishing company altogether. I wanted to strengthen our financial base so we could afford to keep operating it—rather like the way in which all the other bridges leading out of San Francisco are financed by profits from the Bay Bridge. If you get some things going well, then you have a little freedom in other areas."

"Your father eventually came around to your way of thinking?"

"Not entirely, I'm afraid." Grant's fingers stroked his temple, but he barely seemed aware of the gesture.

"At first he was content to let me control our Eastern operations, but once he fully understood the implications of what I was doing he was not at all pleased."

"What did he do, fire you?" Terra was fascinated by the thought she could now ask Grant directly about some of the things she had learned indirectly through the years.

"He probably wished he could, but it wasn't that simple. The business was started by my grandfather, and I inherited almost as much interest in it as my father did, although for a long time he controlled the decision-making positions."

"You didn't try to take control away from him, did you?" Even though she had phrased the question in the negative, Terra felt instinctively the answer must be yes.

"I suppose some people would phrase it that way," Grant said quietly. "From my point of view certain things had to be done, and since he wouldn't support the necessary changes, I felt I had to proceed without him."

Behind his matter-of-fact words Terra thought she could see some of the pain the struggle with his father had caused him.

"He resisted every move I wanted to make right up until the day he died." Grant's voice was filled with regret.

"And afterward many of the old guard felt honor bound to continue the resistance, even after our success proved we were on the right track."

He sighed wearily. "It's taken a long time to get things operating smoothly. Actually, it's only been in the past few months that I've felt able to take time out for myself."

"That's not the impression I got from the

newspapers." Terra laughed, feeling comfortable and at ease with him again. "I find it hard to believe you've been living the life of a hermit."

"No, of course I haven't. But most of the socializing I do is a matter of obligation...all part of the job."

"You don't really expect me to believe that?" She didn't attempt to disguise her amused disbelief.

"What would it look like if I showed up at social functions alone time after time?" Grant countered. "Our society prefers that people appear in couples, so I oblige."

"I certainly admire your willingness to sacrifice yourself for your work," Terra teased. "It's nice to see a person with such a strong sense of responsibility."

Grant responded to her mockery by reaching over and rumpling her hair. She put up her arms to defend herself, and in the good-natured tussle that followed he drew her once again into the circle of his arm. Her heart quickened with anticipation, but Grant was merely playing. He had always teased her when she had been a girl, and he was merely teasing her now. As soon as he sensed the stillness caused by his embrace, he again reached for her hair and gave it a flick with his finger as if to tousle it, but something stayed his hand.

Slowly he entwined his fingers into the soft strands, lifting them and letting them fall, as though for an eternity. With the slightest trace of pressure his thumb rested on Terra's temple, and though the contact involved an area of skin only as large as his fingertip, she felt the power of his touch course through her, pinning her to the spot.

Then his thumb softly outlined the planes of her jaw, and he rested his hand in the space between her shoulder and the base of her throat. Breathlessly she glanced up at him and was shocked to see a faraway expression in his eyes, as if he were not in the room with her at all. His mouth was quirked into a strange small smile as he spoke softly.

"We used to have such fun," he said. "I used to look at you and think it was a shame that such a delightful little scrap of a girl would someday have to become a woman—with all a woman's problems and complexities. Things seemed so simple in those days. I knew that heavy responsibilities awaited me even then, but visiting you and your father was like an escape. My own father was a loving man in his way, but he was stern, and without a wife he had left me in the care of professionals—nannies and housekeepers. I didn't really know what a family was like. So even though I was already a man, I found a little of the family I had missed when I came to your house. I felt like a child again, and watching your antics, I was sorry I'd ever grown up—I wished you would never grow up. Now I've changed my mind."

With gentle pressure he eased her even closer to him. Held firmly against his side, she could feel the heat of his body penetrate the layers of fabric that separated them. It added a warmth to her own already heated skin. Briefly it occurred to her that now was the time to pull back, to break away from the spell that seemed to hold her to him. But her body paid no attention to the demands of her mind. Instead of wrenching herself from him, she snuggled deeper into the curve of his shoulder.

He lowered his head and buried his face in her hair. His lips brushed the tender skin at the nape of her neck, and she felt a little rush of intense pleasure as his tongue found the sensitive area under her ears. Softly, without urgency, his lips continued their gently persuasive journey up the side of her cheek and across to the delicate skin of her eyelids. His lips were warm and caressing, and his breath lightly fanned her closed eyes.

His hands picked up the gentle rhythm of his kisses. With one hand he tenderly explored her throat, his fingers moving with slow sureness toward her shoulder as he coaxed open her collar. The buttons of her blouse gave way one by one as his gently insistent fingers pursued their leisurely path down toward the soft swelling of her breast.

Terra's breath seemed to stop. The featherlight strokes of his powerful fingers were barely perceptible at first. She fought the urge to press his hand with her own, to hurry him in his possession of her breast. But she didn't move at all, and when his hand finally cupped her full roundness and his fingers teased her nipple, Terra gave a rippling sigh of pleasure and consent.

As if waiting for the signal, Grant's lips moved toward hers, tantalizing the corners of her mouth with light kisses. Her own lips began to respond in harmony with his; his urgency increased, and his tongue sought her own. Then his free hand moved down her side to her thigh, following the curve of her body, outlining her with flame.

The gentle waves of feeling that had been stirred in her by his first caress gathered momentum, swelling into a torrent of sensation that threatened to engulf her. As his hand stroked her thigh she felt a deep longing rise inside her. He pressed her closer to him, and she unconsciously arched her back to decrease the small distance between them.

"Terra, Terra," he murmured against her lips. "From the moment I saw you this afternoon I knew we would be together tonight."

Like a sudden dash of cold water, his words jolted her back into awareness, and this time her body reluctantly gave in to her reasoning. She struggled in his arms as if she were drowning. At first, unable to understand the reason for her change of heart, he tried to keep her in his arms, but then he released his grasp. Finally she twisted into a sitting position and, anxious to separate herself from him, moved toward the corner of the sofa.

"So you had this all thought out," she whispered in a voice thick with emotion. "You had your evening's entertainment all planned. No wonder you were so anxious to leave the party. You couldn't wait to get on with the show."

The muscles around Grant's jaw tensed into a hard straight line. His eyes narrowed, but he did not speak.

Taking his silence as confirmation of her accusation, Terra sighed wearily. "If this is what you mean by playing with the big boys, then you're right. I'm not in your league, and frankly I don't think I want to be."

"You didn't want me to stop." It was a statement, not a question.

"No," she admitted, "at least part of me didn't. You're very good, Grant. You can play on my feelings like a master violinist."

"Then why not relax—" he reached over to stroke her hair "—and enjoy the music?"

Drawing her into his arms again, he murmured, "I won't hurt you, Terra. Just let go. You won't regret it."

"I think I might come to regret it quite a bit," she replied, pulling away from him. "I don't think we understand things in the same way, Grant," she said sadly. "I don't want a night of love or a week of love and then loneliness. When I love I want it to mean something, I want it to be more than just the pleasure of an impetuous moment. What we have here is a difference in style...." She tried to sound flippant but realized it wouldn't work. "Let's just forget it, okay?"

Grant stood up and pulled her to her feet in front of him. Holding her hands in his, he stood silent, his dark eyes boring into hers. Then he dropped his hands. "Good night, little girl."

His words carried with them a cutting finality that echoed in her ears long after she had shut the door behind him.

CHAPTER FOUR

TERRA CLIMBED ON THE BUS Monday morning and took her favorite seat by the window. Nodding a pleasant good morning to several other regular commuters, she pulled out her notebook, hoping to get a little work done on the long ride across the bay to the office.

A blanket of dew still covered the lawns, sparkling as the sunlight glanced off the small drops of moisture. Terra resolutely turned her eyes away from the familiar scenery and back to her notebook. She had spent Saturday and Sunday trying to tie up loose ends in her research, trying to come up with something that would at least placate Paul for the time being. But the memory of Friday night hung over her, intruding on her concentration. She had accomplished very little.

Sifting through the welter of confused feelings that Friday's events had stirred in her, she had tried to make sense out of them. She felt she had had many small glimpses into the person Grant had become, but she wasn't at all confident she understood him. Clearly he was a complex, even calculating man who analyzed a situation and then acted on that analysis without allowing his emotions to interfere. The way in which he had struggled with his father over the future of the company demonstrated that he pursued the course of action he thought was right against any resistance, even when that resistance came from those he deeply cared for. That ability no doubt accounted for his amazing success, but it probably also explained the reputation he had acquired for ruthless and unfeeling behavior.

Terra suspected he was not unfeeling at all. Her thoughts of him were colored by memory, but she had seen enough of the present-day Grant to surmise that his feelings could run very deep. As he had talked about his father she thought she had glimpsed a deep love, an abiding sadness over their estrangement. Yet the truth was he had not allowed that emotion to influence his actions. For that reason she felt she had been right in considering him a smoothly functioning machine. Such a man was admirable—but also disturbing and a little disappointing.

Much more disturbing, though, was the other side of his nature, the side she had reacted to instinctively. At first she had denied that Grant could possess warmth and genuine passion. But she could no longer ignore the fact that his sensual forceful attraction had got to her. He exuded a magnetism impossible to escape. His every look and every gesture communicated his underlying awareness, at a level deeper than conscious thought, that he was above all a man. Terra had seen the effects of that sexuality on other women, and now she knew she wasn't immune to it herself.

On a conscious level his matter-of-fact acceptance of sexuality between men and women was more than she could handle. She definitely did not believe in casual physical relationships, and yet Grant seemed to accept them as a natural expression of human nature. His actions on Friday showed her he considered physical love an inevitable conclusion to a pleasant evening between friends.

About his attitude toward lasting love she was a little less certain. From his behavior and conversation she felt he was a thoroughgoing skeptic about permanent love. His interest in female companionship seemed confined to physical pleasure and social obligation, with no concern for a lasting emotional relationship. The avoidance of permanent ties no doubt partially accounted for his reputation as a rake, but why he seemed so set against commitment she didn't know. Fleetingly she considered that an early experience with love might have disappointed him, might have created his cynicism, but nothing she had heard about his past seemed to fit this theory. All she could conclude at the moment was that to Grant committed love was not a necessary prerequisite to physical love.

The bus left Berkeley and hurtled down the

freeway to the Bay Bridge, its jerky stop-and-start motion replaced by a swaying rhythm as the huge machine approached the speed limit. Making good time was difficult in both Berkeley and San Francisco because of the traffic and frequent stops, so the driver made the most of the unbroken stretches of freeway.

When her thoughts turned to her own reaction to Grant, Terra felt at loose ends. Although the memory of Friday night's interlude on the sofa caused her to shudder with embarrassment, she forced herself to analyze her own actions objectively. It was true that the past had given Grant a powerful hold on her emotions, but childhood infatuation could not account for the abandoned way in which she had responded to his caresses. Looking back on the event, she could see how he had gradually led up to the embrace by the fire. In retrospect the whole evening seemed a prelude to the moment in which he had taken her in his arms.

Yet even so she had to acknowledge it was her own explosive desire for him that had tipped the scales toward passion. He had released feelings in her she hadn't known she possessed. At each step of the way he had invited her gently to go with him, and without forcing her, he had waited until she had signaled her willingness. And she had seemed, at least for a while, to abandon all effort to resist him.

Reluctantly she concluded she had underestimated the power of what Grant would call "animal instinct." There appeared to be no other way to account for the feelings that overwhelmed her. She could not be in love, she felt sure. As a girl she had often thought herself in love with Grant, but she knew better now. Her anger at him had faded over the weekend, but she still intended to be wary of him. She did not approve of what she felt were his manipulating tactics, his lack of emotion in dealing with others and his blasé way of treating women. She did not always understand his motives, she admitted that. But his assumption that he knew best in every situation annoyed her. Most distressing of all was the dark emotionless mask that could fall over his face at will, hiding his feelings totally. "Little girl" he had called her when he left, as though those words had nothing to do with the past they had shared, as though he had had, in that moment, no personal feeling for her at all.

Despite the fact that love with Grant would be an impossibility, Terra couldn't shake the memory of his touch. Her body responded to his with a force that defeated understanding. Her logical mind could make list after list of reasons why she should not be so strongly attracted to him physically, yet she knew she was.

Never before had she been so powerfully affected by a man. She felt she would never forget the feelings of intense desire that he had coaxed from her. Because he had got to her once, she knew he could get to her again. And the next time she might be too late in marshaling her resistance. Despite the pleasure to be had in not resisting, she set her mind firmly against the possibility. Grant could not love her, and she had decided long ago that in the end only heartache could be expected from physical passion without love. Therefore the only course of action would be to avoid Grant. She had come to this same conclusion several times over the course of the weekend, and she was certain it was the most prudent decision she could make.

Having once again settled the thoughts that were plaguing her, Terra glanced out the window at the approaching skyline of the city. This view, with the early-morning sun glinting off the metal-and-glass giants at the edge of the bay, never failed to excite her. The city had so much energy, so much life. She felt she had hardly begun to discover the joys of San Francisco, even though she had lived in the area all her life.

The bus approached her stop, and Terra closed her notebook and put it back into her purse. As she walked the short distance to the bookshop she noticed that remodeling had been started on another of the old buildings. Many buildings in the area, including the one that housed Fosters', dated from the 1880s and were among the few structures to survive the disastrous earthquake and fire of 1906. Several years earlier the historic value of this prefire neighborhood had been discovered by both preservationists and real-estate agents. Intensive renovation had begun immediately, and the area had developed into a very desirable location, housing designer shops, specialty firms and professional offices.

The facade of Fosters', with its charcoal gray woodwork complementing its red brick exterior, was probably one of the most attractive on the street, Terra thought as she approached the shop. Until Paul had inherited the bookstore it had been almost conspicuously shabby next to its remodeled neighbors, but Paul had begun the face-lifting as soon as he had taken over, and now the Foster building commanded attention on a block where old and new were gracefully combined. Terra liked the new look very much but was secretly annoyed about the expense, especially during a period when book sales seemed to be declining.

She inserted her key into the iron gate that barred the passage to Fosters' front door, pushed the gate open and hurried down the narrow covered walk that ran alongside the building. Before Paul had called in the decorator this passage had been a gloomy prelude to the stores that opened off both it and the small courtyard and alley beyond, but as part of the renovation it had been refurbished and landscaped. Plants in wrought-iron holders hung on the walls and brass fittings gleamed in the dim light. Beyond the flagstone path in the center of the courtyard a fountain gurgled cheerfully. Although she shuddered at the expense, Terra was grateful for the effects that had been achieved. It perked her up just to walk along the passage as she made her way to the back of the building.

Unlocking the heavy wooden rear door, she looked around the deserted shop and smiled, thankful she had arrived before the others. Although she was sure she couldn't avoid a discussion with Paul, at least she wouldn't have to face him before she had had a few moments in which to prepare for the ordeal.

She hurried upstairs to the third floor, aware the others would arrive at any moment. Safe in her office, she took off her pale green jacket and inspected her plants. Her first responsibility on Monday morning was the one she enjoyed most, and as she made the rounds of her plants, checking the moisture in the soil and watering where needed, she felt ready to begin the day.

Her gardening done, she took her papers out of her bag, groaning once more at the small amount of progress she had made over the weekend. With determination she spread her notes out in front of her and picked up her pen. Paul would expect a report sometime during the day, and right then she had nothing to show him. She had scratched out two attempts at an opening sentence and was beginning a third when she heard footsteps on the stairs. Seconds later Margaret appeared, a steaming cup in each hand and a newspaper tucked under her arm.

"I thought you might like some coffee," she said, setting the mugs down on the desk.

"Thanks," Terra acknowledged, waiting for the inevitable questions.

"How'd you like your taste of high life on Friday night?" Margaret asked, slowly sipping her coffee and studying Terra carefully.

"We went to the Gardens. The food was terrific," Terra said, knowing Margaret was not interested in what they had eaten.

"I'm not talking about the restaurant, silly," Margaret replied, setting down her cup and leaning closer to Terra's desk. "Tell me about the Dukes' party. I can hardly believe you had a chance to go just like that. Come on, tell me what it was like."

"How did you know I went to the Dukes' party?" Terra asked in surprise.

"Are you kidding?" Margaret's eyes widened. "Everybody knows about the Dukes' summer open house. People wait for years to get their names on the list—except Grant, of course. He has a standing invitation. You were with him, and he was invited, so.... Didn't you see yesterday's paper?" She spread the newspaper in front of Terra with a dramatic flourish. Grant's face, surrounded by those of several attractive women, leaped up at her.

The older woman shook her head in despair at Terra's amazed reaction. "What am I going to do with you? I would have been leaning in front of the camera, and you didn't even know the photographers were there.'' She paused. "Well, what was it like?''

Terra shook her head slowly, still overwhelmed. "It was elegant—and boring. I can't see why it merits so much attention. It was full of people I had never met, didn't meet and, thank goodness, will never again have the opportunity to meet!'' She pointed to a picture of a group of what appeared to be businessmen. "Look, here's Paul.''

"Business as usual,'' Margaret commented disdainfully. "Did you meet her highness, Stephanie Duke?''

"We were introduced,'' Terra replied absently as she continued to stare at the picture of Grant. Glancing up, she went on, "She wasn't at all friendly. She spent most of the time hanging on to Grant as though she'd fall over without his assistance—like a tomato tied to a stake. Impressive.''

"My, aren't we getting catty in our old age!'' the other woman joked. "I guess she's still trying to get him back again. They were engaged a long time ago, but apparently she broke it off. Said she couldn't stand the New York scene. But I've heard there was a bit more to it than that.''

"Oh?'' Terra said, as though she were merely speaking to be polite. "Like what?''

"Well, I think Grant was less than happy to have her there with him on the East Coast. Maybe he was preoccupied with business—or maybe he was less interested in her than she was in him. He may have changed his mind by now, though—that was several years ago. Stephanie came triumphantly back to San Francisco, announcing she was home to stay. Evidently she didn't stick around long enough to convince Grant her presence was indispensable. There are those who say she's regretted it ever since, but who knows? Maybe she'll have another chance. Grant's not the type to burn bridges. Mainly because he's not the type to build them in the first place.''

''I thought Stephanie was almost engaged to Paul,'' Terra remarked thoughtfully.

''Such a little innocent you are! Of course she is. But my guess is she found out Grant was coming back for an extended stay and she pushed things with Paul to let Grant know what he's missing. She'll marry Paul, too, if she can't get Grant back. It's obvious she's trying to make him jealous by using Paul. Even marriage wouldn't stop her if Grant so much as crooked a little finger in her direction.''

''Doesn't that upset Paul?'' Terra was not sure she believed what she was hearing.

''Why should he care? He's in love with her rich book-collecting relatives, not her. All he wants is a nice little marriage license that makes him heir-in-law to all those gorgeous rare books her grandfather keeps under lock and key.''

''Come on, Margaret, you're exaggerating. Paul wouldn't be that crass!''

''Wouldn't he?'' Margaret chuckled. ''Sometimes I don't believe you're for real. How a beautiful girl like you got to be twenty-four yet remain so naive is beyond me.''

''I'm not all that innocent, Margaret, so quit making me sound like a child. I just don't happen to believe that everyone in the world is out for either sex or money.''

Margaret folded up the paper, a big grin on her face. ''You may think you know a lot, Terra, but you've still got a few lessons coming. Try to enjoy them now, and maybe they won't hurt so much later.''

Terra wasn't exactly sure how to interpret the older woman's statement, but after she had left and Terra had had a moment to think things over she could see that, discounting Margaret's cynicism, what she had said made sense. It seemed pretty obvious that Stephanie was still in love with Grant. Even Paul's indifference to her flirting seemed understandable in the context, Terra admitted to herself, feeling a twinge of conscience at the thought. She really didn't relish disloyal thoughts about Paul. It made working for him even more difficult.

A broken engagement might explain Grant's avoidance of serious entanglements. Terra didn't think he seemed in love with Stephanie, but he was such an expert at hiding his feelings she couldn't tell for sure. He must have cared for Stephanie at one time or they wouldn't have become engaged. The possibility that they might get back together made Terra renew her resolve not to get involved with Grant.

She put aside these troubling reflections and settled down to work. After several hours of concentrated effort she sat back, stretched and glanced at the clock. Realizing she had just half an hour before she was supposed to meet Jeff Baxter for lunch, she quickly put away her notes and headed downstairs.

On her way out the door Paul stopped her. "What did you think of the Dukes' party? Nice the way rich people live, isn't it?"

"The party was lovely," Terra answered, surprised at how nervous her voice sounded.

"I'm glad you had the chance to go. It's good for the staff to socialize with the customers once in a while." His eyes narrowed. "But of course relations with customers have to remain entirely on the impersonal level. You understand that, don't you?"

"Don't worry, Paul," she said, hiding her annoyance, "I've enough business experience to realize that." She anxiously consulted her watch, aware that time was slipping away.

"Before you leave—" Paul grasped her arm a little harder than Terra thought necessary "—tell me what you've done on the brochure first."

She tried to pull away from his grip but realized she couldn't do so without causing them both some embarrassment. His manners seemed to be getting worse by the day.

"I've started writing, and it's going fairly well." This was not the exact truth, but at least it should satisfy Paul until she could show him what she had been doing. "I'm sure it will be done by Friday."

"That's what I like to hear, Terra. I know I can count on you." His fingers eased their hold on her arm, and she slipped away.

"I'll see you later, Paul," she said as she moved toward the door. Once outside she quickened her pace. She hurried through the passage and out into the alley. She took a shortcut through two office buildings and reached the bus stop just as the bus was about to pull away. Luckily the driver saw her and opened the door. As they jolted over the cable car tracks to Union Square, Terra wished she hadn't promised the brochure to Paul by the end of the week. She honestly didn't know whether she could finish it by then, and if she didn't, she knew she would feel the full brunt of his anger. She realized with a start that she was beginning to be a little afraid of him.

She jumped off the bus and walked diagonally through the park to the opposite corner. Pigeons thronged expectantly around her and then scattered to avoid her brisk steps. As she reached the restaurant Jeff was just approaching, and they rode up in the elevator together.

The Oasis was a tiny Middle Eastern restaurant hidden on the fourth floor of one of the old office buildings that lined Union Square. Its tables were decorated with cheerful yellow cloths and fresh flowers. They were shown to a small table by the window.

Terra had not seen Jeff in more than a week, and the two friends had plenty to talk about. She considered telling him about her problems with Paul and the brochure, but he had had a problem of his own that morning, and she ended up giving him advice rather than seeking advice from him. After a few minutes she had forgotten about her own problem, and for a while that was a relief.

The lunch was a pleasant break in the day. They ate falafel—patties of fried chick-pea meal garnished with salad and spicy sauce and wrapped in rounds of pita bread. It was relaxing to be with Jeff, and Terra felt grateful for his undemanding company. It wasn't until they were just about to leave that he said, "What happened on Friday night with Ingraham?"

"Absolutely nothing happened!" she answered, rather too vehemently. "I wish people would stop asking me that."

"Okay, okay." Jeff pushed the tip under a saucer. "Didn't know it was such a touchy topic. Anyway, nothing much must have happened. He didn't stay the night."

"Jeff Baxter!" she lashed out in indignation, but cooled down when she saw his grin widen.

"Relax, Terra. I'm just teasing. I know you're too smart to fall into his clutches."

She paused before replying. Jeff didn't realize how close she had come to doing just that. Then her thinking took a different turn. "How do you know when Grant left?" she asked.

"Oh, I keep my eye on things," Jeff said lightly. "But don't worry, I'm not sitting at my window watching your doorstep. You and Grant were just ahead of me coming home on Friday night, and Saturday morning when I left for my racketball game I noticed his car was gone." He got up. "Let's go. I've got to get back to that mess at the office."

As she made her way back to the bookstore Terra thought about what Jeff had said. She knew he got up early to play racketball every morning, so his explanation was logical enough. Yet it bothered her that he seemed to be keeping track of her activities. Jeff was becoming more possessive without seeming to realize it was inappropriate.

She and Jeff spent a great deal of time together, eating at each other's houses, going to concerts and plays or just talking. Occasionally Jeff would kiss her—but always affectionately, never with any passion, though lately she had sensed a difference. But they were close friends, and she felt certain they could keep things that way. For her part she knew she'd never fall in love with him. She had always dated other men and never really considered going places with Jeff as dating. Still, she wasn't sure about Jeff's own feelings. If he was seeing other women,

Terra didn't know about them. Could it be he was much more serious about her than she was about him? His interest in her relationship with Grant seemed out of character for him. She couldn't recall that he had ever before shown any interest in the people she went out with.

She was probably making far too much of nothing, she decided. Still, she cared for Jeff very much—in a sisterly way—and did not want to see him hurt, especially if she could do something to avoid it.

Deep in thought, she was halfway down the alley before she noticed the silver Mercedes parked between the two laurel trees. She could feel the tempo of her heartbeat pick up. Why had he come? Although she was firm in her resolution to refuse all further invitations from Grant, she had not expected to test it so soon. With a little warning to herself to remain calm she pushed open the door and went in.

The front area of the store was deserted. From down the hall she could hear voices, and she hesitated before going upstairs. Usually the receptionist was at her desk noting who had returned from lunch, but she, too, was not to be seen. It would have been proper to wait for the receptionist to return, but Terra didn't want to run the risk of meeting Grant as she stood waiting. Quietly she made her way toward the stairs, and as she passed the specialized book room she tried to identify the voices inside. She could hear Paul and Margaret, and above their familiar tones a low feminine voice she had heard previously. She tried to sneak discreetly past the door, but Margaret caught sight of her.

"There you are," she called. "Paul asked me to find you, but I didn't think you'd come back from lunch."

Paul, Margaret and several other members of the staff were clustered around the mahogany reading desk, bending over a woman who was no stranger to Terra. Several books were spread out on the table, and Margaret had obviously been showing them to the woman. Terra searched the room quickly for Grant. He was standing away from the others, coolly watching the activity. His eyes locked with Terra's, causing her heart to skip a beat, but they soon dropped, offering no friendly greeting.

Paul quickly reintroduced Terra to Stephanie Duke, who acknowledged her with the merest of nods. Terra's glance flew instinctively back to Grant. However, he was not looking her way.

"Stephanie has decided to do a bit of collecting herself—in the family tradition," Paul said with unctuous politeness. "She thinks she might be interested in some first editions of L. Frank Baum's *The Wonderful Wizard of Oz* and other Oz books."

Stephanie glanced at Terra. "I don't know anything at all about rare books," she drawled, "but Grant and I got to talking at lunch about the copy of *The Wonderful Wizard of Oz* I had as a child. That was a reprint, but I've always thought it would be nice to own an old copy. Grant agreed, so he brought me here.''

She looked over at Grant and batted feathery eyelashes in his direction. "I'd always thought granddaddy's collection a bore, but I'm beginning to see now there's more to it than I realized. I always thought one book was as good as another until Grant started explaining things to me." She uttered a silvery little laugh and cast another helpless look at Grant, who smiled.

Paul, too, smiled without the least bit of discomfort. To him a customer was a customer. He turned toward Terra. "Stephanie might be interested in seeing a list of all the Baum books," he suggested. "She might also like to know a bit about how she can identify first editions. Why don't you sit down with her and go over the Baum catalog you prepared last year?"

Paul looked at Grant. "There are a few things I'd like to discuss with Grant, so why don't you stay here with Stephanie, Terra, and we'll join you later."

Stephanie looked miffed, as though being turned over to Terra were absolutely the last thing she had planned on. But Grant nodded his agreement, and the two men left without protest from the "customer."

Wishing that Margaret had been assigned the task of entertaining the charming Ms. Duke, Terra nonetheless politely pulled a chair up to the desk and smiled pleasantly. Margaret and the others drifted away, leaving the two of them alone.

As soon as Grant withdrew from the room Stephanie's interest in the books in front of her waned considerably. She pushed her chair back and fanned herself with one of the Foster brochures.

"Don't you find it a little warm in here?" she questioned.

"Perhaps a little," Terra agreed, and rose to open a window.

"Is there much I have to know just to buy an old book?" Stephanie asked, a trace of petulance in her voice.

"That depends on what you want," Terra replied patiently. "Are you interested in first editions, or do you want something with a fine binding and color illustrations?"

"I don't know what I want," the woman said idly. "Grant said he was getting back into collecting, and I thought he could help me pick out something." She spoke as if she thought buying a rare book were like buying a sweater or a dress. Then she gave up pretending any interest in books at all.

"Grant tells me you're an old friend of his," she said frankly. "How long have you known him?"

"Several years," Terra answered flatly, not willing to go into detail about her relationship with Grant.

"Well," Stephanie commented, "Grant and I

go back quite a way, too." She pulled out a gold cigarette case and matching lighter from her purse.

Terra cringed. Mr. Foster had never allowed smoking in the store, no matter how important the customer. Even now almost no one lit a cigarette here, though Paul's redecorating scheme had included the purchase of custom-designed crystal ashtrays.

"Yes," Stephanie said slowly, "a very long time, indeed." She blew out a thin stream of smoke, then lifted her green eyes to meet Terra's gaze directly. "But of course it's not the length of time you know someone that really counts. It's what you do with the time you have...."

This bit of suggestive repartee annoyed Terra greatly, and she thought of one or two things she would have liked to say in answer, but they were even more cutting than the bold sentence she finally did offer. "From what I hear Grant Ingraham never spends much time with any one woman—not long enough to have time to marry her, for instance...."

Stephanie appeared not to be moved by Terra's statement at all. "He thinks he hasn't yet found the right woman," she commented, "but I'm sure his mind can be changed."

"I wish you luck," Terra said. "Would you like to see the list of the Oz books?" On noting the insolent shake of Stephanie's red hair, which today was a flaming mass falling onto her shoulders, Terra nodded. "I must get back to work. I'll ask someone to make you a coffee if you like."

After arranging for Stephanie to be looked after, Terra escaped upstairs. The woman was beautiful, no doubt about that, and maybe she would have more luck with Grant than her numerous rivals seemed to have had. Her family's position was definitely in her favor, too. Terra told herself she didn't care who won the wonderful trophy of the person of Grant Ingraham. All she wanted was to stay completely away from him, to forget about him. She figured Stephanie and Grant were two of a kind. They deserved each other!

She sat at her desk and plunged into her work, determined not to let thoughts of Grant interfere. She had just got back into the flow of her writing when Margaret burst in.

"What a woman!" Margaret lifted her eyebrows heavenward. "She's so indiscreet. She's dating Paul, but she even goes so far as to hint about marriage to Grant in front of total strangers!"

"I told you it was shocking," Terra said, referring to their earlier conversation. "She's apparently decided he's been waiting all these years for the right woman when all along she's been right under his nose—so to speak. I think she intends to enlighten him as to what he's been overlooking."

"She may learn better," Margaret said, "but on the other hand she may just be right. I would guess that Grant will never marry, but if he decides to, Stephanie's the most likely bet.''

"Why do you think that?'' Terra asked.

"It's a natural. They've known each other forever, and he's so close to her parents. Of course, he'll have to do something about Paul, but that won't be much of a problem.''

Terra shook her head. "It's none of my business, and I'm tired of thinking about it. Now I really have to get back to my work.''

"It'll have to wait a little longer,'' Margaret said. "I came up here to tell you Grant wants to see you downstairs. He's in Paul's conference room.''

Hiding the fact that she was shaken by the prospect of facing Grant at close quarters, Terra followed Margaret back downstairs. Hesitantly she gave a soft knock at the door of the tiny room to which Paul, during his spate of reorganization, had given the label "conference room.''

"Come in,'' answered the deep even tones of Grant's voice. He was sitting at the oval table, and when Terra entered he rose and pulled out the chair beside him. "Sorry to make you come all the way downstairs, but your office is not exactly equipped for conferences, so Paul suggested this, though this conference is only going to involve you and me. . . .''

Terra's heart fluttered and she couldn't imagine what he meant, but from the cold tone of his voice she soon realized he was talking business.

"How did the work on the brochure go over the weekend?" he asked.

"Not very well," Terra admitted. "The problem is in writing down the information I do have but eliminating references to what I don't have without being dishonest. Not an easy task."

"Paul's getting a little worried..." Grant began, and Terra almost laughed out loud at his understatement. "So," he continued, "he's written out a draft for you. He wanted me to see it and then talk to you about it."

"Why didn't he tell me so himself?" Terra looked at Grant suspiciously.

"Maybe he thinks I have some influence over you." His eyes mocked her. "I said I'd give it to you." He pushed the typewritten pages across the table.

Glancing at them, she could almost hear Paul speaking. The account was written in the same flamboyant style he used when talking about the pamphlets. Reading it quickly, Terra knew she could not sign her name to this kind of writing. It was thinly disguised salesmanship, not at all the scholarly review of the facts she was working on.

"You've given me the draft," she said ungraciously, "now what?" She knew she shouldn't be angry at Grant. She didn't think he expected her to accept something like this. Her eyes drifted down to the pages in disgust. Or did he?

The impersonal curtain had fallen over his

eyes. "You have to make your own decisions, Terra," he said. It was a dismissal, and she accepted it as such.

For the next few days Terra's work occupied all her time and used all her energy. She stayed late at Fosters', fixed a quick dinner when she got home and continued working, sometimes until midnight. Again and again she went over her notes. Time after time she thought she had found a slant that would allow her to present limited information in a convincing but truthful way. If all her efforts had brought her closer to the end of her task she wouldn't have been so exhausted, but by Thursday evening the pile of discarded drafts was several inches thick, while only one finished page of copy lay on top of her desk.

Sitting in her father's study, she tried to force herself to begin one more version of the section that described the lost edition's history. When no words would come, she once again read over the dramatic account of the discovery of the pamphlets. She had taken down word for word what Paul had related to her. The evidence sounded so conclusive, but she still felt that same uneasiness about it. "I don't care what anyone else thinks," she said aloud. "The facts just don't make sense!" She slammed her fist down hard on the desk, then slumped over onto her folded arms, startled at her own outburst.

The pressure must be getting to her, she decided. Late as it was she had no chance of writing anything decent that night, so she thought she might as well stop working and try to relax. That way she would at least be calm when she had to face Paul the next morning.

She started to gather the notes she had strewn all over the study but then stopped. Ordinarily she would never have left a mess like that, but she didn't have one ounce of energy left. With a defiant shake of her head she doused the light and shut the door on the whole problem.

Upstairs she pushed the yellow swag curtains back from the tub and drew a warm sudsy bath. Afterward she spent a leisurely half hour brushing her hair, doing her nails and generally pampering herself. The silken feel of body lotion, followed by the delightful scent of powder, reminded her there was more to life than hard work.

Dressed in a short summer nightgown and a matching filmy robe that revealed more than it concealed, Terra turned her attention toward choosing her clothes for the next day. The confrontation with Paul was certain to be unpleasant, and she wanted to wear something that would bolster her self-confidence.

She pushed aside first one hanger then another, and her eyes fell on a splash of bright peach. Several weeks earlier she had been lured into an exclusive dress shop in Maiden Lane by a sale sign in the window and had finally succumbed to the temptation of a stunning but full-priced silk suit. The gored skirt accented her slim waist and complemented the graceful curve of her hips; the snugly fitting jacket had the blend of sophistication and soft femininity that Terra knew suited her well, but it was the blouse that had sold the suit. The tiny floral print in all the colors of the rainbow picked up the rich peach color and made it sing.

She had not yet worn her treasure, preferring to save it for something special. Although the meeting with Paul was definitely not the kind of occasion she had had in mind, she decided to dress in the suit, feeling certain she would need the lift such an outfit would give her. She hung it on the closet door and laid out the rest of her things. Then, having assured herself the house was locked up for the night, she threw off her robe and climbed into bed.

Under the sheets she stretched her legs sensuously against the smooth cool material and let her thoughts drift. The weekend was approaching, and she longed to do something exciting and not connected with work at all. She considered shopping in San Francisco and having lunch at Fisherman's Wharf, but although that seemed a pleasant prospect, it didn't thrill her. A picnic in Golden Gate Park, a ride on the lake in a rowboat, tea at the Japanese Tea Garden— these were things she really wanted to do, but they weren't much fun alone. She considered asking Jeff to go with her, but somehow that didn't seem wise.

As she lay there, a picture of Grant as he

would have looked stretched out casually on the grass at Golden Gate Park floated into her mind. She could see him smiling up at a female companion, but she couldn't imagine the woman's face.

"If he goes picnicking with anyone," Terra muttered, flinging herself over on her stomach, "it isn't going to be me."

CHAPTER FIVE

WITH AN EFFORT Terra tried to shake off the heavy veil of sleep that hung over her. The alarm clock was ringing wildly, and she needed to stop its raucous summons before it woke the whole neighborhood.

She was on her feet and halfway across the room before she realized the insistent sound was not coming from the placid little clock on the dresser but from the doorbell. Bewildered, she pulled her robe around her, acutely conscious it would not be much of a barrier to prying eyes. She glanced quickly toward the closet but didn't see her longer, more respectable terry-cloth robe in its usual place. Meanwhile the doorbell was still ringing as if the caller intended to rouse the whole world. With a sigh Terra headed for the stairs, determined not to open the door wide enough to be seen. As she passed the living room she noticed the mantel clock said six.

Standing on tiptoe, she peered through the door's tiny window. The ringing stopped, but the sound that took its place was equally disturbing: the voice of Grant Ingraham.

"Good morning, Terra," he said cheerily.

"Are you going to let me in, or are you just going to stand there admiring me?"

"What are you doing here at this hour of the morning?" she hissed through the door.

"You'll have to speak up a bit. I can't hear you," came the full-voiced reply.

"I can't let you in. I'm not dressed," she whispered back as loudly as she dared. In two minutes everybody on the block would be gaping out the window.

"I'm afraid I still can't hear you very well. Did you say you were undressed?" Even through the door Terra could hear him chuckle, and the sound delighted and infuriated her at the same time. Desperate that he not repeat any reference to her state of dress for the benefit of the neighbors, she opened the door a crack.

"I'm not decent," she said in a voice she hoped was low enough to imply the necessity for discretion. "And please keep your voice down."

He made a move as if he were going to ask her some other embarrassing question.

"What do you want?" she cried out quickly before he could comment further on the state of her clothing.

"I'm certainly not going to stand here and whisper through this crack," he replied, finally lowering his voice. "Open the door and stand back, because I'm coming in."

The no-nonsense ring in his command made her realize she had to do something fast. "If you'll just stay put for one more minute I'll be right back," she whispered, and then she turned and ran for the stairs, hoping to be safe in her room by the time he realized she was no longer barricading the door.

Halfway up the stairs she heard the deep chuckle and knew it wasn't coming from the front porch. Conscious that the morning light from the upstairs window probably silhouetted her slim figure despite the short robe she wore, she bounded up a few more steps. From the bottom of the stairs she heard Grant say, "Slow down, Terra. A female body is not such a novel sight to me that I'm going to rush after you."

Flushing with anger and embarrassment, she ran up the rest of the way and flung herself into her room. "I'll bet it's not an unusual sight for you," she muttered. Her heart was thudding uncontrollably, and she thought it ridiculous to be so self-conscious. After all, Grant couldn't have seen that much. Yet her fingers trembled as she searched for her terry-cloth robe. It took ages to find, but finally she spotted it on the closet floor. Shaking the robe as if to remove the wrinkles, she glanced at it. What a mess! How was she going to face Grant dressed like that? *Well,* she thought to herself, *as old Aunt Hattie used to say, "Uninvited guests dine potluck."* Defiantly she belted the robe tightly around her and stalked down the stairs.

Grant stood at the foot of the staircase, looking solid and thoroughly respectable in his pin-striped suit. In fact, he struck her as so appealingly handsome that Terra was instantly ashamed of her own appearance. "It would serve you right if I had called the police," she fumed.

"Considering your sleepwear, I doubt I'd be the one who'd get hauled into the station," he said, laughing. "Do you always sleep in such insubstantial garb?"

"I don't sleep in that robe," Terra protested unthinkingly.

"Oh?" Grant said, raising his eyebrows. "How interesting...."

"That's not what I meant," she sputtered, not at all amused by his teasingly suggestive grin.

He stood looking at her for a moment, and his grin changed to a soft smile. Then his eyes lost their amusement and his voice its teasing lilt. "You'd better get dressed in proper business clothes, Terra. We haven't got much time."

"Much time for what?" she wanted to know, planting her feet firmly. It would take much more than an imperious demand from him to make her move. "I have no intention of dressing until you tell me why you've barged in on me at this hour." That didn't sound quite right, and she feared she had laid herself open for another smart remark, but it did not come.

"We've no time to waste because we have an appointment at the Blansford Library at eight o'clock. An hour and a half is just barely enough time to make it through the city and down the peninsula to Woodside. If you don't get a move on, we'll embarrass ourselves by being late.''

"The Blansford!'' Terra could hardly believe her ears. Going there would offer her whatever faint chance she still had of finding evidence to prove the authenticity of the lost edition before her deadline. Just one reference, one tiny mention of Robert Waltham's reason for not selling the ten copies, would banish her doubts and enable her to finish the brochure. As soon as she remembered the brochure she also remembered her promise to Paul—and hope vanished.

"I can't go. I have a job, remember? If I don't show up for work today, Paul will probably fire me.''

"Give him a call. Since the time you'd be taking would be spent on the lost edition, I'm sure he wouldn't object.''

Terra didn't share Grant's certainty in the least; Paul wasn't famous for being reasonable. But she didn't want to miss an opportunity that wouldn't come again. She called Paul at home. When she explained why she was disturbing him so early, his reaction was even more explosive than she had expected.

"Damn it, Terra. I thought I made it clear to you the research is over. I'm paying you to write, not to waste your time in libraries. You've had all the time I'm going to give you. Either that copy is finished today or you are.''

His voice dropped lower and became insinuating. "You're not fooling me one bit. You just want an excuse to take a day off with Grant. You say he's there?"

"Yes, he's here," Terra said, barely able to control the anger in her voice.

"Well," Paul replied, "isn't that cozy—at six o'clock in the morning!" Before she could answer he demanded, "Put Grant on the line."

Silently she handed the phone to Grant and winced as the loud squawking on the other end proved that Paul was still raging.

By contrast Grant's voice was calm and in control. "I know time is running out, but if the printer can wait until this afternoon he can wait until Monday morning."

He paused, listening to what were clearly further objections from Paul. Then he continued coolly, "Yes, she does think she'll be able to write it immediately if she has a chance to look at the material at the Blansford. I'd strongly recommend letting her go."

Paul talked on at length, but when Grant finally hung up he said, "It's all set. You can go. But I promised Paul you'd have that brochure completely finished by Monday, so no matter what you find today, you'd better be able to deliver after the weekend. Can you?"

"I can," Terra said, vowing to herself to make use of the time that would be available.

"Then that's settled. Go get dressed. And hurry. I'll wait outside."

She fled upstairs and threw off her robe, fighting down a momentary surge of annoyance that Grant had not bothered to let her know about the appointment in advance. His arrogance was unbelievable; to show up at six in the morning and expect her to take off with him with no preparation. Yet she had to admit she was grateful to him. Although she knew she shouldn't count on finding conclusive evidence at the Blansford, it was her one hope of getting something more concrete than the information she already had.

She wondered why Grant would bother helping her in this way. Her last conversation with him had been so brief, so formal, she had been quite sure that any interest he had had in her had been fleeting, if not a figment of her own imagination. It had almost seemed silly to her that she had resolved not to see him, since she couldn't foresee then that she'd have a chance to exercise that resolution. Now that the chance had arrived she had agreed to go with him without even remembering she had vowed to stay away from him at all cost. So much for determination! But of course, this was business, purely business, and if Grant had no difficulty separating business from pleasure, neither should she. With luck he would leave her at the library and she could catch a bus home when she was through.

Quickly she dressed, grateful she had laid out her things the previous night. Before going downstairs, she took an extra second to appraise the silk suit in the mirror. Her insides were churning—and not only from excitement at finally being able to get into the Blansford. Yet despite her inner turmoil, the woman who stared back at her from the mirror was calm and poised. She locked up the house and joined Grant where he stood on the walk.

"You could use a bit of work on that roof," he commented. "I wouldn't mind lending a hand. Wouldn't be the first time I was up there."

Terra was too stunned to answer. Perhaps Grant had forgotten himself. She couldn't imagine the head of Ingraham Corporation with roofing nails in his mouth and a hammer in his hand, though she could remember a younger Grant helping her father.

"I have professionals to handle jobs like that," she said, not wanting him to think she wasn't able to take care of her home. Grant merely nodded.

Glancing at her watch, she realized that Jeff might already have left for his racketball game. She hoped he hadn't noticed Grant's car. She was tired of explaining herself to Jeff.

Walking toward the car with Grant, she felt at a loss for words. It was hard to understand his going out of his way to get her the appointment, and she should have thanked him, but somehow words of gratitude didn't come. "I would have been better prepared to make use of any material I might find today if I had had a day's warning," she commented in a tone formal enough to rival any he ever used.

"Unfortunately," he replied also in business-like tones, "that would have been impossible. All the details came together very late last night."

"At least you could have called, even very late, to see if I had any objections to all the plans you were making for me," she persisted, still a little angry at his high-handedness.

"How could you object when the plans were in your own best interest? You wanted to get into the Blansford. I'm getting you in. I don't see any point in discussing the matter further."

There it was again—his arrogant assumption that he knew best. But in this case Terra had to admit his logic was irrefutable.

They got into the car, and Terra stared silently out the window as they drove through Berkeley to the bridge. When Grant didn't speak a wicked impulse seized her, and she asked, "How is your protégée doing?"

"My protégée?" he repeated, genuinely confused.

"Yes, your initiate into the pleasures of book collecting."

"Oh, Stephanie." Grant smiled when he uttered the name, and Terra wasn't sure why. He paused a moment before saying anything more. "Stephanie has had a lifelong opportunity to take up an interest in book collecting. Somehow she hasn't shown much enthusiasm until quite recently," he declared thoughtfully. "I trust that she's genuinely interested and not just giving in to one of her whims.''

"And are you one of her whims?'' Terra asked. As she spoke she couldn't believe what she had said, but the words had slid out of her mouth before she could stop them. She cringed inwardly, expecting a cutting remark in return for her insolence.

Grant's eyes left the road for the briefest of moments and captured her own. There was no anger or shock in his gaze; in fact, amusement twinkled in the dark depths. "I've really got to teach you not to play games with me,'' he said.

"I'm not playing games,'' she replied with mock seriousness. "I'm genuinely interested in knowing how you and Ms. Duke are getting along—in the book-collecting department, I mean.''

"Jealous?'' Grant asked, well aware Terra couldn't care less about Stephanie's new hobby.

"Absolutely not,'' Terra insisted. "Stephanie Duke is obviously a refined and cultured woman, and she seems to be willing to accept attentions from you. You could do a lot worse,'' she added wickedly.

Their banter was improving her spirits, and the mood was light and carefree. She wondered how he would respond to what could only sound like an attempt at matchmaking.

"Where did this sudden interest in my welfare come from?'' Grant inquired good-naturedly. "If you've got ideas of finding the 'right woman' for me, forget it. I decided long ago no such person exists.''

"Oh, pardon me," Terra teased. "I quite forgot the world-famous bachelor doesn't believe in love. How careless of me not to have remembered."

They had reached the toll bridge and were gradually inching up to the gate. Even at this early hour it often took almost as long to pay the toll as it did to get across the bridge. But Terra didn't find it irritating to be stalled in the long line of cars. In fact, so engrossed was she in the conversation she hardly noticed where they were.

"I certainly do believe in love," Grant stated emphatically. His eyes gleamed impishly. "You and I just happen to have a different definition of love."

"I'll say we do. Real love is not something that conforms to the latest style and can be tossed out when the fashions change. It grabs you and holds on to you for life." Terra's voice rang with conviction, but Grant was still in a teasing mood.

"Ah," he said, "another pronouncement from the chairman of the Love Is Glue committee."

She turned to him, a laugh in her eyes, but it faded as she saw his own smile fade. He became serious with lightning swiftness, which seemed to be his way.

"I'll believe in your kind of love, Terra," he said, "when I find someone who can convince me it exists." His tone seemed to imply the odds of that happening were about a million to one.

They had passed the toll gate and were now whizzing along the upper deck of the bridge. Beneath them the bay was a deep gray-blue and the waves rolled and swelled with an inexhaustible energy.

"What will you be looking for at the Blansford?" Grant's question drew Terra's eyes away from the vast expanse of water.

"At this point anything I can find," she said with a note of desperation.

"If you don't have a more organized plan than that," he commented, "I'd say this trip will be a total waste."

Belatedly Terra realized he had expected a more serious answer to his question, so she proceeded to outline for him the various courses of action she had contemplated. She spoke hesitantly at first, not sure exactly how much detail he cared to know, but his questions revealed he had a thorough grasp of the subject, and soon she was pouring out all her thoughts and concerns. Although many book collectors were not experts in the ways of distinguishing one edition from another, Grant was an exception. He was able to offer suggestions she felt would prove very valuable, considering the limited time she had in which to make use of the Blansford's resources.

She pulled her notebook from her bag and began to jot down some of Grant's recommendations. Wistfully she reflected that this was the kind of guidance she had once got from Paul's father and was what she missed so much in working for Paul.

The thought of former days marked her face with sadness. Noticing her expression, Grant said, "What are you thinking about?"

"Oh, about Paul," she replied absently, and did not look up. Had she done so, she would have seen that Grant's face, too, was washed with a wave of sadness at her answer.

She continued scribbling in her book and was so immersed in thoughts about first editions she was only vaguely aware of their progress through San Francisco and onto the freeway that led down the peninsula. When she finally did stop writing and look up, they were leaving the freeway and turning onto a narrow road that made its twisting way up to the top of a ridge. From this vantage point Terra could see for miles over shrub-covered hills, occasionally glimpsing the startling blue of a mountain reservoir.

"I'm always amazed this much wild country exists so close to San Francisco," she commented.

"Some of this land is watershed," Grant replied, "and much of the rest belongs to people who want to preserve its unsettled character. But for real wildness I prefer the land up north."

"The satisfied bachelor's northern hide-away?" Terra joked.

"Yes."

Grant slowed the car and turned off the main

road into a lane marked Private Drive. They followed it through a grove of trees to an imposing gatehouse. An elderly man came to the door and, on seeing Grant behind the wheel, waved them through the open gate. The lane was flanked by two rows of tall eucalyptus trees, whose thin curving leaves cast patterns of light and shadow on the road in front of them.

Quite suddenly they rounded a bend and swept into a large open courtyard with a fountain in the center. Well-manicured lawns bordered by beds of primroses stretched out from the fountain hub. Beyond the spectacular spray of water stood an enormous Palladian mansion.

"This can't be just a library!" Terra exclaimed in amazement.

"Oh, no," Grant laughed. "This is the Blansford family home. The library is housed in one wing. That's why they limit access to the collection except when special arrangements have been made."

They parked the car near the fountain and walked toward the marble portico.

"Blansford has talked about moving the library to a building of its own in another location so it could be opened to the public, but he's reluctant to get that far out of touch with it."

"Does he actually select the books himself?" Terra asked.

"For years he has. Now that the collection is fairly well established he'd like to turn some of the responsibility over to someone else. He was hoping one of his children or grandchildren would inherit rare-book fever, but so far the only one who has shown any interest of note is his potential grandson-in-law.'' He cast a sideways look at Terra.

"At least that's someone to take an interest in the collection,'' she replied, glancing around at the extensive gardens.

"True.'' Grant's voice was dry. "Blansford has recently hired a distant cousin, a librarian, to oversee the library in the meantime.''

"And you're a friend of the cousin?'' Terra asked, picking up on the one thread she thought might explain how Grant was able to get a privilege for her that had been denied to others.

"No,'' he answered, "not exactly a friend, although I have met him a couple of times. We won't be seeing him today, though. He's off making some arrangements for the annual exhibition they hold here in connection with the bookfair.

"Exhibition!'' Terra exclaimed. "Do you mean the library is going to be open to the public?''

"Yes,'' Grant acknowledged. "Most people will be coming to see the exhibits, but scholars and dealers who want to take a look at the books and manuscripts can make advance arrangements.''

"I wish I had known,'' Terra remarked. "I wouldn't have had to presume on your kindness....''

"It's no presumption, Terra," Grant said softly. "Besides, that won't be for another week or so, and Paul needs the brochure before then. In fact, I believe they're planning some kind of publicity about the lost edition during the Blansford exhibition. The brochure will be part of the publicity material."

As he spoke he pushed the door chime, and Terra's attention was distracted by the liveried doorman who answered their ring. They were shown into an ornately furnished drawing room and advised that someone would be with them shortly. The doorman had scarcely withdrawn when the door opened again and a distinguished-looking but spritely, white-haired gentleman entered the room. Although Terra supposed he must be in his late seventies, his erect carriage and snapping eyes belied his age.

"Grant, my boy, what a pleasure!" He shook Grant's hand with a great deal of energy.

"Terra—" Grant turned toward her "—I'd like you to meet Nathaniel Blansford."

Terra's widened eyes revealed her astonishment. In a daze she shook the hand of the world-famous industrialist who had amassed a fortune and then used it to assemble one of the greatest book collections in the world.

"I'm delighted you two could come so early and on such short notice. When Stephanie called last night she said you wanted to visit as soon as possible, and today was the last time for a week or so I could be here to show you around."

Smiling at Terra, Blansford continued, "I admit I wasn't expecting such an attractive visitor. I got the distinct impression from my granddaughter that Grant was bringing an older, somewhat more—uh—shall we say, serious-looking woman."

Terra was taken by surprise. If she had heard rightly, Stephanie was Nathaniel Blansford's granddaughter. When she gave a moment's consideration to Blansford's description of the visitor he had expected, she was more amused than annoyed. It certainly did sound like the sort of thing Stephanie would have said about her!

Grant shrugged. "Your granddaughter has met Terra, but perhaps she didn't make the connection that she was the researcher on this project. Terra works for Paul," Grant explained.

Suddenly the mystery surrounding the visit cleared. Grant had taken Stephanie up on the offer of her grandfather's help, but not for himself. His smooth words had covered for Stephanie, but it wasn't hard to guess the woman's displeasure. She had probably only acceded to Grant's request in order to score points with him. If the final arrangements had been made late the previous night, it didn't take much imagination to conjure up the kind of persuasion he had used and why he couldn't interrupt it to call another woman. Terra was disgusted, but then another thought occurred to her.

If Grant had been able to arrange a visit for her by asking Stephanie, why couldn't Paul have done the same? Perhaps he was a little envious of her, especially since some book collectors had made it known they felt the Foster reputation for scholarship was being upheld by Terra rather than by him. But surely his resentment wouldn't run so deep he would compromise a thorough investigation just to keep Terra from getting the credit. No, she couldn't believe that of Paul.

When she thought over carefully what she had said to him concerning her research, she wasn't sure she had insisted strongly enough that she needed to visit the library. It was reasonable of Paul to decide that a visit wouldn't have been worthwhile and then to let the subject drop. Perhaps if she had been more forceful in her insistence, he would have been more cooperative.

What mattered most was that she was there. It wasn't really important in the long run who had made the arrangements. She felt eager to get down to work, and despite the charm of chatting with Mr. Blansford she was happy when the interview came to an end and the old man began to lead them through a maze of marble corridors decorated by huge paintings in ornate gilt frames. Glancing through doorways as they passed, Terra saw rooms filled with antique furniture and elegant objets d'art.

"Does anybody actually live in these rooms?" she whispered to Grant.

Blansford was several feet in front of them,

but he overheard her remark and smiled. "Not anymore, my dear. When our children were growing up we filled the whole house. But now even the grandchildren are grown, so we use most of the house to display our paintings and antiques. My wife loves period furniture, and we've made a little hobby of choosing paintings of a certain period, then furnishing the rooms to match the paintings."

Nice the way the rich live. Paul's words rang in Terra's memory, and she could see his point, though she herself would not want to live in a beautiful but essentially empty house.

Eventually they came to a large two-story room lined with bookshelves. A little balcony ran around the room at the level of the second floor to provide access to the second level of shelving. Massive oak tables filled the center of the room, and leaded glass windows faced out over gently rolling lawns.

Blansford pointed out the card catalog and the tall ladders on wheels that allowed one to reach the top shelves. "If you lack anything, please be sure to let us know." He gestured toward the bellpull in the corner. "Someone is always available."

Terra tried to convey her appreciation of Blansford's kind generosity, but he brushed aside her thanks with a gracious smile. "Don't mention it. Stephanie and Grant are two of my favorite people, and I'm glad to be able to do them a favor." Turning to Grant, he asked,

"Will you have a cup of coffee before you go?"

The younger man nodded. "I have an appointment at ten, but I should have plenty of time."

"Fine," Blansford said, and putting a friendly hand on Grant's back, he led him toward the door.

Terra lost no time in heading for the catalog. The oaken drawers of the cabinet moved with silken ease, and she pulled out first one drawer and then another. Most of the cards were quite specific, noting particular books and manuscripts individually in neatly typed lines. But the cards for the Waltham collection were different. The references were general, not specifying individual works but bearing descriptions such as "one large file of documents." And these cards were not typed but written in a neat small hand Terra imagined would have been quite suitable for a librarian. It was obvious the Waltham material was a new addition to the collection and work on organizing it was just in the beginning stages. Perhaps this was another reason Paul had felt that work done here would not justify the time spent. Nonetheless Terra's notebook was rapidly filled with lists of items to be located and checked.

The hushed atmosphere of the library was perfect for concentrated work, and sitting at the massive table with stacks of books before her, Terra was in her element. The only sound in the room was the soft rustle of paper as she worked her way through document after document, unaware of the passage of time. Despite her quick pace a peace filled her, a quiet joy that wiped all troubled thought from her mind. In this spirit of intense but relaxed concentration she accomplished a great deal of work without even realizing how much energy she was expending or how her few hours there were flying by. When Blansford appeared beside her she jumped. She wasn't even aware he had opened the door and entered the room. And when he asked her if she would like to join him for lunch, she was startled to realize it was already noon.

"Have you had any success in finding out more about the lost edition?" he asked as they walked through the museumlike rooms to the part of the huge house still occupied by the family. "I, of course, can only welcome any evidence that will strengthen the claim of authenticity, though I have it on the best authority that there's little to worry about in this case."

Again Terra was surprised to run into yet another person who was convinced the lost edition was genuine. Choosing her words carefully, she answered the man's question. "I've picked up a lot of new information about the Waltham Press, and I know a little more about the type of customer to whom the press catered. Unfortunately I still haven't been able to track down any exact reference to the ten copies Paul has. I've combed the account books pretty thoroughly. This afternoon I plan to tackle the orders and receipts.''

"That's going to be the hardest part of your job, my dear.'' Blansford's tone was discouraging. "For years I've been buying the records of defunct English presses in order to preserve what I consider to be a fascinating mass of material, but I simply haven't had the time to organize much of what we've brought here. About six months ago I hired a librarian, and he's made a great deal of progress, but I'm afraid we still don't have a complete and accurate listing of everything.'' The elderly gentleman smiled. "I remember when Paul sold me all the Waltham records. They arrived in five huge crates, and even Paul had no idea exactly what they contained. One day we'll get it sorted out, but right now I'm afraid things are rather more of a jumble than suits a respectable library!''

Terra's lunch in the mansion's dining room was more elegant than she could have imagined, but though the food was excellent and Nathaniel Blansford a solicitous host, her mind was really back in the library, and she excused herself as soon as was polite in order to return to her work. On her way back through the house she reflected on what Blansford had said about his acquisition of the Waltham papers. She had known Paul had sold Blansford the Waltham work log, but he hadn't told her there were so

many other papers. Perhaps he had assumed
that nothing there would be of value to her investigation, but since he obviously didn't know
exactly what was there, it was an error in judgment on his part not to have mentioned the
papers to her. He really didn't seem to have a
clear understanding of what was involved in
authenticating a work.

The documents she planned to review that
afternoon were housed in a special temperature-
controlled room beneath the ground floor.
Making her way carefully down the spiral iron
staircase, Terra found herself in a large under-
ground vault. Rows of stacks extended in all
directions; they were filled with gray cardboard
manuscript boxes, each marked with a name.
The boxes seemed to be in roughly alphabetical
order, so it didn't take long for her to find the
ones labeled Waltham, but she was dismayed to
find that that single word was the only iden-
tification the tickets bore. She gazed in disbelief
at row upon row of Waltham boxes and realized
with a sinking heart she would have to open
each box, one by one.

Once she set to work, the task was a little
easier than she had anticipated. As she glanced
through the contents of the first few boxes she
could see that the papers were roughly grouped
by years, even though the dates were not in-
dicated on the outside. Half by luck and half by
shrewd guessing, Terra located the group of
boxes containing papers from 1848. Spreading

them out on the floor, she quickly saw there was
far more information about the printing of the
lost edition than had been included in the work
log. Her heart pounding with excitement, she
began reading and taking notes furiously.

Several hours later she raised her head wearily
and lifted her arms in the air, stretching. She
now knew almost everything possible about the
printing of the lost edition—except the one thing
she most needed to know: how many of the
copies printed had been sent to the Brownings.
She had confirmed that twenty had been
printed, but whether only ten had gone to Italy
and ten had remained in England was still as
much a mystery as it had been previously.

She stood up slowly and replaced the boxes.
At last she seemed to have reached a dead end.
The only other possible question she could think
of trying to answer was why Robert Waltham
had never sold the copies Paul had found. But
trying to second guess where information like
that could be found was next to impossible.

On a whim Terra walked to the end of the
bottom shelf and lifted the lid of the last box.
Amid the papers there lay a tattered brown
notebook. Lifting it carefully, she opened the
book and saw that it was a personal diary written by Robert Waltham himself. "I wonder
whether he kept a diary all his life," she muttered out loud, and began to look through the
boxes in reverse chronological order.

To her delight she discovered an identical

brown notebook that began roughly three years earlier. With renewed energy she worked her way through all the boxes covering the dates of Robert's working life. She ended up with a formidable stack of diaries, beginning when Robert had been seventeen. Settling herself on a low stool, she leaned back against a shelf and started to read.

By the time she had covered the accounts of seven years of Robert's life Terra was thoroughly dejected. It was half-past four, and she had reached only 1905. So far she hadn't learned one piece of relevant information, and she was beginning to wonder if it was worth the effort to finish the diaries. Reading on a little further, she had just about decided she had had enough of the young man's financial woes when suddenly the word *facsimile* struck her eye. Going on, she noted that Robert's latest money-making scheme was a plan to reprint some of the most famous books issued by his father in facsimile editions, using exactly the same type of paper and ink that had been used fifty years earlier.

Terra's pulse began to race. A facsmile edition of the Browning pamphlet would explain why the tests verified the 1848 date. If Robert had been successful in matching the paper, ink and type, the facsimile and the original might be indistinguishable without external proof they were not one and the same. That proof might be in the diary Terra now held in her hand.

From his writing it appeared that Robert's intentions had been entirely honorable. He had had no plans to pass off the facsimile as the real thing. He wrote of printing a new title page that would clearly indicate the date of the edition and the fact that it was a reproduction. This new title page was to be wrapped as a separate sheet around the pamphlet. Even at that time a well-produced facsimile was guaranteed a good sale at a fairly high price, though Robert Waltham would have presumably printed more than ten copies. Had he distributed a large number of the facsimiles, it would have made perfect sense for him to keep a small number for himself.

Terra shut the diary. She felt sure she had found the answer. Robert had printed facsimiles of the lost edition, had kept a small number for himself and, since those were his personal copies, had not added the separate new title page. Paul had, naturally enough, assumed he had found copies of the 1848 edition. Not realizing the existence of the 1905 facsimile edition, he had not searched out other existing 1905 copies, the presence of which would have been strong evidence that his own copies were part of the later printing.

Paul was wrong, and Terra was now faced with the responsibility of informing him of his mistake. He would be greatly disappointed, of that there was no doubt, but she still had enough faith in his integrity to believe he would at least delay introducing the ten copies to buyers until the facts could be checked out in light of the new information she had unearthed.

She replaced the other diaries. Then, collecting the 1905 diary and the manuscript box that had contained it, she climbed the stairs to the library. Other papers from 1905 might provide additional evidence to support her facsimile theory, and she wanted as much evidence as possible to use in convincing Paul his pamphlets were not first editions. Although the lost edition had received much word-of-mouth publicity, nothing official had been written yet, so there was still time to withdraw it from the bookfair and the exhibition. Paul had several other valuable books they could feature, and as soon as she had a chance to talk to him, she could begin working on those descriptions so that she could have an alternate brochure finished on Monday. What incredible luck that she had found out about the facsimiles just in time to save Paul the acute embarrassment of formally announcing a magnificent discovery to the world and then later having to admit he had made a mistake!

Wondering if she could still reach him at work, she glanced at her watch. It was already after five, and on Fridays Paul was usually gone by four. Just as she was debating whether to search for a telephone, the door to the library swung open, and she looked up to see Stephanie Duke standing before her. Instinctively Terra shuffled the diary under her notebook and sat down as though to continue her work.

Stephanie strode toward the table, a less-than-pleased expression on her haughty but beautiful face. "Well," she said, "have you found what you came for? Considering the trouble you went to to get in here, I certainly hope so."

Again Terra had the feeling there was an unpleasant suggestiveness to the woman's remark.

"Since this *is* my grandfather's collection, maybe you'd like to tell me just exactly what you hoped to find by poking around in his papers."

"It's all rather technical," Terra replied in a calm voice. She found it strange that Stephanie would express such interest in her work, unless it was to annoy her. "This sort of thing isn't very much fun for someone who's just starting out in collecting," she remarked, trying to keep from laughing.

Stephanie was in no mood to take Terra up on her comment; in fact, the woman seemed more intent and determined than Terra had ever seen her. Her ordinary manner was f ̃olous to say the least, but at the moment she exhibited a seriousness Terra found vaguely frightening.

"Nonetheless," Stephanie insisted, "I'd like to have a look." She moved closer to Terra and took up a position behind her chair. Again instinct made Terra cover the papers before her with her hand, but though the diary wasn't visible, many other papers were. She could not see Stephanie, yet Terra had the feeling the woman's eyes were scanning the documents spread out on the table. She could almost feel Stephanie stiffen, and there was a moment of utter silence before, without warning, she reached out from behind the chair and made a grab for the notebook and diary.

Terra was startled, but not enough to let the books slip out of her grasp. Without even thinking of the damage that might be done to the diary, she hung on to it. She was mentally calculating the distance to the bellpull when she heard footsteps in the hall. Grant entered, followed by Paul, and both of them stopped short when they saw Stephanie leaning over Terra. At the sound of the men's entry Stephanie had stepped back slightly, relinquishing her attempt to get the diary. But it now lay in plain sight on the table. Paul's eyes darted toward it, then toward Grant.

"What's going on here?" Grant's voice was calm but commanding as he walked slowly toward the women.

Terra was trembling, totally shocked at what had happened and confused because the incident had been so brief. It had abated so quickly she thought she must have imagined Stephanie's lunge toward the material on the table.

The other woman was far more self-possessed. On seeing Grant, she straightened, her body poised and exhibiting none of the tension it had shown only moments earlier. She flashed Grant one of her brilliant flirtatious smiles.

"Grant! So you're here, too. Quite the little crowd, aren't we? Terra here was just showing me another fascinating aspect of old book hunting. I'm really so very glad you showed up. I've got something to ask you. Would you like to come with me into grandfather's study?" As she spoke she moved toward Grant and laid her finely manicured fingers on the sleeve of his jacket.

During this exchange Terra looked up at Paul. He seemed nervous, and his pale features were marked with the effects of shock. Perhaps he was beginning to understand that his fiancée was evidently straying in her affections.

"I'm sure Terra and Paul would be as able as I am to answer any questions you might have...."

"Not this question," she giggled wickedly. "Come along, sweetheart," she said, tugging at Grant's sleeve. "Stop being so stubborn."

Terra would have liked to get Paul's attention, to let him know she desperately needed to talk to him, but he seemed so distraught she wondered whether he would even hear her if she did speak. Nonetheless she ventured, "If Stephanie wants to talk to you alone, Grant, I'm sure she has her reasons. I still have a few things to do here. I'll just wait until you come back."

"See, darling, even your little clerk approves. She trusts me with you all alone." Stephanie shot a withering glance at Terra and began gently pulling Grant toward the door. After a doubt-ful glance at Paul, Grant followed her.

Paul turned to go after them, but Terra caught his arm. "Paul, I've got to show you something."

He spun around, hostile impatience on his face. "Not now."

"Yes, now!" Terra was insistent. "This can't wait. The Browning pamphlets you have aren't part of the real lost edition. They're fac-similes!"

She watched as genuine horror registered on his face. "They're copies! They aren't genuine, and I can prove it!"

He took a step toward her, and Terra edged back away from him. She didn't like the look of pure hatred that shone in his eyes. "You are the most irresponsible person I have ever had the misadventure of dealing with!" he spat out. "If you had one ounce of respect for your profes-sion—or for yourself—you'd learn to keep your stupid mouth shut. How do you expect me to believe that in just a few hours you have figured out how to prove anything. You've worked for months on this, and all your evidence has proved those pamphlets are real. I will not ac-cept the happenstance 'proof' to the contrary that you think you've accumulated in a single afternoon.

"In fact," he nearly shouted, "I'm beginning to get the impression you wouldn't know a fake of any sort if it came up and kissed you on the mouth. I'll never understand why my father hired you, let alone gave you control of the research department. I'm surprised it hasn't occurred to you I'm not as soft as he was. I don't take nonsense, Terra. I don't know what you think you've found, and I don't have the time to waste to find out." Anxiously he glanced at the doorway through which Stephanie and Grant had exited.

"Please," Terra begged, afraid but not allowing herself to be cowed by his exorbitant anger. "It'll only take a minute for you to look at this. I'm sure what you see will change your mind."

"Terra," he said in a calmer voice than he had earlier, "I'm going to ask you to talk to me about this on Monday. Until then I don't want to hear another word." He turned and hurried out of the room.

Terra stared helplessly after him. She felt tears start behind her eyes. He was impossible. The situation was impossible. She didn't need him or his job, but now she couldn't even quit. He was wrong about her being irresponsible— dead wrong. The information she had found that afternoon had increased her responsibilities enormously, for if Paul refused to listen to her, she would be the only one who knew that any customer of his who bought a copy of the Browning booklet would be very badly cheated.

It was all too much. She wished she could sit down, fold her arms on Mr. Blansford's antique table, lower her head and cry her eyes out. Instead she pulled herself together and began to gather the papers. Mr. Blansford had told her not to bother reshelving what she used, and she was glad. In her upset state she wasn't sure she'd be able to put everything back the way she had found it. She simply piled the papers and diary beside the gray box and left it on the table for the librarian to take care of on Monday, as Mr. Blansford had said he would.

The moment she finished, Grant came through the door. As he approached her she could see that his face was somber. "I'm sorry about what happened, Terra," he said. "I came back to ask you whether you were ready to go, but when I heard Paul shouting at you, I decided it would be more discreet to leave you two alone for a while."

"Thank you," was all she could manage through taut lips that threatened to pull down at the corners and reveal the fact that she was still on the verge of tears.

"Are you all right?" Grant asked, bending to get a better look at her face.

"Yes."

"Did Stephanie say much to you before we showed up?"

"No."

He continued to scrutinize her face, concern etched in the fine lines of his forehead. "Are you ready to leave now? I think Mr. Blansford would like to lock up the library."

"Okay."

"Terra—" Grant gently lifted her chin with a strong finger "—you mustn't be so upset about Paul. He's under a lot of pressure these days with the fair and the exhibition coming up. Give him a little time and I'm sure he'll see you're far too valuable an employee and—" he hesitated for the briefest of moments "—friend—to treat in the way he's treated you. He'll come around—you can be sure of it. How can he refuse?" His voice was a soft caress that almost made her forget her anger, her embarrassment and fear.

She raised her eyes to his and saw a kindness there that she found puzzling. Of all the people she knew he would be the only one who could both understand what she had found today and also be willing to listen to her explain it. He might even be able to convince Paul. But it was Paul for whom she worked. He had the right to be the first to know, even if he didn't want to exercise that right. She owed it to Paul and to the memory of his father not to mention anything that would jeopardize the company.

Grant's eyes held hers as though he genuinely wanted to know the things that stirred in the troubled depths of her gaze. But she said nothing, and when he put his hand lightly on her shoulder and turned her in the direction of the door, she walked by his side in silence.

"Where would you like to eat?" he asked when they were outside.

The question surprised her. The time she had

spent with Grant that morning had been casual
and pleasant, despite having got off to a rather
shaky start, but that had only been because they
had discussed business. Now he seemed to be
becoming personal again, and Terra's confidence took a plunge. After the recent shock of
discovering the facsimiles she didn't think she
could cope with warding Grant off. Nor could
she cope with sharing an enjoyable evening with
him, then having him pretty much ignore her as
he had done that week. She wanted solitude and
time to think.

"I have to go home," she said without offering further comment.

Putting his arm firmly around her, Grant
steered her toward the car. "We both need to
relax. We'll go someplace quiet for dinner, and
then I'll take you right home if you still want to
go." Once again his eyes bored into hers, as if
they were looking into her soul. "Are you sure
something else isn't bothering you?"

"No, of course not." She pulled away from
him, climbed into the Mercedes and shut the
door with a decisive bang.

Grant eased behind the steering wheel. "Try
to pull yourself together, Terra. I know Paul
isn't treating you in the way you deserve, but
I'm sure that will change as soon as things
become less hectic at the store."

With a blank face Terra let Grant continue to
talk her into accepting the fact that even rare-
book dealing could be a high-pressure occupa-

tion. She wasn't even thinking about rare books. She was thinking about the fact that once again she had been trapped against her will into an evening with Grant. Not only did she have to go, but she had to pretend to be merely fatigued from the day's labors and piqued at her treatment by Paul. True, those things bothered her, but not nearly so much as the implications of what she had learned that afternoon. She didn't want to arouse Grant's suspicions, to give him reason to pry into matters she just didn't feel she ought to discuss. Already he had shown an awareness that the encounter with Paul held more than met the eye. He seemed not to believe that an argument with her boss had been sufficient to account for her white face and shaking hands.

"I know where we'll go." Grant swung the car around the fountain and headed down the tree-lined drive toward the main road. "We'll have to telephone first, but we can stop in Sausalito and call from there. It's a little late to make reservations, but if we give Maurice a few minutes' warning I think he'll find us a table. He'll fuss, but he'll find us a table."

CHAPTER SIX

EARLIER IN THE AFTERNOON the ocean fog had spilled over the hills, and now it lay like a blanket over the peninsula. As Grant and Terra wound their way toward higher ground, the trees by the side of the road seemed insubstantial in the mist. Terra rolled down her window and let the cool moist air pour over her, filling her senses with the smell, sight and feel of the forest. The quiet of the woods, scarcely disturbed by the smooth purr of the Mercedes, soothed her apprehensions, and she felt herself relaxing. Grant, too, seemed lulled by the misty silence, and they drove for miles without speaking.

All too soon the road widened and the silent trees gave way to rows of houses perched on the hillside. Instead of turning off onto the freeway that cut through the city, Grant followed the parkway beside the ocean. The sea breeze whipped through the open windows, and Terra shivered involuntarily.

"Would you like me to close the windows?" Grant asked, speaking for the first time since they had left the Blansford estate.

"I am a little cold," Terra admitted, "but I love the fresh air, so let's leave the windows down a little longer."

Grant reached into the back seat and pulled out a gray-and-red plaid car blanket. Gratefully Terra wrapped it around her shoulders. Snuggled in its warmth, she turned her head toward the view and let the ocean air buffet her face and billow in her hair. They whipped along the coastline, past long stretches of sandy beach and groves of windswept pines. Leaving the seaside, the road climbed up the face of a cliff, taking a series of steep switchback curves, then running along the cliff's edge.

"We might as well stop off at my place first," Grant said as he turned off the coast highway and headed into the city. "I'll telephone Maurice from there and find out when he can take us."

"Can't we just go on over to Sausalito?" Terra asked. "If we can't eat at Maurice's, I'm sure we can find somewhere else."

"Do you have any objections to going to my house?" Grant questioned. "It's right on our way, and I'd like to drop some things off and make a few telephone calls "

Terra felt uneasy about the prospect of being alone with him in his own home, but she couldn't think of a logical excuse to refuse. He had decided what he wanted to do and, in typical fashion, didn't seem about to welcome any attempt to change his mind. "Whatever you want," she replied coolly, "but I hope we'll be able to eat soon. I'd really like to get home early."

"Don't worry, little girl," Grant grinned. "We won't stay out past your bedtime—unless you want to, of course."

Despite her initial reluctance to visit Grant's house Terra's curiosity began to grow. She knew very little about his personal life other than the rumors and gossip that filtered through Margaret, and the chance to understand a little more about how he lived excited her.

The ascent to the top of the hills of San Francisco was accomplished in stages. The streets rose at forty-five degree angles for one block, then leveled off temporarily at each intersection. As the car slid effortlessly onto each flat cross street Terra felt a temporary respite, only to hold her breath again as the car nosed up another stretch of hill. No matter how many times she rode up and down those hills she always experienced a tingle of apprehension at the incredible angles.

Arriving at the top of the hill, Grant parked alongside the curb. As she got out of the car, Terra tried to guess which of the larger buildings that lined the street housed Grant's apartment. The Pacific Heights district, the location of San Francisco's largest mansions, was still its most fashionable residential neighborhood, but because of rising costs a number of the palatial homes had been converted into apartments.

This area, with its stately houses, beautifully landscaped gardens and magnificent view of the Golden Gate, was exactly the kind of neighborhood she would have expected Grant to choose.

The house immediately in front of them was a classical mansion set back from the street. A gleaming white stairway curved gracefully up the ivy-covered hillside to the front door. Tall Doric columns guarded the entrance, lending both strength and elegance to the architectural line. Opening the wrought-iron gate, Grant led the way up the stairs. When he had unlocked the front door, he held it wide for her. Stepping inside, she saw a spacious hallway flanked on one side by an elegant living room and on the other by a large formal dining room. The wind blew in from the open door, and the twin crystal chandeliers in each room tinkled cheerfully.

Before Terra could relay her delight at what she saw, a plump matronly woman of about sixty hustled down the hall. Terra thought she must be the superintendent and was a little puzzled when Grant said, "Terra, this is Mrs. Edwards, an absolutely indispensable friend."

The woman smiled warmly at the compliment and took Terra's hand in a friendly grasp.

"Mrs. Edwards, meet Terra Scott. We've just stopped by for a moment on our way to dinner," Grant explained. "Perhaps you might show her around while I do some things upstairs. I'll be down in about twenty minutes."

There was something immediately likable and

reassuring about Mrs. Edwards, and Terra
didn't object when the woman took both of her
hands and declared, "You're cold as ice. Why
don't you come back to the kitchen and I'll
make you a cup of tea. It won't take but a
minute."

The younger woman accepted gratefully and
followed Mrs. Edwards down the long hall that
led to the kitchen. Stepping through the door,
she gasped with pleasure at the magnificent
view. The large kitchen looked out over the city
to the Golden Gate. Although the hills beyond
were barely visible in the fog, Terra imagined
that on a clear day the unobstructed panorama
of the bay and Marin County must be spectacular.

Taking a seat at a trestle table in front of the
window, Terra waited while Mrs. Edwards put
the tea kettle on the stove. As she glanced
around she saw that one whole wall of the room
was brick and on it were hung dozens of gleaming copper pans. It must have taken years of
careful use to preserve the smooth shining finish
of the pans while imparting to them the look of
something that was not mere decoration. Care
was evident everywhere in this room, from the
crisply ironed gingham curtains at the window
to the sparkling white dishes visible behind the
glass doors of the huge, old-fashioned cupboard
to the row of herbs growing in terra-cotta pots
on the top of an antique pine dry sink. It was a
comfortable friendly place, and Terra remem-

bered an old embroidered sampler she had once seen that said, "The kitchen is heart of the house." She was sure that anyone who lived in a house with a kitchen like this must have his heart in the right place.

"This is my favorite room in the house," Mrs. Edwards commented as she joined Terra.

"I can certainly understand why," Terra agreed. "But everything else is lovely, too. How long have you lived here?"

"Many, many years." Mrs. Edwards chuckled. "When I first came here in 1940 I thought I'd be staying a year or two at the most. Of course, I didn't figure I'd fall in love. Once I married Mr. Edwards neither of us wanted to leave."

"I don't blame you," Terra said. "You couldn't ask for a more magnificent view or a lovelier home."

"Yes, the house is beautiful. It's changed through the years, but I think I'm happiest with the way it is now. My only worry is that Grant will get tired of such a big place and want to move."

Terra looked at the woman in consternation. "Surely you can rent his apartment to someone else if he leaves?" she asked, unable to imagine any dearth of tenants. Even if the rent were high, there would be plenty of people who would welcome the opportunity to live in a building like that one.

Mrs. Edwards leaned back in her chair,

laughing heartily. "This isn't my house. It belongs to Grant, and he stays here whenever he's in from the East, which lately has been quite often. I've been the housekeeper here since before he was born."

Terra's surprise was so fully evident from the look on her face that Mrs. Edwards felt obliged to explain. "Many of the old houses around here have been converted, and when Grant inherited the house I assumed he would do the same thing."

The tea kettle whistled shrilly, and Mrs. Edwards hurried over to the stove. "But, bless his heart, he had something else in mind." She continued to talk as she prepared the tea. "He made himself a complete apartment on the second floor, and he asked Mr. Edwards and me if we'd live in the rest of the house and take care of it for him. When I lost my husband I was even more grateful to Grant for giving me a home."

The housekeeper set cups on the table and poured the tea. "He's so good to me. He doesn't even want me to cook for him, though I do every chance I get."

Terra took in this information without comment. She was beginning to question her harsh judgment of the man she thought Grant had become. Maybe she had been rash in thinking him much changed. But this was neither the time nor the place to ponder such matters.

They drank the tea, and when they finished Mrs. Edwards showed Terra around the house.

Terra's favorite room was a large solarium next to the kitchen. The floor-to-ceiling windows faced the bay and also overlooked the gardens at the side of the house. A long flight of steps circled its way through the trees and shrubs down to the next street below. These public pathways were part of the charm of San Francisco's hilltop neighborhoods, and the one bordering Grant's house was by far the nicest Terra had seen.

As Mrs. Edwards led her from room to room, Terra could tell that Grant encouraged the woman to live in the whole downstairs as though it were her own. As a result, even though the rooms were large and formal, they felt lived in and welcoming. Although the homey atmosphere seemed to suit Mrs. Edwards, Terra found it hard to visualize Grant living there. She wondered whether her tour would include the second floor, and was disappointed when Mrs. Edwards led her to the living room to wait for him. A few minutes later he came down the stairs, and after a brief goodbye to the house-keeper they left.

The sun had descended into the heavy bank of fog that lay over the ocean, and the billowy mass was afire with shades of red and orange as they crossed the Golden Gate Bridge. The car swept down the steep hill toward Sausalito, a tiny town nestled between the coastal ridge of hills and the bay.

Leaving the bayside village, they followed the

highway north for a short distance and then turned left and threaded their way up steep twisting lanes toward the crest of a hill.

"Maurice thinks he'll be able to squeeze us in, especially if we don't mind a short wait," Grant said.

"It must be a busy place," Terra commented.

"Normally reservations for Maurice's are made months in advance. But he's an old friend, and tonight he tolerated my lack of foresight." Grant grinned. "I told him this was a very important occasion."

"Did he ask why?" Terra questioned, because she wondered why herself.

"Oh, no. Maurice is the soul of discretion. He's also so curious he won't hesitate to draw his own conclusions."

They reached the top of the hill and swung into a spacious driveway. Several other cars were parked there, but all Terra could see of the building was a wooden deck and stairs leading down the hillside. Next to the stairway, almost covered by the verdant shrubbery, a tiny carved sign announced Chez Maurice. Looking over the side of the hill, she got her first glimpse of Maurice's. Like many other buildings in this region, it clung tenaciously to the steep grade, with only the driveway and garage visible at the street level.

Maurice, Grant told Terra as they started down the stairs, had been one of the most famous chefs in Europe before his retirement several years earlier. When he had been a young man he had worked in San Francisco as an apprentice, and he had returned there to retire. Talented and vigorous, he found enforced leisure monotonous, so he had opened a very tiny exclusive restaurant on the top floor of his magnificent Marin County home.

"Actually he doesn't call it a restaurant. He says he entertains a handful of carefully selected friends each night. These 'guests' are only too willing to pay for the privilege."

"Does he do the cooking?" Terra inquired.

"Oh, no, he's the host, although he has been known to create a special dessert on rare occasions. Younger chefs consider it an honor to serve an apprenticeship here, and some of the finest French chefs have spent time with Maurice."

Grant pushed the doorbell, and they were greeted by a slight elderly man with longish, snow-white hair.

"Hello, Maurice," Grant said with a broad smile.

"Grant, my friend!" The old man clasped Grant firmly by the shoulders and shook him playfully. "I am so glad to see you." His gaze traveled past Grant and rested on Terra. "And you have brought your charming friend."

Grant introduced them, and Terra blushed when the older man uttered, "Delightful!"

With a gallantry that suited him perfectly, Maurice held her hand to his lips and bowed ever so slightly. "It is always a pleasure to see you, Grant, but even more so when you bring such a beautiful companion. Welcome, my dear, welcome." And he bowed again.

He showed them in and, once inside, continued to chatter as he studied his reservation book. "Such a treat to see you. Such a gift."

His smile and glance focused so obviously on Terra she laughed warmly in response.

"Such a treat," he repeated to Grant. "But if you had called earlier, even last week, I could have done better for you. Now you will have a short wait. I am sorry, but it cannot be helped."

Maurice continued to hover over the book, calling on the advice of several waiters and murmuring in French more rapidly than Terra's four years of high-school training in that language enabled her to follow.

Finally he looked up and beamed. "There. It is worked out. You will have the porch—our finest table—but it cannot be ready for about an hour." He leaned over conspiratorially and whispered to them, "Even at that I will have to shuffle Mr. Portman off without dessert. He will not suffer from the lack, I think."

Laughingly Terra protested against inconveniencing anyone for their sake, but Maurice silenced her. "Hush, my dear. It is all settled. So until your table is ready you will come downstairs to my quarters for a drink."

"That's very kind of you, Maurice," Grant

thanked him, "but we don't want to disrupt your work."

"Pierre can manage without me. In fact—" he smiled fondly "—if the truth be known, I do not think I am needed at all. These fellows—" he flung an arm to take in all the black-suited waiters "—they say, 'Oh, Maurice, do not go away.' But that is just to make an old man feel good. All runs well with me or without me." He chuckled softly and led the way down the stairs.

Terra had started after him when she felt Grant's hand at her elbow, detaining her and allowing Maurice to get out of earshot.

"I think I ought to prepare you. Maurice is quite capable of making outrageous remarks. He believes that honesty is a prerogative of old age, and so he says exactly what he thinks. Some people have found his comments rather blunt."

"Thanks for the warning. I'll try to smile no matter what he says."

Maurice's living room was exquisitely decorated in shades of soft blue and cream. Elegant tapestries hung on the walls, and graceful eighteenth-century chairs looked surprisingly inviting.

He poured drinks for them, and they sat in front of a large picture window, looking out over the blue black water toward the lights of Berkeley.

While Terra relaxed amid soft velvet cushions, sipping sherry and admiring the view, Maurice and Grant talked about days gone by.

Like Stephanie and her family, Maurice had
been a close friend of the Ingrahams. Grant, it
appeared, had spent several summers during his
adolescent years at Maurice's home in Paris.
From the madcap adventures the two men were
recalling Terra decided Maurice had been
Grant's self-appointed tutor in the pleasures of
Paris, at least such pleasures as a teenager might
enjoy.

Noticing Grant thoroughly relaxed and obviously enjoying the company of his old friend,
Terra felt she had never seen him appear so happy. The wary look he so often had was gone
from his eyes, and in its place she saw content-
ment. She found it difficult to understand how a
man who so obviously nurtured long-standing
relationships with his friends could reject the
idea of a permanent relationship with one
woman.

The Grant she was observing in this room,
and the one to whom Mrs. Edwards was so
devoted, seemed very different from the impersonal business executive who was governed by
expediency rather than emotion. She warned
herself not to be taken in by the sudden appearance of this gentler side of his nature. The
soft gleam in his eyes would no doubt soon be
replaced by the hard shrouded gaze she was sure
was a more frequent expression. When that happened the magic would fade, and she would be
back to facing the reality of her situation with
regard to Grant.

Yet even that reality had a strangeness to it. Somehow, when she had nearly forgotten about the very existence of Grant Ingraham, he had unexpectedly stepped back into her life. She wondered for a moment whether she would even have recognized him had his physical appearance not remained essentially the same, for his personality seemed so changed from what it had been when he was younger.

Glancing at him now, though, it occurred to her that his physical appearance had changed considerably. He was very much at ease at the moment. Sitting comfortably in conversation with his old friend, Grant lounged in a chair that seemed too small to contain him. His broad powerful shoulders made a mockery of the delicate wooden tracery against which they rested. His large strong hands were spread out on the velvet arms of the chair, and the living strength of sinew, the warmth of tanned skin, contrasted sharply with the soft pale fabric of the upholstery. His long legs, stretched out and crossed at the ankles, were the legs of a man fully mature in his masculinity. They were not the sprightly limbs of a youth. And for the first time Terra noticed that the dark fall of his thick hair, glinting in the low light as he nodded to Maurice, was sparked here and there by the tiniest glimmer of silver.

Looking at him this way, studying him without his paying the least attention to her scrutiny, Terra felt a warmth begin to spread through her until it reached her face and made her blush deep red, embarrassed, even though she had not been caught in her intense observation. She looked away from Grant, focusing on a silver vase that held a spray of perfect yellow roses. Maurice certainly had taste—in his business, in the appointments of his home and, presumably, in his friends. Grant was one of those friends, a man sophisticated and knowledgeable in the ways of the world. So Grant Ingraham had grown fully into manhood. That was no surprise. What was a surprise was that the fact should suddenly have become so important to one Terra Scott.

Lost in speculation, she was only vaguely aware the topic of conversation had shifted away from reminiscences.

"You are a fortunate man, Grant, to share the company of such a beautiful and loving woman."

Terra jerked herself to attention, denial ready on her lips, but before she could speak, Grant commented with a smile, "Yes. She certainly is beautiful, but unfortunately I have no right to claim a knowledge of her more intimate than that of an old friend—and business acquaintance."

"Ah, yes," Maurice sighed. "I have difficulty keeping up with the fashions in words. Between a man and a woman what knowledge is there, what business is there, other than love?"

Terra colored again instantly. She had

blushed more in the last half hour than she had in the previous year. Seeing the delicate flush on her cheeks, Grant smiled and shrugged almost imperceptibly, his eyes saying, "I warned you."

She took a deep breath. "I'm afraid you've misunderstood, Maurice. I don't know Grant very well at all."

The old man smiled benevolently. "Do not be embarrassed. Love is often best between near strangers. Time has a way of mellowing passion into great love. Do not worry."

Turning an even deeper shade of crimson, Terra interrupted hastily, "No, no, you still don't understand. I don't even like Grant!"

She stopped in confusion as Grant started to laugh and Maurice's eyebrows shot up questioningly.

"I mean, we aren't even good friends. He's just been helping me with a problem," she rushed on, desperate to check Maurice's obvious train of thought. She wondered whether her behavior had made Maurice think she was Grant's lover or whether the old man just naturally assumed that any woman who shared Grant's table also shared his bed.

Maurice turned and looked sharply at Grant. "Is this true?"

Grant nodded, a look of barely controlled amusement on his face.

"Grant, ah, Grant," Maurice said, slowly shaking his head as though a great sadness had come upon him. "Have you learned nothing of what I tried to teach you about love? A woman like this.... Where are your eyes, my boy? Where is your heart?"

"Maurice," Terra broke in, trying to curb him. "It's not that Grant doesn't...." She paused again, not sure where the completion of that sentence would lead her. "Grant," she pleaded in frustration, "will you please explain the situation to him?"

Grant had been slouched in his chair, his eyes lazily taking in the scene before him as though he were watching a humorous play. When Terra appealed to him he straightened and looked at her with a mock-serious gaze.

"The young lady is concerned, Maurice, that you will think we are lovers. Terra is a very honest woman and would not intentionally mislead anyone."

Terra frowned. That wasn't exactly what she had wanted him to say.

Maurice smiled confidentially. "At last I understand. You two are so coy. You did not tell me, but now I see. You have had a lover's quarrel and think your affair is over, so now you have come to Maurice's for fine food, fine wine, the chance to talk and perhaps to say farewell."

He sighed nostalgically. "Ah, passion. I remember its ways so well. So sudden to flame, so quick to burn out of control, so impossible to quench."

Terra opened her mouth to object and then

shut it once more, finally grasping the futility of disagreeing with Maurice. When she spoke again it was with amused resignation.

"I'm not going to argue with you anymore, Maurice."

Their host picked up the crystal decanter and walked over to offer her more sherry, smiling his acceptance of her truce. As he leaned over to pour the wine he whispered softly for Terra's hearing alone, "It is not Maurice with whom you argue, *mon chou*. It is yourself."

Before she could reply, a waiter appeared and beckoned to his employer. After a short conversation with the man Maurice returned. "I have to leave you now. When your table is ready I will call. It won't be long."

When he was well out of hearing Terra slumped in her chair, sighing loudly. "He is *impossible*!"

"When Maurice gets wound up on the subject of love it's difficult to stop him," Grant commented with a note of amused affection in his voice. "I was afraid we were going to hear his lecture on 'the mystery of great passion.' That waiter showed up in the nick of time." He moved over to a chair closer to Terra. Reaching across the small distance between them, he took her hand in his own.

"He liked you, though. That was obvious." He looked deeply into her eyes, and Terra had the uncanny feeling that she had just passed some sort of test, that it was important to Grant she hadn't failed him.

Under the intensity of his dark stare her own eyes fell, and she cleared her throat before lightly remarking, "Well, I'm certainly glad he did. I'd hate to hear what he says to someone he doesn't like!"

"I like you, too, Terra."

Her eyes flew to him and saw there soft beguiling desire. Such a simple statement from such a man had an impact far stronger than the impact of a more forceful utterance from someone else. For a wordless moment they sat facing each other, and in the tiny space between them blossomed a whole world of possibility and promise.

Grant's lips parted, and Terra leaned ever so slightly toward him. "Getting hungry?" he asked, and she nodded blankly, as though she had forgotten they were in a restaurant.

On cue Maurice appeared and waved them up the stairs. "Mr. Portman has finished his meal." He led them through a series of rooms to a glassed-in porch that overlooked the same view they had seen from the living room. The single table was set with a pale pink linen cloth on which were displayed rose-toned china plates and cups. Tall crystal glasses with delicate stems and flatware that gleamed softly in the low light added to the fresh yet elegant setting, and in the center of the table, in a crystal bowl, floated two perfect orchids, their inner petals picking up the blush of the cloth. So intimate was this very private room that it did not seem to be in a place of business.

As she sat down Terra noticed a tiny envelope on her plate. She regarded it doubtfully for a moment, then lifted it. The stiff creamy paper felt cool between her fingers as she hesitantly opened the flap. She extracted a small card and read, "May you prosper in your love." Her eyes sought Grant's, and he held out his hand for the card. Skimming it, a teasing smile danced on his lips, and he looked up at Maurice, who beamed like a child who has just performed a new trick. Impulsively Terra got up and kissed him on the cheek. He was incorrigible, no doubt about that, but he was also thoroughly charming.

"Tonight," Maurice said as he held her chair for her, "you are my guests. Relax. Enjoy each other. Trust me to make your evening a special one."

The dinner progressed at its own leisurely pace, which so calmed and relaxed Terra she forgot everything that had been on her mind. Waiters appeared first with a salmon pâté on a silver platter garnished with limes and capers. Then came a consumé, delicately seasoned and graced with a hint of sherry. It was jellied and chilled, and it sparkled beneath a sprig of fresh mint. As a prelude to the main dish Maurice served them a cool champagne sherbet to clear the palate for the tastes to come—the tastes of Chateaubriand smothered in mushrooms, accompanied by a bevy of lightly cooked fresh vegetables.

The food, the soft strains of music in the background, the golden gleam of the candles that lit the room—all these overwhelmed Terra's senses like powerful drugs. It was as though she had discovered a new world. And at the center of that world was Grant, smiling intimately at her, talking softly and, every now and then, stroking the back of her hand when she rested it on the rose-colored tablecloth. His presence seemed to wrap itself around her, to urge her gently to follow him. But where and into what she did not know.

Staring dreamily at the two orchids, Terra thought that Maurice had created the perfect atmosphere for falling in love. For a moment she allowed herself to imagine what it might be like to love Grant. He was enigmatic, hard to understand with his swift changes from warm personal openness to cool business demeanor. He was assertive and powerful in his own world, but he was gentle, too—or so it seemed. And, Terra had to admit, despite the fact he was president and chairman of the board of a huge multinational corporation he was fun!

He was also the world's most confirmed "confirmed bachelor." He made no secret about the rules of his game of love. He would want a woman to love him, but only until he was ready to move on. With an effort Terra forced herself to shake off her romantic musings. If she did not think clearly now, how could she hope to keep her balance when she was alone with Grant?

She looked up to see Maurice approaching with a wheeled cart. While they watched he began to blend exotic-smelling liqueurs with fresh fruit in a skillet over a low flame. He touched a match to the mixture and it flared dramatically. Spooning the bubbling filling onto a thin crepe, he rolled it deftly and placed it on a plate before Terra. When he had repeated the performance for Grant, he folded his hands and beamed at them.

"It is time for this old man to go to bed. You may wish me pleasant dreams, but I will wish a sleepless night for both of you."

Terra could do nothing but laugh at such outrageous frankness, and she bade him a fond good evening.

They finished dessert, and Grant poured the last of the wine into her glass. She sipped it and gazed at him across the table. The dreamy wonder of being with him in this fine place filled her again, but when he spoke the spell was shattered.

"Terra," he said, "what did you find at the Blansford today?"

Terra knit her brows, trying quickly to rally her thoughts. The afternoon seemed faraway, as though it had been spent on a different continent. Then gradually the candlelight and flowers receded, and the image of a woman reading documents flashed into her mind's eye, as if that woman were someone other than herself. Shuddering, she relived her discovery, Paul's horror and her own sense of helpless frustration.

"I can help you, Terra. Tell me what you found. Unless I know what the problem is, I can't help you to solve it."

Like suddenly released water spilling over a dam, words rushed out. Detail by detail she laid her suspicions and her discovery in front of him. In response to his questions she gave him as many details concerning the facsimiles as she could remember without her notes.

When he stopped asking questions she said, "It's all so unbelievable, such an amazing coincidence. If I hadn't accidentally stumbled on those diaries, Paul would be claiming that our copies are part of the genuine lost edition, and he'd be wrong."

Grant remained silent and thoughtful.

Terra fidgeted with her wineglass and then folded and unfolded her napkin, waiting for his support. She really wanted him to go with her on Monday to convince Paul, but she didn't want to ask; she wanted him to offer.

"Grant," she began tentatively, "what are we going to do?"

He looked at her solemnly. "We aren't going to do anything, Terra."

"Nothing at all?" She was incredulous. "We can't stand by and let Paul make a mistake like that. He'll be the laughingstock of the book world. We have to convince him the copies he discovered are facsimiles."

"We still don't know that for sure," Grant replied quietly, as though trying to calm her. "I know you're excited about your discovery, but try to keep things in perspective. Do you honestly think experts wouldn't be able to distinguish between a genuine first edition and a reproduction?"

Terra hesitated. "If the type, paper and ink were all the same, it's possible the experts would be fooled, isn't it?"

Grant shook his head slowly. "The possibility of anyone's duplicating the 1848 edition so exactly is remote enough to be practically nonexistent."

"Under ordinary circumstances, yes," she agreed, "but we're not talking about ordinary circumstances. The second printing would have been done by the same printer as the first. That means the typeface might still have been available. Even if it had passed out of use for other books, it might have been kept by Waltham. The same with the paper. Granted, it would have been exceptional for the press to have held on to fine paper like that for more than fifty years without using it, but it's not out of the question."

"No," Grant said, beginning to seem a little on edge, as though what Terra was saying had more validity than he wanted to admit, "it's not out of the question, not impossible—just one hundred percent improbable—which amounts to the same thing.''

Terra sat back, unable to answer, and Grant continued, ''You've said yourself you haven't found any evidence that the facsimiles Waltham planned had ever been printed. All you really have is a description of a plan to make money, a plan conceived of by a young man who was in financial straits. Did you find mention of the booklets going to press?''

''No.''

''Did you find catalogs listing the facsimiles for sale?''

''No, but—''

''Did you find customer orders for them, correspondence requesting copies?''

''No. No, I didn't. I didn't have time, Grant. Who knows what else is in those files? That's the whole point—the proof is there. I just know it. I just need time to find it.''

''Terra,'' Grant said softly, ''time is a factor in every business. You have to learn when to stop. Take publishing. If my people waited to put out a book until it was absolutely perfect, we'd never publish a damn thing. Nobody has infinite time to work on a project, no matter how important it is. The author looks at his manuscript and he says to himself, 'this is the best I can do and still fulfill my contract.' The editor looks at her deadline. The same with the marketing people, the same with the bookseller. Time is a factor always, and it's always limited. You have to stop somewhere and say, 'This is the best I can do.' You've done your best, and you should let it go at that.''

Terra was impressed but remained uncertain. ''I still think it's possible the pamphlets are facsimiles. It would explain everything.''

''Now you're committing a basic error in research,'' Grant chided. ''You're letting your fondness for your theory color your judgment. I had a feeling this was happening. I wanted to give you every opportunity to convince me you were able to support your suspicions with hard facts. You've got facts, but they do not exclusively explain what you're trying to prove.'' His eyes held hers. ''All you have is more suspicion—based on logic, true, but not based on irrefutable proof. This could go on forever, Terra. . . .''

She didn't argue any further. What Grant said about lack of conclusive proof was certainly true. The scenario that would explain the booklets as facsimiles *was* the less likely one. Perhaps she was trying too hard, jumping to conclusions on insubstantial evidence. Yet she still felt convinced the pamphlets were not from the 1848 edition. If she couldn't convince Grant, who seemed to be on her side, how was she going to convince Paul, who was dead set against her?

Grant leaned against the table and took both her hands in his. For a fleeting moment she

thought the conversation was over. She thought
Grant would speak of matters more suitable to
the surroundings. She thought he was going to
say something to Terra Scott, woman, instead
of Terra Scott, researcher. A little thrill of expectation sparked in her as he breathed, "Terra,
I want you to make me a promise."

Without answer, she raised her eyes until she
met his. "I want you to promise me you won't
mention your theory to anyone."

It took quite a bit of effort to hide her disappointment when she was looking directly at him.
She didn't know whether she had managed it,
but apparently she had, for he continued without a pause. "The rare-book market is extremely volatile. One whisper of doubt and the value
of the lost edition could come tumbling down.
You have no real proof, and until you do it
would be unfair to jeopardize the reputation of
the edition, not to mention Paul's reputation—
and your own."

"But I've already mentioned the theory to
Paul."

Grant seemed shocked at this, but his loss of
composure was so brief, so nearly imperceptible, Terra thought she must have imagined it.

"On Monday," he said evenly, "you'll tell
him you've thought things over and you realize
you have no proof. You do realize that, don't
you?"

She nodded mutely.

"And," he continued, "if you also finish the

brochure as promised, he'll be convinced you've changed your mind. Otherwise he'll assume you're sticking to the facsimile theory.''

Terra understood all of this. She had not changed her mind, but the late hour and the wine were having their effect. She could not decide now what had to be done. Grant released her hands, and she withdrew slowly from his grasp. She felt as though a perfect evening had been totally spoiled, and she wished it were over. It was impossible to argue with Grant's position, and she was tired of trying.

''I don't think I need to mention,'' Grant said coolly, ''that our conversation should remain between us. I don't think Paul needs to know we've discussed matters.''

''Of course,'' Terra answered succinctly, hoping to close the topic once and for all.

When they reached the car she slumped gratefully against the comfortable leather seat. The whole day crashed in on her with sudden force, and she drifted into an uneasy sleep.

The next thing she knew the car had stopped and Grant's large hand was gently shaking her shoulder. Sleepily she opened her eyes and let him lead her toward her house. She fumbled for her key, and he took it from her. Once inside he closed the door and guided her toward the couch.

''Shall I make some coffee?'' he asked. ''I think I can manage to find everything.''

Terra would have preferred him just to leave,

but she was too sleepy to argue. She told him where to locate the coffee and the cups, and before she could say more he was at her elbow with a steaming mug. She had again fallen asleep. He sat beside her and propped her up with his arm across her shoulders. Handing her the coffee, he began apologetically, "I know I should just let you go to sleep, Terra—you've had a hard day. But somehow I didn't think it appropriate to waste Maurice's good dinner."

At those words she shot totally awake, as though the coffee had been ice water and he had thrown it in her face. What did he mean? Was he going to extract payment for having taken her to the elegant restaurant. Was he really that crass?

"What?" she said hoarsely.

"I took you to see Maurice for a reason, Terra. For a selfish reason, a presumptuous reason, I admit. I think I wanted his approval."

"Oh?" she questioned. "Does he check out all your prospects? Sort of a screening process, is it? I guess it's like the first readers at your publishing company. I take it they look at anything that comes in and get rid of the dross before the bigwigs waste any of their precious time."

"Come on, Terra," he said, on the edge of anger, "stop being such a child. I'm telling you this because it's important, because you are the first of my dates Maurice has ever met."

"But surely you've taken other women to his place."

"Only relatives."

Terra wasn't sure what was going on here. Perhaps there had been more to the fuss Maurice had made than she had understood at the time. Perhaps her dinner with Grant really had been a special occasion. She felt ashamed of her impolite reaction to his admission, but she was still not ready to examine the implication of his words.

"Do you mean you've gone to Maurice's alone?"

"Often," Grant replied. "I suppose it seems strange to you that the bachelor-rake, the bon vivant, should sometimes choose to dine alone?"

"No."

"I don't prefer to dine alone, Terra," he said, and his voice had become a little huskier than it had been. He moved closer to her on the couch.

She would have moved away; she was not at all confident of the wisdom of even having let him come in, let alone sitting so close. She would have moved away, but something in his eyes stopped her. They seemed darker than ever, a dusky light emanating from their cloudy depths. He raised a single finger and drew it along her cheek. She sat perfectly still, as though a dangerous animal were investigating her at its leisure. Perhaps if she didn't move it would lose interest and go away.

His finger retraced the same path, and her skin tingled under his touch. Slowly he cupped her face, the slight roughness of his male skin brushing the silky femininity of her own. The contrast sent a shiver racing through her, and her slender shoulders trembled.

"Oh, my, Terra, you *are* tired," he said, and made a slight movement as if to rise, to leave.

Without even realizing she was about to do it, Terra reached out her hand and put it on his thigh to stop him from standing up. He almost started as her gentle fingers touched the muscled strength of his leg. He did not relax; in fact, he seemed to become tenser. His eyes bored into hers, and she saw that the cloudy depths had cleared, that the light that burned there now was the clean flame of desire. She couldn't bear the intensity of his gaze. Her eyes fell, but only so far as to stare at his wide mouth, his lips curved with a sensuousness that was compelling, tempting.

Suddenly she felt she had to know again the taste of those lips. She tilted her head, raised her chin ever so slightly. But the movement was a declaration, and its meaning was clear to the man at whom it was directed. Instantly his lips seized hers with a power she had forgotten he had. A jolt rocked her, and in response he pressed his eager mouth even more firmly against her own. His swift tongue teased hers, agile as flame, and willingly she ran her own tongue along the contours of his fine white teeth.

His strong tanned hands held her face, and

they were so warm, so fiery, it seemed they had retained something of the sun that had browned them. Her own pale fingers reached for the darkness of his thick hair. Its springy vitality almost resisted the tousling of her fingers, but she persisted until both her hands were buried in the softness.

At the touch of her hands on his head, Grant pulled back his face until he could look at the woman in his arms. With breathless anticipation Terra opened her eyes, afraid that when she did so there would be no one there. But she was wrong—gloriously, wonderfully wrong. This was not a phantom or a dream. This was the man whose physical presence had imposed upon her all evening. She knew now why she couldn't take her eyes off of him at Maurice's. It was because she wanted to have her hands on him. A feast for the eyes was a stingy feast indeed. She almost giggled at the thought, and seeing the smile in her eyes, Grant smiled, too. "Terra?" he said. "Terra...."

And his arms encircled her in an embrace that left her breathless and not caring whether she ever breathed again. Once more his lips claimed hers. They were not questioning. Their hot pressure asked nothing, simply stated that he was a man and she was a woman. His mouth did not explore hers. It knew its territory well, and the heat of his kiss burned across her senses like a brushfire across a wide field.

With an abandon she had never known before

Terra gave in to the feelings rushing through her. She was dizzy; she was elated; she was transported by the sensation that every nerve in her body was alive, was responding to the passion of the man whose own passion was undeniable, inviting, enticing as a candle to a moth.

Deftly, Grant removed her silk jacket. His hands grazed her neck, her arms, her breasts, and she cursed the thin fabric of her blouse that prevented his flesh from touching her own. But the blouse, too, soon met its fate, and when Grant's fingers slowly, teasingly, stroked light as a breeze between her naked shoulders and the dusky cleft of her breasts, Terra shuddered and arched slightly to meet his questing fingertips.

As soon as he saw her nearly imperceptible movement toward him he withdrew his hand, and Terra's body, involuntarily expressing disappointment, sank back against the cushions of the couch. But once more his fingers reached for her, this time beginning their inexorable journey of flame at the base of her breast and rising in their touch toward her nipple, which hardened in anticipation. Again she thrust herself toward the power of his hand; again he pulled away. A soft moan escaped from her throat, and instantly Grant's lips stifled her small weak sigh.

The warmth of his kiss enveloped her, and this time when she arched her back toward him, his hand grasped her with a gentle but firm clasp that sent her head reeling. She could feel with heightened senses her swollen nipple against the slightly rough skin of his palm, and his large strong fingers held her quivering breast, radiating a searing heat that spread to the farthest reaches of her sensitized body.

"Oh, Grant!" she whispered in the one brief instant in which his lips released hers. But then, they again descended to silence the plea in her voice. Her hand, trembling with eagerness, searched for the buttons of his shirt, and feeling her shaking fingers on his chest, he guided them toward the goal she sought. One by one she fumblingly pulled the smooth buttons from their holes, and when she had released them down to his waist, he gave a skilled shrug that opened the shirt almost completely, exposing the bronzed expanse of his muscled chest.

Again Terra's hand reached for him, and this time she touched not the stiff white cloth of the shirt but the pliant vibrant silkiness of his skin, skin that exuded a warm manly muskiness. Her hand seemed small against him, but it had a power of its own, for when he felt her fingertips tentatively touch the hot skin near his nipple, then hesitantly burn a path to the strong curve of his shoulder, he drew in a tremulous shuddering breath. He pulled her so close she could feel her soft breasts flatten against the throbbing wall of his chest; his arm behind her lay hot on the skin of her waist, and the moist breath from his sensuous lips fanned her closed eyelids.

She put her slender arms around his broad back, glorying in the feel of his nearness. She

held him so hard she thought her arms would go
numb from the effort—but she didn't care. His
hair brushed her forehead, and so alive was she
to his presence it seemed she could feel each
strand separately. Her lips grazed the tender
skin at the place where his neck met his
shoulder, and unable to resist the impulse, she
darted her tongue toward the spot. His skin was
salty beneath her mouth, and again she flicked it
with her tongue. He stiffened and drew back his
head.

Her eyelids felt heavy; it seemed to take
forever to raise them to stare into the dark eyes
that were now bearing down on her own. His
gaze was unclear. Passion clouded his expression, but a slow tender smile spread from his
wide lips to the eyes that held Terra's own with
riveting power.

Yet even as she watched she could see his expression change. His face began to harden as a
pond hardens with the first freeze of winter.
Terra shuddered, but it was not the quivering of
passion that shook her frail frame. He was still
so close to her she could feel his heart beat
against her own. Yet there was again a distance
coming between them, and she knew he was not
going to kiss her in the way that had transported
her only moments earlier.

And she was right. Lifting himself, he
brushed his lips against her forehead. He
reached down and picked up her blouse, gently
putting it over her shoulders. She did not leave it

that way but hastened to draw it on, to cover herself, to protect herself from his gaze. She could not understand what had happened, what she had done to change the situation between them, and as Grant was silent, she thought she might never know.

But then he spoke, and though she remained disappointed, his gentle voice soothed her and his words made sense, though reason was not what she most wanted at the moment.

"Terra," he said softly, "oh, Terra, you are more beautiful, more desirable than I even imagined. But we can't. We can't let our first lovemaking be just one more trauma in a traumatic day. You've had all you can take today, and I can't let myself add one more crisis to the score. I want you to go shower and go to bed—alone. You have enough to think about without my adding another burden."

Wordlessly she shook her head, but her protest had no effect on Grant.

"Come along now," he said, making her feel like a child. He picked up her silk jacket and folded it over his arm, standing and urging her to stand, too, which she did on shaking legs.

He led her to the bedroom, and when they reached the door she expected him to say he would go back downstairs and let himself out. He knew the way; he knew the whole house. Instead he said something that shocked her.

"Terra," he breathed, "I'm staying tonight."

Instantly she snapped out of the lethargy that had weighed down her thinking.

"Oh, no. You can't. I . . . ."

"I'll use the spare room. My intentions are one hundred percent honorable," he grinned, much to Terra's indignation. "I have to be in Berkeley first thing tomorrow, and it doesn't make sense to drive all the way across the bridge and back again when it's already so late. I've spent many nights in the spare room here, and one more won't matter."

She could have pointed out to him that all those other nights had been at a time when her father had been alive—and present. Instead she said, "Oh, Grant. No one ever stays here. I have a reputation to uphold. I have to face the neighbors tomorrow, you know. I'm sorry, but it's impossible."

What was really impossible was to imagine him being under the same roof with her and not continuing what had been started so brief a time ago. Terra's head was beginning to clear, and she knew it wouldn't be long before regret would start to set in, regret that she had acted in so abandoned a fashion with a man to whom she meant nothing except another conquest. She didn't trust him; she didn't trust herself. She didn't want him to stay in her spare room. Or rather, she was afraid he *wouldn't* stay there, that she would awake to find him in her own room and that she wouldn't ask him to go away.

"Grant, you've got to understand. I really—"

"Terra, I'm staying. Now go to bed." He turned and went down the hall toward the spare bedroom.

She stood motionless for a few moments. She was so tired. It had been an incredible day, and she was worn to the bone with exhaustion, too tired to fight, rapidly becoming even too tired to worry.

She shrugged and began to undress, casting an occasional glance toward the doorway. Her nightgown lay on the bed where she had tossed it in her haste that morning. She wondered if she ought to try to dig out a flannel nightdress from her cedar chest but decided against it. It was a little silly to be wearing a flannel nightgown in California in the summer! Besides, she was not going to accommodate the man down the hall by being uncomfortable on his account.

She took a quick shower. Then, turning out the light, she climbed into bed and closed her eyes. But she could not relax. She shifted from one position to another, her ears straining to hear sounds from down the hall.

She tried to think about all that had happened that day. Thoughts of Grant seemed to wipe out all other thought, but even so fatigue overcame her. She had begun to drift off to sleep when a sound outside her door jarred her awake. Her heart pounded, and she drew in a ragged breath. Then she heard a soft knock at the door.

"Terra?"

A jolt charged through her, leaving her tingling. She lay as silently as she could, but the pounding of her heart seemed to fill the room with sound.

The door creaked a little as he pushed it open. Closing her eyes, she held her breath, knowing that he was moving closer. Yet when he spoke she realized he was still standing close to the door.

"Terra?" he repeated. "Are you awake?"

Holding the covers up to her chin, she whispered a response. "Yes."

"I meant every word I said at Maurice's. Don't tell anyone about your suspicions. If you speak indiscreetly, you will hurt a lot of people, including yourself." Without waiting for a reply, he left the room and shut the door. Sighing, Terra rolled over on her stomach and buried her head in the pillow. If she had needed any proof she was a stupid fool for nearly giving in to Grant, she had it now. What a sweet good-night from one lover to another—"don't speak indiscreetly about business matters." She was planning just what she would say to that in the morning when sleep claimed her and wiped out all plans for revenge.

WHEN SHE AWOKE the next day, the sun was shining resplendently and she was filled with a joy she couldn't understand. It took her a moment to remember the rapture of Grant's caress and another moment to remember it had come to naught. Yet she wasn't really disappointed.

Grant had been so tender, so passionate, she knew the unfinished business between them was more than a matter of a few Victorian pamphlets. In the bright light of morning the events of the previous night appeared in a different perspective, and Terra was almost certain she had put a false emphasis on the note of warning she had heard in Grant's last remark. She had thought, in the moments before she had fallen asleep, that he had had his own interest at heart, but now she saw things more clearly.

He had no personal interest in the pamphlets, had expressed no intention of investing in the edition. If he *had* warned her, he had probably been sincere in his concern for her professional reputation. It was certainly true that she ran the risk of mistaking a theory for a fact. Nonetheless she had no intention of letting the matter drop. She couldn't prove the booklets were facsimiles, but then she still couldn't prove they were genuine, either. She decided to continue to play by ear. It wasn't going to be easy, considering Paul's reaction to her revelation, but it was all she could think of for the moment.

More pressing was the matter of her overnight guest. Straining to hear sounds from down the hall, she concluded that Grant must still be asleep. She jumped out of bed and pulled on a pair of snug blue jeans and a striped jersey top. Quickly she ran a comb through her hair and splashed water on her face.

She made as little noise as possible as she

descended the stairs and headed for the kitchen. On tiptoes she approached the cupboards and was about to open a door when she noticed a cereal bowl and a juice glass in the sink. She turned and ran back up the stairs to the spare room. Standing in the open doorway, she saw that the bed had been neatly made. The room showed no sign of having been occupied.

For a reason she couldn't explain she felt drawn back downstairs and toward her study. A sense of uneasiness crept over her, a vague sense that something was very wrong. Entering the study, she walked over to the desk, and as she looked at the jumble of papers before her goose bumps began to rise on her arms. The picture of the room as she had left it, papers flung all over and the door shut, flashed into her mind, and she realized instantly that all her papers had been moved. In a neat pile in the middle of the desk were several sheets of paper covered with what could only have been Grant's handwriting, and beneath them was a typed copy of the same material. Reading it, she realized he had written the brochure for her. The prose was much more polished than Paul's version had been, but the story was essentially the same. The last sheet contained only three words: "Remember your promise."

Terra's heart sank. So Maurice's good dinner hadn't been wasted after all. The terrible truth struck her like a blow to the stomach. She wanted to cry, to lash out at Grant and at herself. She had foolishly misread his intentions entirely. The special occasion of the previous evening had been a special opportunity for Grant to sneak into her house and make use of her notes. She couldn't understand his part in all of this, but she could understand that she had been used—and the knowledge was crushing. She should have followed her instincts. She should have remained convinced that Grant had changed. She shouldn't have fallen for his tender manner. She should have realized it was false, a ploy. She should have...she shouldn't have.... The words spun in her head, and for a while she could only sit at her desk in silent misery. How could she have been so gullible? How could she have been?

CHAPTER SEVEN

AFTER SHE HAD FORCED HERSELF to drink a cup of coffee and eat a piece of toast that seemed as palatable as paper Terra plunged into her Saturday-morning chores. She dusted the bookshelves and the furniture and vacuumed the carpet with much more care than usual, eager to keep herself occupied. For two hours she busied herself with cleaning and polishing, until finally she ran out of things to do. She made herself another cup of coffee and considered trying to eat a sandwich, but changed her mind as soon as she had taken the bread and meat out of the fridge.

Sitting at her kitchen table, she could see her own garden and, beyond that, Jeff's lawn and flower beds, bathed in the noonday sun. Jeff's parents lived in that house, too, but they had been away for several weeks visiting his sister, who had just had a baby. Idly she noticed that both his lawn and hers needed mowing. When Jeff got around to cutting his, he would do hers, as well. In return she gave his roses the same care she gave her own.

It was a comfortable arrangement, just like

everything about their relationship. She felt completely at ease with Jeff, not at all as nervous as she felt whenever Grant was around. She should have learned from that fact. She should have known that the predictable comfort offered by a man like Jeff was preferable to the seesaw of emotions she experienced with Grant. She should have known better, but she hadn't...didn't now.

She shifted her glance inside, staring into her cup at the little pool of dark coffee without really seeing it. The memory of dinner at Maurice's floated across her mind, and despite the bitterness with which she ought to have remembered it, the thought of the dinner wrapped her in a momentary haze of pleasure. She could still see the gleam of the silver, the pale orchids vibrant against the rose linen, the spectacular panorama of the lights beyond the bay, and she could still sense Grant's presence, as though something of him lingered, like a fine elusive perfume. But she had realized, even while it was happening, that the evening had had a fairy-tale quality about it. It had been a dream. And now she was awake.

With the wisdom of hindsight Terra knew the evening had obviously meant something entirely different to Grant. In the cold light of morning it had become more than evident to her that she had mistaken Grant's romantic interest in her. It should have been clear to her from the beginning...it *had* been clear—she had just chosen to ignore the facts.

When Grant first visited the bookstore—only
a week ago—she had wondered briefly why he
should suddenly appear after all those years, but
the question had been buried in the rush of
events that followed. Nagging doubts had
sprung up when she'd met Dan Forbush and
then again when she'd spoken to Dr. Duke. But
she had been oblivious to the biggest clue: the
attention that Grant had paid to her.

With painful frankness she again went over
events in her mind. Her "romantic" dinner with
Grant had probably started off as an appropriate and polite conclusion to the research trip. It
had provided Grant the opportunity to ask her
what she had discovered at the Blansford. It
seemed pretty clear to her now, though, that he
hadn't really expected her to find anything important. He had seemed slightly shocked at her
argument in defense of her facsimile theory. In
fact, it was then that he had probably formulat-
ed the plan to stay overnight at her house!
Obviously the Browning-pamphlet notes were a
much more compelling reason to get into her
home than she herself. The thought tore at her
heart, but she forced herself to continue to
review the facts calmly.

All of a sudden she set down her cup with
such an abrupt movement that a sharp clang
rang out as it hit the saucer. How could she have
been so blind? The key to all this had been staring her in the face, but she hadn't noticed it until
that very minute. Grant must have been official-

ly investigating the lost edition from the very start! That alone must have been his reason for suddenly appearing at Fosters' as if out of the blue. Paul himself would never have thought it necessary to call in an outsider, but Grant could easily have given in to the request of an interested friend—Forbush or, more likely, Mr. Blansford. There was really no telling who might invest in the edition, who might benefit from Grant's assurance the pamphlets were what Paul Foster claimed them to be.

Grant hadn't been actively involved in collecting for some time, but that didn't mean that his opinion wasn't an informed and valuable one. Naturally once he discovered Terra was officially in charge of the investigation he would want to keep tabs on her. What better way than to renew her acquaintance, taking advantage of the old friendship between her father and him?

Grant, if he was acting on behalf of friends who wanted Paul's information checked out, would not logically stifle any attempt to prove Paul wrong. That meant he must honestly be convinced the booklets were real—which was very convenient considering the fact he would find it embarrassing in the extreme to have to prove Paul wrong after having known him for so many years. Perhaps Paul understood what Grant was up to and that was why he had reacted so violently to the suggestion Terra had information that might change Grant's mind.

It was ironic, Terra thought unhappily as she

washed out her cup and saucer, that after going to so much effort to find out what she knew, Grant had ended up rejecting her conclusions. His reaction to her discovery still bothered her. She had wanted and needed his support and had been stunned when it was not forthcoming. Up until the discussion at Maurice's he had seemed to be keeping an open mind about the possibility the pamphlets were not genuine. Yet in thinking back, she realized he had never given any indication he supported her suspicions; he had merely encouraged her to try to prove them. He must now feel, she reflected, that all available evidence had been uncovered, that he could go to whomever he was working for and tell them Paul was offering the real McCoy.

In his own typical fashion Grant had taken the last step into his own hands; he himself had written the sales brochure, completely bystepping Terra's doubts and hesitations. But the brochure was still with her. He must trust her as well as Paul. Why? He must have had quite a bit of confidence in his performance as a lover to think she would see things his way just because he had kissed and caressed her. Terra shuddered in disgust that rapidly changed to sadness. What had seemed to promise so much had meant so little. . . .

She dried and put away the breakfast dishes. Then she stood on a kitchen chair and took her long-spouted watering can down from the top shelf of the cupboard. Although many of her plants needed water at various times during the week, she always took a few moments on the weekend to inspect each plant and gave it as much attention as it needed. In addition to watering she dusted leaves, pruned away dead growth and checked for any problems that might threaten the plants' health. On that particular morning, however, she went about her tasks so absently a whole army of aphids might have escaped her notice. She was totally preoccupied with the events of the previous day and night.

Grant's insistence that she keep silent about her suspicions now made much more sense than it had. Once he felt convinced the pamphlets were genuine he would be very anxious to protect the interests of Dan Forbush and Nathaniel Blansford and would not want anyone stirring up trouble by raising ungrounded suspicions. In Grant's eyes Terra must appear to be an amateur scholar who had formed a theory based on a hunch and who then refused to give up that theory despite having had it pointed out to her that her ideas were implausible. He probably even thought she presented a danger—at least in the financial sense. Her doubts, once expressed, had the power to knock down the price of the edition. That fact had been mentioned previously—and it was an important one.

If only she had been able to make a stronger case for the facsimile theory! If she could have convinced Grant, his manipulation of her would have been unnecessary. She would have been spared the insult of being used by him. Of course, she would also never have known the powerful magic of being in his embrace. But she didn't want to consider that angle. She had to keep her head on business, and the fact remained that had she been more skilled at getting her point across, she would have saved Paul the embarrassment of being wrong. She was still convinced the facsimile theory was correct. Suddenly she realized she was now in a position to make not only Paul look foolish but Grant, as well. For a moment it seemed to her it would serve him right, but she got no pleasure from that vindictive thought.

She finished working with the plants downstairs and proceeded to the second floor. Plants hung near all the upstairs windows, and almost every sunny shelf and table sported a pot of African violets. After carefully inspecting each one, she rotated the pot a quarter of a turn to ensure that the flowers grew symmetrically.

As she returned one particularly beautiful plant top-heavy with purple flowers to its saucer, Terra reflected that in all probability she would have no further chance to talk to Grant about the lost edition—or about anything for that matter. Once the brochure was in Paul's hands his mission would be complete. And his confidence that Terra would indeed give Paul the brochure was well-founded. What choice did she have?

With a sigh she left her prize violets and went back downstairs. She replaced the watering can and pushed the chair she had used back under the table. All of her movements were slow and ponderous; there was no joy in the simple tasks that had always given her pleasure previously.

The second chapter in her association with Grant was now closed. She didn't want things to end this way! She had feared that meeting Grant would change her life—and she was right. For years the memory of him had satisfied her, but now that she had felt the power of his kiss, the strength of his embrace, she could be satisfied with nothing but the man himself. Now that he had come back she didn't want to let him go. Yet she had no choice, and the sooner she could readjust her feelings and return to her former state of mind concerning the changes that had taken place in him, the better off she would be.

From outside she could hear the buzz of a gasoline engine. Looking through the window, she saw Jeff start the lawnmower and begin to push it back and forth across the lawn. When he had nearly finished the backyard she stepped over to the window and waved. But Jeff had his face averted and he couldn't see her. Tired of her own thoughts and anxious to be outside, she walked out of the side door toward Jeff. As she approached he ducked his head lower and kept on mowing.

"Hi, there," she called to him above the noise of the machine.

He nodded slightly to show he had heard her but kept on mowing. Puzzled, Terra called again.

"When you're through would you like to come over for a sandwich?"

Jeff looked as though he were about to refuse but then shouted, "Okay, if you insist."

Terra shrugged at his almost unfriendly response and went back inside to fix their lunch. After about fifteen minutes the sound of the motor stopped and she could hear the crunch of gravel as Jeff wheeled the machine down the driveway to the garage. Minutes later her screen door slammed and he walked into the kitchen.

Terra's cheerful greeting was cut off by the look of anger on Jeff's usually bland face. "What's the matter with you?" she said instead.

"I'm surprised you have to ask," he responded cryptically.

"Come on, Jeff," Terra protested. "I'm not going to play twenty questions with you. What's wrong?"

"You went out with Grant Ingraham again!" The statement sounded like an accusation.

Terra was surprised he knew about her outing on Friday, but then she remembered Grant's car had been out front Friday morning. Jeff must have seen it when he left to play racketball. She was sure he hadn't seen Grant leave on Saturday morning, for Jeff always slept in on the weekends.

"It wasn't a date," she explained, "more like a business obligation."

Jeff's expression turned more disapproving than ever, but he remained silent.

"We went to the Blansford Library," she commented.

"I thought you had more sense than to get mixed up with a bastard like that." The young man's face was screwed up into a deep scowl.

"Jeff!" Terra was outraged. "I won't let you talk that way." It wasn't hard for her to think that Grant deserved the title, but she couldn't bear to hear him maligned by anyone else. "What's Grant ever done to you?"

"What's he done to you? That question's more to the point," Jeff countered.

"He hasn't done anything to me," Terra protested, hoping the lie didn't show in her eyes. Grant had caused irreparable damage. He had knocked down a closed door, churned up her emotions, then walked out again. But that was a secret she planned to keep well hidden.

Jeff's eyes darkened at her denial. He opened his mouth to speak but instead stepped close to Terra and put both his hands on her shoulders.

Startled by the roughness of his manner, she raised her hands to his chest and pushed against him. His hold on her tightened, though. His face momentarily lost its young attractiveness, and his skin seemed flushed with heat. His rapid breathing was disturbingly audible.

"Jeff," Terra managed to choke out before

his mouth closed over hers. Unlike any of his previous kisses this one was urgent and demanding. His hands moved heavily down her back, and his moist lips searched her tightly closed mouth.

"Jeff, stop it," she cried as soon as she could squirm away from his embrace. But her words were smothered when once again his mouth descended toward her own. His hands fumbled with the buttons of her shirt and Terra began to struggle in earnest, suddenly afraid. This was not the Jeff she had known for years but some wild stranger. Her struggles seemed to excite him more, and he pushed her back against the kitchen wall, pressing her to him.

"You stop that this minute, do you hear?" she shouted, and mustering all her strength, she finally managed to pull away from him. He staggered backward but paused for only a moment, as though gathering his strength, before again reaching for her.

Evading him, Terra called out in alarm, "What's got into you? What do you think you're doing? Stop it this instant!"

The panic in her voice seemed finally to register. Jeff stopped in his tracks, the odd look slowly fading from his eyes. "I'm sorry, Terra."

He turned abruptly, as if to hide from her the expression on his face, then moved toward a chair and placed his hand on the back of it to steady himself, but he did not turn around again

to face her, even as he began to speak in a subdued voice.

"I love you, Terra." He slowly shook his
head. "I've loved you for a long time, but I've
always thought I would never have a chance to
let you know—a chance to make you love me in
return. For one wild moment I thought that
after last night things might be different. I'm
sorry," he repeated.

"What do you mean, after last night? Why
should anything be different? What are you
talking about?" Terra was shaken and angry.

Jeff turned to face her, and she was shocked
at the misery evident in his eyes. "I thought the
fact that you spent the night with Grant meant
you would be more accessible. I was stupid.
Knowing his reputation, I thought there
couldn't be anything serious between you.…"

For a moment Terra was speechless. Then her
anger spilled out. "Let's get one thing straight,
Jeff Baxter. What I do is none of your business—old friends or not. But for the record I
did not sleep with Grant Ingraham last night or
any night."

"You don't have to lie to me, Terra," Jeff's
eyes were now soft and pleading. "I saw his car
here this morning."

"You're a regular little early bird, aren't
you?" she asked contemptuously. "Someday
you're going to learn to mind your own business!"

"I'm not judging you," Jeff countered with a

note of desperation in his voice. "I was furious at first, crazy with jealousy. But then it occurred to me that for once I might have a chance. I thought maybe the time had come for me to let you know I want to be in the running, too."

"This isn't a race," Terra began angrily, but then the full significance of Jeff's words hit her. She pulled out a chair, sat down and looked up at him, saying softly, "I care about you, Jeff, I always have. But caring is only one kind of loving. If it's not the kind you want from me, I'm sorry, but it's all I can give."

He nodded as if he knew full well that what she was saying was the truth.

"You're not in love with me, either," she continued, her voice gentle because she was embarrassed for him. "We've just become a habit with each other. Lately we've been together so much that you haven't had a chance to do other things and meet other people."

"There's no one else I want to meet." Jeff pouted.

Reaching up to take his hand, Terra laughed. "Come on, now, don't be silly. You haven't given anyone else a chance."

"We'll still do things together, won't we?" he asked.

"We're not going to let an old good friendship fade," she answered. "But you need to go out with other people. Why don't you ask someone to go to the concert with you tonight?"

"I thought you and I were going together,"

Jeff said. "We don't have to start this separation movement right away, do we?"

Terra smiled. "I could use a quiet evening at home. Work has been really tough this past week, and I need to relax."

Jeff looked at her sharply. "Is it work that's bothering you, or is it Grant?"

"I don't know what you mean." She got up and went to the kitchen sink for a glass of water.

"You're crazy about that guy. I can see it in your face, hear it in your voice when you mention his name. I wish I could help you, Terra. I would hate to see him walk all over you. If the creep had any sense at all he'd see what he was passing up."

"You're jumping to too many conclusions. There's nothing between Grant and me at all." She fought to keep her tears under control. That was really the whole problem—if Jeff wanted to know the truth.

"Okay. I won't force you to admit anything you don't want to." Jeff returned to the table, sat down and put his napkin in his lap. "Let's eat something before we keel over from hunger."

Terra put the sandwiches on the table and sat down, too. He talked about his job and joked about the problem he was having with his car, but although the topics of conversation hadn't changed, Terra knew that things were different between them. In a way she was sorry they couldn't go on as they had been, but even as she was regretting the change, she knew it had been inevitable. When Jeff finished his lunch and left, Terra felt another door in her life had just closed.

The rest of the afternoon and evening passed with punishing slowness. Terra prepared an omelet for dinner and, after washing the dishes, took a leisurely bath and put on a pair of lounging pajamas. She selected a predictable symphony on the radio, located the mystery she had brought home from the library and propped herself up in bed. This was the kind of quiet evening she had wanted, and yet she found it difficult to concentrate on her book.

The afternoon's scene with Jeff replayed itself over and over again in her memory—but now with a different focus. At the time she had hardly noticed Jeff's pronouncement about her feelings for Grant, but now it echoed through the recesses of her mind, forcing her to listen to it. *You're crazy about that guy. I can see it in your face.*

Involuntarily Terra's hand moved to her cheek. How could Jeff have come to such a conclusion? She had never even thought of the word *love* in connection with Grant—not seriously, anyway. She had actually spent only a few hours with him—or so it seemed. Yet when she was really honest with herself she had to admit she had never stopped thinking about him, not since her first crush had begun so many years earlier. Her feelings for Grant had gone through many

changes, from a child's adoration through a
teenager's idolatry to a mature admiration. But
that admiration was not love; in fact, it could be
said it was the opposite. Admiration was a cold
objective feeling; it was based on the man's ac-
complishments, his hard-nosed success. Love
could only be based on what Grant *was*, not on
what he had accomplished.

But what was he? Terra's head was spinning.
She thought about the Grant who had warned
her to keep her suspicions to herself—a cold-
blooded businessman. And she thought about
him as he had been at Maurice's—a warmly
alive, deeply attractive person. He was a mystery more puzzling than any she would find in
the open book in her hand.

Perhaps she would never find out who the
real Grant Ingraham was. Perhaps she didn't
really want to. And yet, in her confusion, images of him sped before her closed eyes—images
of the handsome youth who had been her
father's friend, images of the strongly virile
adult who had held her in his arms. Perhaps, as
with Jeff, he could become her friend. No. They
could never be friends. There was only one relationship Terra wanted with Grant, she now
reluctantly admitted to herself, and friendship
wasn't what it was called.

Oh, but to love him, to have him love her in
return was just impossible! He was such a
sophisticated man—a New York publishing executive. He had a social life that made Terra's

own look like a quilting bee! She could well imagine the long line of women parading after him, eager for his attention. She had no intention of joining the queue.

She felt confused and angry. Why had he had to come back? Things had been complicated enough already, considering what she had been going through at the store. Of course Grant was involved in that, too. It was really too much, but one thing was certain: she would be a fool to let her heart get in the way of her head. She had to think clearly.

Jeff was wrong. She wasn't in love with Grant—though to be fair, she would admit there was a slight possibility she might be tempted to love him. Well, temptation was made to be resisted.... With that determined thought Terra snapped off the light and closed her eyes.

THE NEXT MORNING unhappiness hung over her like a cloud, but Terra decided she wasn't going to give in to it. She walked to the store for the Sunday paper and greeted the clerk with automatic cheerfulness.

As she was opening her front door on her return, Jeff stuck his head out his window. "Good morning," he called. "Did you enjoy your quiet evening alone?" His voice sounded as though he didn't quite believe she had been alone, but he seemed in good enough spirits.

"It was lovely," Terra lied. "How about you? Did you get to the concert?"

"I took your advice," he replied. "I went with Marsha Davidson. Remember her?"

"Of course. And how was it? Did you have a good time?"

"It was great," Jeff said in the tone of voice of one who had just been asked how he had enjoyed a funeral. Yet something in his demeanor gave Terra hope. He was a resilient young man, and if Marsha wasn't his heart's desire, at least dating her had been a step in the right direction.

"I'll see you," she called up, waving goodbye as she went inside.

She spent the morning reading the paper and doing the crossword puzzle. After lunch she wandered around the house, trying to think of something to do that would occupy her thoughts. She had reread Grant's manuscript for the brochure. He certainly hadn't missed his calling—in either his profession or his hobby. His prose was stylish and grammatically perfect. His description of the pamphlets spoke directly and enticingly to exactly the collectors for whom it was intended. Reading his effort, she herself almost believed the lost edition was the most authentic document since the Declaration of Independence. Almost believed. . . .

She had vaguely intended to try one more time to write the brochure herself but instead had spent the weekend putting off her decision on what to do with the manuscript Grant had prepared. She had almost come to the conclusion the best thing to do would be to present it to

Paul as a fait accompli. She would tell him Grant had worked on it. When he saw what the manuscript said, Paul wouldn't care who had written it. All that would matter to him was that it was done.

But it mattered very much to Terra that the brochure was still her responsibility, and she could not in conscience stand behind what was written in Grant's pages. She had hoped that by not thinking about matters directly she could relax enough to decide what she should do.

Late in the afternoon she remembered that a Mexican ballet company was doing a program of folk dances at the Greek Theater on the University of California campus. She didn't want to go alone. In the past she would have asked Jeff, but she couldn't fall back on old patterns just as he had made a first tentative step toward independence. She decided to call Margaret to see if she was interested in going to the performance. Margaret lived on the other side of Berkeley, and the two of them occasionally went to a play or a movie together.

Margaret was free that evening and was delighted at the suggestion. She offered to drive by Terra's house and pick her up, but Terra declined, feeling she would enjoy the walk, so they agreed to meet at the theater.

At half-past six Terra arrived at the box office. The Greek Theater, a traditional part of Berkeley life, was outdoors, set in the middle of a grove of eucalyptus trees. The seats were stone, arranged in semicircular tiers around a stone stage. Because the outdoor stage couldn't have all the customary theatrical equipment, the performances were often unusual and filled with original touches designed to compensate for the lack of sophisticated apparatus.

Terra and Margaret had decided to meet early since they had not purchased their tickets in advance, and when the two women entered the theater they were among the first arrivals. Choosing seats halfway up and directly in the center, they spread their blankets on the stone seats and sat down. Knowing they would have forty-five minutes to wait, Terra had brought a thermos of coffee and plastic cups with her.

As usual Margaret was full of chatter. She had gone to the opera the previous night, and she was certain Terra would be interested in hearing about every detail of her evening. Terra listened patiently, making a comment or two when Margaret paused, but for the most part she sat quietly, enjoying the refreshing evening air.

"I first saw him down in the lobby and I thought he might have been with you, so I followed him up to his seat—without his knowing it, of course."

Terra pulled her mind away from the haunting beauty of the eucalyptus trees in dusky shadows and forced herself to pay attention to Margaret. "What did you say? I'm afraid I didn't hear," she apologized.

"I said I saw Grant at the opera last night," Margaret repeated in exasperation. "I thought he might be there with you, but he was with Stephanie Duke. I've never seen anyone look so smug in my life. You'd have thought she was at the altar with Grant rather than at the opera."

Terra groaned inwardly. She had put Grant out of her mind and had hoped to keep him there. She should have known better. Margaret never missed a chance to talk at length about one of her favorite subjects.

"Maybe he likes her," Terra said with no interest at all in her voice. She wanted to get the inevitable discussion over with as quickly as possible.

"Or else he likes her family's money. I've heard the Dukes are thinking of investing heavily in the Ingraham Corporation, so maybe Grant is simply taking care of business. But still," she continued, "he might be getting interested again. In the past little while they've been out together at least three times that I know about, and that's nearly a record for Grant."

Terra remained silent.

"I was surprised he switched from you back to her so quickly," Margaret said tactlessly. "They way he looked at you at Fosters' made me think you'd last longer than some of the others."

"Maybe now you'll believe we were just old friends having a nostalgic evening together.

There was nothing personal in it at all." Terra looked around at the people filling the theater and wished the show would begin.

"I know that's what you keep saying," Margaret laughed. "But I happen to believe no woman is immune to Grant Ingraham. I know I'm not."

"Well, then," Terra responded lightly, "why don't you go after him yourself instead of worrying about me?"

"I've already had my turn," Margaret said, "and with Grant you don't get seconds."

Terra didn't quite understand Margaret's meaning. "You've gone out with Grant?" she questioned.

"I guess you could call it that," Margaret replied breezily. "How did you think I knew so much about him?"

Terra shook her head wordlessly.

"It happened about four years ago, before you started working at the shop. He had come back for a few weeks, so it didn't last long—not that it would have anyway. It was brief, but it was glorious—just like a fireworks display." Margaret stood and stretched. "These seats feel hard already, and the show hasn't even started."

"Why don't you fold your blanket over once more to make a softer cushion," Terra suggested.

As she did so the older woman picked up the thread of the conversation. "I thought you knew all about Grant and me," she said. "When I first met you he seemed to be all we talked about."

"I remember," Terra said. "Since Grant was a friend of my father's and a friend of yours, too, it seemed a natural thing to discuss. I didn't realize what sort of a friend he had been."

"Well, I guess I wouldn't have wanted to let on about what had happened. I was pretty angry for quite a while after it was over. But I've become philosophical about it. When you see it happening to others around you it doesn't hurt so much."

Terra didn't think she could ever be as cool as Margaret, but she didn't comment. "Were you in love with him?" she asked.

"I thought I was," Margaret answered. "And I thought I could make him fall in love with me. Like everyone else I was vain enough to believe I was the one woman who could convince him to settle down. It took me quite a long time to see he had no intention of letting any relationship become permanent."

"That makes me so angry!" Terra said vehemently, despite her resolve not to encourage Margaret's comments about Grant. "It's just not fair for a person like him to get someone else seriously involved when he's just playing around himself. I know that's the style these days, but I can't help it, I don't like it at all!"

"It's not as if he's dishonest about it," Margaret laughed. "He made it clear right from the start love was not going to be involved. I just refused to listen to his words. Right up until the end I thought I could change his attitude." Margaret shook her head. "But I know now he'll never change. He's a born loner, and any woman who thinks she can change him is a romantic fool."

The bright spotlights began to dim, signaling the start of the show and saving Terra the necessity of replying. As the lights over the seats faded, spotlights flashed into brilliance on the stage and lines of dancers dressed in gaily colored Mexican costumes whirled out to greet the audience. The lively sounds of the orchestra swelled out on the evening breezes, and the stage became a dazzling blur of sound and color.

Despite all the things coursing through her mind, Terra forgot everything and let herself be swept away by the romance and excitement of the folk dances. Each presentation was an authentic dance representing some custom or ritual of village life. In the hunting dance, two men, one wearing a headdress of antlers, enacted the perennial struggle between man and beast. In another dance sequence a wedding was celebrated, and the young bride and groom were honored by special dances, after which they performed the touchingly beautiful wedding dance. Caught up in the illusion, Terra found herself deeply moved as the two lovers exchanged their solemn vows.

She was genuinely sorry when the show was

over. Clapping enthusiastically as the dancers took their bows, she wondered what their lives were like offstage. When the dancers who played the young bride and groom came running out hand in hand, the glow of the wedding dance still hung over them, and Terra hoped that in real life they were in love. Grant would laugh at such thoughts as foolish nonsense. He would have pointed out that the stage wedding was a fantasy, just as he probably thought that true love in real life was a fantasy.

As Terra and Margaret joined the crowd of people edging slowly toward the exit, Margaret looked at her watch. "It's early. Why don't we stop off at Casey's on the way home. Lots of people I know are usually there on Sunday night."

"Ten o'clock isn't exactly early for me," Terra said. "Tomorrow's a workday, remember?"

"We won't stay long," Margaret promised. "You need to get out more, meet more people. I think you'll like the Casey's crowd."

"Okay, I'll come," Terra acquiesced, "but I can't stay long."

Casey's was a small bar in North Berkeley with beamed ceilings and banners bearing coats of arms hanging on the walls. Margaret was greeted raucously as they entered, and amid the clamor she introduced Terra to the people standing nearest them. Then Margaret was scooped into the arms of a tall, well-built man, and Terra was left on her own. Before she could decide where to sit she was surrounded by a group of young men, all vying for the chance to show her to a table. Looking to see where Margaret had gone, she spotted her in a corner booth, wrapped in the embrace of the tall man. Terra allowed herself to be led to a table and concentrated on her new companions' names.

Banter flowed, and she soon felt very much a part of the crowd. They were all jammed together at the small table, and several times Terra felt her thigh bump against the person next to her. Each time she moved away, trying to allow room for everyone. A young man only a few years older than her was seated next to her, and soon she found herself talking mostly to him. As they spoke his hand moved along the back of her chair. When she made some little joke in response to a comment of his, he swung his arm around her shoulders and drew her toward him, laughing and squeezing her. She let the momentum of his hug subside and then with a relaxed motion eased away from him and shrugged off his hand.

He looked momentarily annoyed, but the frown passed from his face, and minutes later his arm was back around her. Her shrug was more definite the second time, and he seemed to get the message.

Conversation continued, and after a while Terra began to tire. All the noise and smoke were starting to give her a headache. She looked around again for Margaret. Catching her eye, Terra pointed to her watch, and Margaret replied by beckoning Terra to her booth. Terra said goodbye to her companions and walked over to Margaret.

She was introduced to Margaret's friend, and after a few polite words she suggested to Margaret they should be getting home.

Displeasure showed clearly on the other woman's face. "But we just got here!" she protested. "Relax, honey, and have a good time. You won't turn into a pumpkin."

"I'm leaving, Margaret," Terra stated, realizing now she should have asked Margaret to drop her off at the house on the way to Casey's. "Why don't I just walk home? It's not far."

"I don't think that's a good idea," the tall man with Margaret joined the discussion. "No city's streets are completely safe at this hour. Why don't you stay here and enjoy yourself. We'll take you home in an hour or so."

"Thanks, but it's really getting too late for me," Terra insisted. "I think I'll be all right if I stay on well-lighted streets."

"I'll take you," a voice at Terra's elbow interrupted. She turned to see the young man who had been sitting next to her at the table.

She was about to protest that an escort really wasn't necessary when Margaret interrupted. "Good. I'm glad that's settled. See you at work tomorrow." She turned back to her friend.

Terra hesitated a moment longer, then nodded her acceptance of the stranger's offer. It was a short distance to her place, and she thought it would be safe to walk with him. Outside he introduced himself as Frank and gestured toward his car.

"Why don't we walk," Terra suggested, determined not to get into a car with someone she didn't know. "It's not far."

"What are you, some kind of physical-fitness freak?" Frank asked, but he matched his stride to hers as she started off.

Terra didn't feel much like talking, and Frank, too, was without much to say. When they were about halfway to her house she felt his arm wrap itself around her again, and with a quick little side step she eluded him once more. Arriving at her porch, she thanked him for taking the trouble to accompany her home, then said good-night.

"Hey," Frank protested in a louder voice than necessary, "after I walked all this way aren't you even going to ask me in?"

"Maybe next time," Terra declined politely. "It's awfully late and I really have to go to bed."

"That's just fine with me. I'll come, too." Frank had followed her up the porch steps and now pushed her against the door, his hands grabbing at her and his lips seeking her mouth.

Terra turned her head away and tried to push him off. "Please, Frank, stop it. I'm going inside."

"Not so fast," he puffed. "Give me a little reward for being so nice to you." Again his mouth sought hers.

Next door the porch light snapped on and a voice called out, "Terra, is that you?"

Frank released her and looked suspiciously over at Jeff's house.

Relief in her voice, Terra called back, "Yes, Jeff, I'm just getting home. How was your evening?" she asked, hoping he would not turn off the light until Frank left.

"Just fine." Jeff now appeared on the porch. "I was staying up to offer you a ride into San Francisco tomorrow if you wanted to wait until nine."

"Thanks for the thought, but I need to be in early." Terra paused and then in a firm voice thanked Frank for seeing her home. He hesitated and finally muttered goodbye before he turned and stomped off. When he was well down the path, Terra thanked Jeff for coming to her rescue.

"Who was that?" Jeff asked.

"A friend of Margaret's," Terra answered.

"Well, anytime you need help, just call for Uncle Jeff," he kidded. There was just the tiniest hint of bitterness in his voice, but he smiled warmly at Terra and waited until she was safely inside before going back into his own house.

As she got ready for bed, Terra decided she should have known she wouldn't really have enjoyed Margaret's crowd. Their outlook on life was different from her own. The way Margaret had reacted to Grant was an example. Margaret had been hurt, but she had bounced back, and not only had had many relationships since then but would have been eager for another chance to get close to Grant if she thought she could have.

Terra's convictions were different. If she had loved Grant, that love would never have faded completely, even though she would have tried her best to rationalize it away. Even if she loved him deeply she could not accept a casual relationship with him. If she wanted that kind of a relationship, she felt sure Grant would be interested. All she would need to do would be to indicate her willingness. And she had no doubt it would be marvelous—until it ended. Then something in her would die; she knew herself well enough to be certain of that fact. It would be far better to keep her feelings locked in and hope that, with time, their strength would fade. Of course, the whole question was academic. She didn't love Grant then, and she wouldn't love him in the future.

She felt sure about her resolution not to get any further involved with him. Yet it was easy to make such a resolution when there was no opportunity to act otherwise. Grant had disappeared on Saturday morning as though without a trace. He hadn't called. If he had been interested in her at all, he would have at least picked up the phone. She was glad he hadn't. She might never have to face him again, but if she did, she hoped she would have the strength of will to be cool and unemotional. Aloofness was essential unless she wanted to give in—like Margaret.

She laid out her clothes and prepared for the next day. Glancing at her briefcase, thoughts of the lost edition rushed over her. Important as her discovery at the Blansford had seemed on Friday, now that Monday was fast approaching she didn't see any way to make use of what she had found. It was almost as if she had forgotten all about it. Of course, that was just what Grant had nearly ordered her to do, and she couldn't think of any alternative except to acquiesce.

She had been convinced her discovery warranted further investigation, but she had failed to get Grant's support. Even so, his refusal to acknowledge she had important new clues didn't mean they didn't exist. Others might be interested in her theory. Perhaps the chance would come for her to seek out more proof. If she had real reason to suspect the genuineness of Paul's booklet, she was under an obligation to inform him about it, even though he would not be any more receptive to her ideas than he had been on Friday.

Perhaps she was faulting him prematurely. Surely he would be anxious to avoid a possible scandal. And if his pamphlets were facsimiles, he could still hope for a respectable profit, even if it were not as much as it would have been. Paul might be willing to settle for less, would have to settle for less if his reputation was at stake.

She walked over to the chair where her brief-case lay and clicked the briefcase open. The neat pages of Grant's typing stared up at her accus-ingly. She might be young, but she had already spent years in her profession. She felt her whole future depended on what she did with these few pages of Grant's writing. A whole weekend of distractions—including her disturbing personal thoughts about Grant—hadn't cleared her mind, hadn't allowed her to forget her integrity was at stake. Maybe Grant truly thought her discovery proved nothing, but she was not so sure. There was really only one thing to do—as there had been only one choice all along. First thing in the morning she would go to Paul and try once more to explain the significance of her discovery. If he got angry, so be it. As for Grant, if he was genuinely interested in protect-ing the investment of his friends, he could only gain from Terra's professional carefulness— though she was sure he wouldn't be around to thank her for it.

CHAPTER EIGHT

WHEN TERRA OPENED THE DOOR of the bookstore on Monday morning, one of the junior clerks called to her from his desk.

"Terra, Paul wants to see you right now."

Terra nodded. A confrontation was inevitable. He wanted the finished brochure, and she was planning to convince him the pamphlets were facsimiles. "I'll put my things upstairs and be right down."

The clerk frowned. "Paul said you were to go to his office the minute you got in. He seemed quite upset. Why don't you just give me your handbag. I'll put it in my desk drawer until you're finished with Paul."

"Oh, all right," Terra answered. She slowly made her way toward Paul's door, wishing she had had a few minutes to organize her thoughts. On the other hand, she reflected, it was just as well to get the difficult interview out of the way as soon as possible. She was as ready as she'd ever be.

She knocked confidently on Paul's closed door and entered at his gruff summons. He must have arrived only moments earlier; the blinds of his windows had not yet been drawn. The dark orange shades blotted out the daylight, giving the room a somber glow. Paul was standing behind his desk but sat down the minute she entered, not bothering to raise the shades. He motioned for Terra to take the seat opposite him. His expression was severe, and when he spoke his tone was resentful and angry.

"You've given me a bad weekend, Terra." He paused, staring stonily at her, and Terra's hopes lifted a little. She was sorry to have worried him, but if he had taken time to think about what she had hurriedly told him on Friday, perhaps he would be prepared to listen.

"Did you tell anyone else about this crackpot facsimile theory of yours?" Paul demanded.

Terra shifted her weight in her chair and clasped her hands together, stalling for time. Grant had warned her Paul would not want her to have told anyone about her suspicions. She didn't want to lie to Paul, and yet she also knew he would be furious at her for confiding in Grant.

"I wanted to talk to you first, Paul, before I spoke to anyone else. . . ." Terra said evasively.

"Thank God for that," Paul said. "At least you have some sense." The unveiled anger and contempt in his voice startled her. "Now you listen to me. That facsimile theory is ridiculous. No facsimile in the world could be so true to the original that the experts couldn't tell the difference."

"Yes, but—" Terra tried to interrupt.

"Shut up and let me finish," he went on rudely. "That theory is hogwash. Don't you realize that if you tell that to anybody who knows anything about rare books you'll be laughed out of the book trade? Everyone will know right away you're grasping at straws. I don't know why you're so determined to discredit the lost edition. Maybe you just want to make a big name for yourself."

He stopped momentarily, and his hands moved over the papers on his desk, aligning them into neat little piles. "But it won't work. People will laugh at you, and the lost edition will sell anyway." He stood up abruptly, placed his hands on the desk and leaned forward. "I'm warning you, Terra. Keep your stupid ideas to yourself—for your own sake."

The buzz of the intercom prevented Terra from replying. Paul stared at it for a moment, then sat down and picked up the receiver. "Yes," he said sharply. Then his tone evened out. "Oh, sure. Send him in."

He looked across at Terra. "Grant Ingraham's here to see me, so we'll have to continue this discussion later," he said, dismissing her. As she rose he added, "You can forget about the brochure. I've already sent that copy I wrote to the printer."

"Paul, you can't...!"

"Don't you tell me what I can or cannot do. I'm not finished with you yet. We'll talk about this later. Until then you better keep your mouth closed.''

He had walked around the desk and was now crowding her out the door. Reluctant to leave when she still had so much to say, she stood in the hallway, facing Paul uncertainly and trying to think of something that would force him to listen.

"Good morning," a smooth deep voice rippled in her ear, and she turned around to find Grant standing right behind her. He was so handsome in the dark pin-striped suit and immaculately white shirt that Terra momentarily lost her breath. She had heard Paul say that Grant was coming. Yet the sight of him seemed almost like a total surprise. Instinctively she reached out and put her hand on the wall for support. She felt as though she might faint.

Grant greeted them both pleasantly, his eyes holding Terra's so long she was afraid Paul might think it strange. But he noticed nothing. His face was strained with the effort of hiding his anger from Grant. "Shall we go, Grant?" he said in clipped tones, nodding toward Terra in a gesture that said, "Get out of here."

Before she could move away Terra felt Grant's strong hand at her elbow. His touch radiated warmth, but it also started her heart to erratic beating. It was almost as though her body remembered his touch and was responding to it without her conscious mind giving consent. For a few seconds she thought time had stopped, that they had been frozen there with just that slight touch of Grant's fingers on her arm uniting them irrevocably.

Then Paul smiled tightly and motioned toward his office door, breaking the spell. Terra regained her balance and tried to step backward away from Grant. As she moved she felt his fingers tighten, as if he didn't want to let her go.

"Sorry to bother you so early on a Monday morning," he said, following Paul into the office and leading Terra along, "but I thought I'd just drop in on you for a moment if you can spare the time."

"Of course. Glad to see you anytime." Paul waved his hand toward an overstuffed chair. "Come on in and sit down. Terra was just leaving."

At these words she turned to go, but found Grant blocking the exit. Expecting him to step aside, she started forward, almost colliding with him when he remained firmly where he was.

"I'd like her to stay if she can leave her work for a while." Grant moved into the room, forcing Terra to step inside, also. "I actually came to talk to both of you."

Terra stiffened, wondering what was coming next.

Paul glanced uncertainly at Grant, then accusingly at Terra, as if he suspected she knew something about the reason for Grant's visit. She wished she did. Grant seemed unaffected by the tension in the room, but Terra wanted to run.

"Do you mind if I open the blinds?" Grant asked smoothly. "It would be a shame to waste the light of such a beautiful morning."

Paul nodded his silent agreement, and Grant pulled on the cords to raise the shades. The sunlight flooded in, and for an instant Grant stood silhouetted against the window. His broad shoulders, narrow waist, the fine shape of his handsome head, even the outline of his large hand as it held the cord, burned into Terra's eyes like the afterimage from a flashbulb. She was filled simultaneously with desire and regret. She wanted him and she didn't want to want him—then or ever.

He moved from the window, and sunlight filled the room, changing the dreary atmosphere and sparking a little hope in Terra—hope that Grant might have changed his mind about the facsimile theory.

The three of them sat down, Paul taking the chair behind his massive executive desk, but it was Grant who assumed control of the meeting. He smiled and crossed his legs in a relaxed manner, apparently unaware that both the other people in the room were nervously waiting for him to begin.

"First, I wanted to tell you, Paul, that I think you made a very wise decision in letting Terra take the time to go to the Blansford on Friday."

Terra held her breath. Had Grant changed his mind? Was he now going to discuss her discovery with Paul? It seemed highly unlikely, and yet Terra could not imagine where else such a remark might lead.

"As I'm sure she'd told you, she had a chance to go through all the printing records for the lost edition, and what she found confirms that the Waltham Press printed the lost edition in 1848."

Terra let her breath out slowly. If Grant was leading up to a disclosure of the facsimiles, he was certainly doing it very gently. There had never been any doubt the Waltham Press had printed the original. What had been in doubt was whether the booklets Paul had were actually part of that original edition. Terra watched Grant, who paused in his explanation only long enough to return her glance. His eyes seemed to say, "Don't speak," and Terra felt she was witnessing something she couldn't quite understand.

"I, for one, was delighted to have the lost edition verified beyond any doubt," Grant continued, leaning back in his chair as though comfortable and at ease. His casual manner did not have any effect on Paul, who was still sitting ramrod straight in his chair.

"Whenever any big discovery like this one breaks, doubts always arise, and since several close friends of mine are planning to invest in the lost edition, I was glad you allowed Terra to continue searching until all possible questions were answered."

In spite of her apprehension over what Grant

would say next, Terra smiled inwardly when he acknowledged he had been checking on the authenticity of the booklets on behalf of his friends. She had been correct in her analysis of his motives, she thought to herself. And it also seemed now that she was right about Grant's being utterly convinced the pamphlets were genuine. She could see that all chance of convincing Paul otherwise had flown out the window.

Paul looked at her suspiciously. "Terra has told you she has no further concerns about the genuineness of the lost edition?" His disbelief sounded clearly in his voice.

"She showed me the extensive evidence she found supporting authenticity," Grant confirmed, oblivious to the insinuation in Paul's tone. He turned to Terra. "As I recall, you said you had discovered one or two things you needed to think about and check on at home. They were resolved to your satisfaction, weren't they?"

Grant's innocent gaze captured hers and held it, demanding a response. What was he trying to do? He had maneuvered her into a position in which she was forced to accept the authenticity of the pamphlets or else defy him and tell Paul about her doubts in Grant's presence. Was he challenging her, or was he trying to protect her somehow?

Paul was watching her intently, barely concealing the rage flashing in his eyes. Terra knew with certainty that if she mentioned the facsimiles now, in front of Grant, she would be fired. There was nothing to gain by bringing up her suspicions. Unknown to each other, both men had rejected her ideas, and she could see that nothing could be accomplished by trying to convince them both at once. Whatever Grant's intentions, he had her trapped. For now, she had to appear content with accepting Paul's pamphlets. If she wanted to pursue her theory, she would have to do it on her own.

At least Paul didn't suspect she had spoken to Grant. Her best course of action would be to appear to acquiesce. She could continue her research privately on her own time, and when she had conclusive proof to back up her theory she would confront them both.

"You are now completely convinced the pamphlets are genuine, aren't you?" Grant prodded.

Terra searched the depths of his eyes, looking for the slightest hint the situation was more complex than he was pretending. But he was a consummate actor. Even though she knew better, she found herself believing he had never heard her doubts. And indeed he might as well not have known about them, so completely did he appear to reject them.

Terra held her chin high, but her smile was conciliatory. "You're right." Her glance took in both men. "The evidence for authenticity is overwhelming. It's almost impossible to argue with it."

Paul's shoulders sagged slightly, and a relieved smile spread over his face. To Terra her words had still carried a measure of her defiance, since she had avoided stating directly what both men wanted to hear, but evidently her short speech had satisfied Paul. Grant, too, seemed pleased that all parties were in full agreement.

Grant began to talk about the opening of the bookfair—now only three weeks away—and about Paul's plans for the first public display of the lost edition. As Grant asked questions, Paul's annoyance seemed to disappear, and soon he was describing the Foster exhibit in a lively and animated manner. Seeing him gesture dramatically as he talked about the upcoming event, Terra recognized some of the old enthusiasm that had once been characteristic of Paul. Perhaps now that he thought the issue of the pamphlets was settled his good humor would return.

Terra watched him, and her face softened into an expression of reminiscence. She had spent so many happy hours at Fosters'. It nearly broke her heart to think that what had been so good had gone so sour. Her feelings of regret showed clearly in her face as she stared at the man who had once been a good employer but who now seemed to be becoming an ogre. With a sigh she reflected that things would never be the same in the store. Grant, hearing that sigh, glanced at her, and a look of regret crossed his own watching face.

As the men talked, Terra tried to find a break in the conversation that would allow her to leave gracefully. Yet whenever she started to rise and excuse herself, Grant directed a comment toward her and she was compelled to respond. Paul was apparently unconcerned about her presence, so after several unsuccessful attempts to escape she sat back and listened to the discussion.

"I thought I'd have all the pamphlets on display on opening day of the bookfair and then transfer several of them to the exhibition at the Blansford," Paul was explaining. "Stephanie's grandfather suggested we might have one on display at the library when their exhibition opens next week, but I think it's better to show the pamphlets for the first time at the fair. Besides, we won't have the brochure ready until just before the fair opens." He looked pointedly at Terra. "But Nathaniel is planning some exhibits featuring other material from the Waltham Press, so I think we can generate interest in the lost edition, even though copies won't be on show until two weeks into the Blansford exhibition."

Grant glanced carefully at Paul, as though he had been waiting for just the right moment to say something important. "I'm glad you mentioned Blansford's exhibition, Paul," he said. "It relates directly to the reason for my dropping by to see you this morning."

Paul stared at Grant in surprise. Obviously

he, like Terra, thought Grant had come to reassure Paul he had no doubts about the pamphlets. Terra sat forward a little in her chair.

"Jamie, the librarian at the Blansford," Grant said, "was setting up the display of the printer's work records and supply ledgers for the exhibition yesterday, and he couldn't locate some of the Waltham Press records he had planned on using."

Terra stiffened slightly, and Paul cocked his head inquisitively at Grant. "Couldn't locate the Waltham papers? What do you mean?" Paul asked.

"You know how chaotic all that material is," Grant continued. "They don't have a precise listing of what's there, but Jamie does remember that when he was grouping the papers roughly by date he saw detailed accounts of the purchases, supplies and products of the press during its entire existence, and now certain years are missing."

Seeing Terra's apprehensive look, Grant smiled reassuringly. "They've got misfiled somehow, I'm sure," he explained. "I don't know how anyone finds anything in that collection with all the material they have. As I told Nathaniel and Stephanie at dinner yesterday, it just proves the importance of getting the collection cataloged as soon as possible. The missing papers are bound to turn up when they go through the collection box by box."

Terra digested this information absently. Her

mind hooked on to the one detail that had nothing to do with business. So Grant had had dinner with Stephanie on Sunday—and he had gone to the opera with her on Saturday. Anyway you counted, that added up to the whole weekend. No wonder he hadn't called her. He had better things to do with his time. Remembering Stephanie's vulgar comment about the importance of what one did with one's time, Terra cringed. Then she brought her thoughts back to the matter at hand—but not soon enough apparently. When she glanced up she noticed Paul was staring at her, his brows knit in a puzzled frown.

"Nathaniel is sure the manuscripts will be located eventually," Grant continued, "but he had his heart set on exhibiting a complete run of Waltham papers, so he asked me to stop by and find out whether, by any chance, Terra remembered seeing the work records for the press's later years. I know you were looking at documents before 1900—" he turned to Terra "—but Nathaniel thought perhaps the papers from the later years might have been slipped in with some of the earlier material."

Grant looked at his watch, and a slight flicker of impatience crossed his face. "I told him it was a long shot, but he wanted me to check with you, since I've taken an interest in all this...."

Both men had turned to face Terra, expecting a response. Grant's glance was friendly, and

Terra couldn't help but feel warm at the smile in his dark eyes, but Paul's expression was threatening.

Terra's mouth felt dry and she moistened her lips. "What years are missing?"

"They can't seem to locate several papers from 1905 and 1906," Grant commented.

At this bit of information Paul almost seemed to jump in agitation, but he relaxed and sat back in his chair, waiting. For the second time that morning Terra felt trapped, although this time it was because of circumstances and not because of Grant's manipulation. She desperately wanted to know more about what the librarian thought was missing. Yet she couldn't ask too many questions without angering Paul further. He would immediately think she was referring to her facsimile theory.

She wanted to help Nathaniel Blansford if she could, but it was too dangerous to mention, in the presence of Paul and Grant, that it had been the 1905 papers that had first aroused her suspicions. Grant was obviously prompting her to deny any knowledge of the later papers, and the dark looks Paul was giving her were blatant signals to remain silent about anything she had seen at the library. She had no idea why the papers might be missing. Perhaps Stephanie. . . . But no; she was sure the episode with Stephanie had merely been an exercise in pique—misplaced jealousy. Nor could she have said what papers had been there to begin with; she hadn't had time to go through them as carefully as she had wanted to.

Aware the seconds were ticking away, Terra decided to continue her waiting game. Perhaps she could talk to Grant later in private, give him what little information she had and find out more for herself. Speculations and questions whirled through her mind, but she realized that wasn't the time to sort them out or bring them into the conversation. She shook her head. "I went through quite a bit of material, but I don't remember having seen anything misfiled. Nor did I notice any lapse in material that had been arranged in sequence."

Grant brushed his hands together as if he were glad to have that bit of business out of the way and anxious to move on to other things. "I didn't think you could help much, but thanks for answering Nathaniel's questions." He stood up. "Blansford thoroughly enjoyed meeting you, by the way, and urged me to bring you out for another visit soon."

Moving toward the desk, Grant shook hands with Paul. "Sorry to take up so much time...."

"No problem," Paul muttered in response, seemingly preoccupied. The three of them moved across the room to the door.

"I certainly hope the manuscripts turn up before the exhibition," Terra commented as they walked into the hall. "From what you said they were an important part of the display."

"You're right. They're the central focus of

Jamie's exhibit,'' Grant answered. "But even if the originals aren't discovered before next week, the exhibit won't be ruined. Most of the later papers were photocopied several months ago by a professor at Stanford who needed them for research. As soon as Jamie realized he couldn't locate the originals, he called Professor Brown. The man couldn't offer any suggestions as to how to find the missing material, but he did make arrangements for Jamie to borrow his copies.'' Grant paused in the hallway. "Nathaniel would prefer to show only original items, but the copies would do. Some original material will be on display in locked cases, and the photocopies will be accessible to people who want to thumb through them.''

Grant continued to talk to Paul, but Terra stopped listening. If photocopies of the missing documents were available, then the information in them wasn't lost and the situation wasn't as critical as it had seemed at first. Although she didn't know whether the missing documents contained information relevant to the facsimiles, they covered the years during which the facsimiles would have been printed. If the photocopies were going to be on public display, she would have the opportunity to examine them carefully without alerting either Paul or Grant.

Grant shook hands with Paul once again, but as he did so his eyes strayed to Terra's. He was acting the perfect businessman today—the per-

fect Mr. Executive Ingraham. Yet as his gaze
met her own, his eyes softened and a small smile
lit his sensuously molded lips, a smile different
from the flashy, easy one he offered to Paul.
For a moment Terra's breath fluttered. Unbidden,
an image of those lips descending toward
her own filled her mind. And in that brief
instant she cared nothing about Paul, about
Fosters', about books. Nor did she remember
the countless times she had told herself Grant
wasn't interested in her personally. *She* was interested
in *him* personally, and that was all that
mattered. Her eyes took in the whole massive
frame of him, and her fingers tingled to touch
him, to run again through the dark forest of his
hair. She wanted to trace with those fingers—
no, with her tongue—the curved planes of his
striking face. She wanted him—oh, yes, she
wanted him. She recalled for the hundredth time
the low voice saying, "Terra? Terra..." as
though her name had had no sound, no sound at
all before his lips had formed the word. She
wished he would again ask her to dinner as he
had the first time he had come to Fosters'. She
wished the magic would start all over again,
weaving her into the enchanted web that surrounded
him wherever he went. She didn't care
how many others had been lured there and
caught.

But Grant did not ask her to dinner. He
turned and walked toward the front door of the
shop. Terra's heart fell, and something of her

disappointment must have shown on her face, for Paul grunted in disapproval as she made to move away.

"Just a minute, you." Paul swung her around roughly by the arm, and her eyes flew open in astonishment at his treatment of her.

"Get into my office," he ordered. "We've got some talking to do."

Completely baffled by his unexpected harshness, Terra preceded him down the hall and once more took a seat in front of his ostentatious desk. He strode through the door and slammed it shut with a force that caused a book to go flying off the shelf and land awkwardly on the carpet. Despite her fear Terra wondered whether the book's binding had been ruined by the fall.

"What's the matter, Paul?" she asked, collecting herself.

"Don't try that wide-eyed innocent act on me." His voice was a growl of anger. "What happened to those papers?" he demanded, looming over her. "I want to know what you did with them."

"Paul, I don't know what you're talking about." Her voice was firm, reasonable, confident, but under her cool manner she was seething. She had had just about enough of this whole situation. Who did he think he was, accusing her?

"Oh, yes you do know what I'm talking about. You're responsible for the disappearance of the Blansford papers. You use the Waltham Press material on Friday, and on Sunday some of it is gone. That's not a coincidence and you know it."

"Paul, you know I wouldn't do such a thing. Grant said those papers were misplaced."

"Grant doesn't know what I know, does he? He doesn't know you went through those papers with a theory in mind, a theory you must have thought those papers could prove. You were in the library by yourself all day Friday. You had plenty of time to choose which documents you wanted to disappear."

"How can you accuse me of stealing documents?"

"I didn't say you stole them," Paul answered, unpleasantly emphasizing the word *stole*. "That would have been too risky. But it wasn't necessary, was it? All you had to do was hide the critical papers in other boxes. That collection is so vast it could be years before all those papers are cataloged, years before anyone discovers the so-called proof of your facsimile theory is no proof at all. You think you're clever, Terra, but you're not clever enough."

Terra could hardly believe what she was hearing. Paul's accusation made no sense at all. "What possible reason could I have for hiding those papers, Paul?"

He whirled on her. "The same reason you've had all along—to discredit the lost edition. I'm not stupid, Terra. I know that ever since I brought the pamphlets back from England you've tried to prove they were forgeries. Now you've come up with a cock-and-bull story about facsimiles and have very conveniently managed to do away with all the evidence that could prove you wrong."

Paul approached her chair and pointed a finger accusingly at her. "You thought you hit a gold mine when you found Robert Waltham's mention of those facsimiles. And then you ran across the records of late 1905 and early 1906 that proved Waltham had abandoned his scheme. But you couldn't give up the chance to destroy me, could you? So you hid all the evidence that could contradict your theory and then planned to 'discover' Waltham's reference to the facsimiles. Once that was made public it wouldn't matter that you had no proof. Unless I could show positive refutation of your charge, the doubts would always be there, and the commercial value of the pamphlets would be destroyed."

He backed away and shook his head sadly. "You've resented me ever since I stopped dating you years ago. When I went back to England you began undermining my position, making my father depend on your judgment rather than on mine. It was a nasty shock when he died and I took control, wasn't it? I wouldn't let you continue to run the business into the ground, so you decided to ruin me. I played right into your hands by turning the investigation of the lost edition over to you."

He walked around his desk and sat down, staring threateningly at Terra. "You almost got away with it. If Blansford's librarian hadn't remembered seeing those papers you hid, I wouldn't have stumbled on your tricks. But I've had my eye on you all along."

Paul stood abruptly. "I'm on to you, Terra. The party's over. You're through here—fired! And I warn you, if you so much as whisper a word of that facsimile idea to anyone I'll expose you as a thief. If I were you I'd get out of the rare-book field altogether. There's no future for people like you in this business."

Terra was stunned. As if in a dream, she stood up, facing Paul. "You're wrong, Paul. I've been as loyal to you as I was to your father. You may think you have the right to treat me this way, but you're going to find you're wrong. My lawyer will get in touch with you. I'll leave as soon as I can get my things together." Her hands were shaking, she was perspiring and her throat was as dry as dust, but she kept her cool, even when Paul surprised her even further.

"You'll go now," he demanded. "Everything in your office belongs to me except those stupid plants you've got all over the place. All your work was done on my time, and it stays here." He clamped his lips together and with a stern expression escorted her out of the office. In the foyer he informed all the staff within earshot that Terra was leaving Fosters'.

"Margaret will bring you any personal belongings you've left in the office," he said coldly, then turned and went upstairs. It didn't take Terra long to figure out he was locking the door to the third floor, and when he came back downstairs the key was still in his hand. Without a further word he disappeared into his office.

"What happened?" Margaret asked in a loud whisper. "Are you really quitting?"

Terra didn't answer. She retrieved her purse, grateful she had left it downstairs. At least her notes were still in her possession. Or were they? Panicking, she hastily pulled open her bag. Nothing had been tampered with.

Margaret watched her, concern evident in her features. "What happened with Paul? Why are you quitting?" she persisted.

"Not quitting, Margaret. Fired. Paul and I had a difference of opinion. Since he's decided my presence is dangerous, he doesn't want me to go upstairs, where I can latch on to something valuable and walk off with it. So I'll have to ask you to bring my plants home for me. I hope that won't be too much trouble."

"Of course not," Margaret replied. "But at least tell me what happened," she repeated urgently. She wasn't fooled by Terra's collected manner.

"I've told you all I can," the younger woman answered with a note of weariness in her voice. "Paul was unhappy with the way I handled the investigation of the lost edition. That's all."

She walked toward the door, making it clear she had nothing further to say about her disagreement with Paul. "Give me a ring, and I'll come pick up my plants from your house," she said as she reached the door.

Stepping outside, she paused. She stood on the sidewalk for a moment, feeling as disoriented as a stranger in an unfamiliar neighborhood. Everything had happened so quickly—and none of it made any sense! She should have stood up to Paul, should have told him his accusations were absurd. *Had I known I'd be fired anyway,* she thought, *I'd have told the beast exactly what I think of him a long time ago! I missed my chance!* There was a grim humor in the thought, and Terra began to laugh, though tears stung her eyes. She composed herself just as Margaret came bursting out of the shop.

"Thank goodness I caught you," Margaret gasped. "I was so stunned I forgot I promised Grant I would give you this as soon as you finished talking with Paul. She pressed a sealed envelope into Terra's hands, then ran back inside.

Terra opened the envelope. It contained a folded sheet of paper that said only, "Call me."

CHAPTER NINE

TERRA PUSHED HER MONEY into the coin slot and dialed Grant's number. As the telephone rang, she questioned again her wisdom in running to him like this. There were a million reasons why she shouldn't be seeking his help, but at the moment she couldn't remember a single one.

"Good morning, Ingraham Corporation."

Reluctantly Terra asked to speak to Grant and was told he was in a meeting. With relief she thanked the receptionist and started to hang up.

"May I tell him who called?" the cheerful voice persisted. Terra gave her name hesitantly. "Please hold, Miss Scott, I'll connect you." The telephone whirred and clicked, and in a few seconds Grant's low melodious voice came over the wire.

"Thanks for calling, Terra," he said, "I'd like you to have lunch with me today."

Just minutes before she would have jumped at the invitation, but suddenly she felt numb. She glanced at her watch. It was only half-past nine. Lunchtime seemed a long way off, and she didn't know how she'd feel by then. It seemed an effort just to get from one minute to the next.

"I'm afraid I won't be in the city at noon,"
she said. "I'm on my way home."

"So early?" Surprise sounded clearly from
the other end of the line. "Why? What's happened?"

"I was fired," Terra replied, deciding there
was no point in trying to conceal the truth.

"So you insisted on trying to convince Paul
his pamphlets were facsimiles. I warned you he
would be angry."

"I didn't even mention the facsimiles after
you forced me into agreeing the booklets were
genuine!"

"Then why did Paul fire you?" Grant asked.

Terra sighed wearily. "It's too complicated to
explain over the phone. I don't think he trusts
me anymore." She smiled a little at the understatement.

"Where are you now? Still at the store?"

"Hardly," she replied. "Paul wouldn't even
let me go back up to my office. I'm at a phone
booth down the street from the book shop."

"I need to talk to you, Terra. I can meet you
at the Redwood Park in five minutes."

The park was a lovely landscaped garden in the
shadow of one of San Francisco's tallest sky-
scrapers. It was only a few blocks from Fosters',
and Grant could reach the park in five minutes
because of the light traffic. Terra hadn't realized
he had been so close all these years. But of course
he probably had spent much more time in New
York than in San Francisco.

"I'm exhausted. I think I'd better go home."
She wanted to see him; in fact, she wanted to
throw herself into his strong arms and weep on
his broad shoulders. But the events of the morning had left her shattered. She felt unsure of
herself, unable to speak to Grant in a way that
would do her credit. "Can't we talk some other
time?"

"No," he responded, "I have to see you this
morning—now. Five minutes, Terra."

As she made her way to the park she wondered why Grant had insisted on seeing her right
away. What would he think when she told him
about Paul's accusation? Was there any chance
that he, too, would suspect her of hiding evidence that did not conform to her theories? He
had once suggested she was willing to sacrifice
logic for the sake of a theory. Surely he
wouldn't think she was willing to stoop to dis-
honesty. For the first time it occurred to her she
might be in real trouble. Then she dismissed the
thought as ridiculous. She hadn't tampered with
the documents; she had left them for the librarian to file, just as she had been instructed.

She walked down Montgomery Street toward
the park, not even noticing the colorful San
Francisco sights that usually gave her such
pleasure. There was almost no wind, and the hot
sunshine offered a welcome change from the
damp chill of the past few days. It was a bitter
coincidence that on the most beautiful day San
Francisco had seen in weeks she had lost her

job. She was sure the full implications of what
had happened would hit her soon, but at that
moment she moved as though in a daze. An unfamiliar feeling began to stir in her, and it took
her a minute before she could put a name to it.
Relief! She felt so relieved she wouldn't have to
confront Paul again she could almost feel her
spirits lift.

Reaching the park, she sat on a weathered
wooden bench tucked in the shade of a circle of
redwood trees. As she was breathing in the
sweet forest scent, she saw Grant come through
a gate toward her. He was a large man, but he
moved with a certain masculine grace, an easy
rhythm that emphasized the power of his body.
The motion of his walk tousled his hair, and he
lifted a tanned hand to push an errant lock back
into place.

Sitting down beside her, he cupped her chin in
his hand. His skin felt cool, soothing, and his
dark eyes stared critically at her upturned face.
"You don't look like a young woman who's just
been fired," he commented. "In fact, you look
almost happy."

"I guess I'm a little relieved not to have to
argue with Paul anymore. He's changed so
much in the last year...."

"Tell me what happened," Grant said. His
voice was as warm, as gentle, as it had been the
evening of the dinner at Maurice's.

Suddenly Terra felt like crying. Never before
this moment had it occurred to her how alone

she had been since her father's death. There had
really been no one to talk to all that while. But
now, despite anything she might think about
him, Grant was there, and he was willing to
listen. Under his gentle urging she gave him a
detailed account of her final interview with
Paul. When she related that Paul had accused
her of concealing the documents, she watched
his face carefully. She could see no suspicion
there, just thoughtful concentration. The only
detail she omitted was Paul's assumption that
she had been smitten by him.

Grant was silent for a moment. Then he gently took Terra's hand between both his own. "I
know how much you care about all this," he
said softly, "but I think the time has come to
stop fighting, to admit that Paul, after all, is in
charge of the operation. You've done what you
could, even if in your own eyes it's not
enough."

Terra remained silent. She wasn't about to
give up yet, but for all his understanding she
didn't think Grant would understand that.

"We have something very serious to consider
here."

"We?" Terra asked.

"We." His dark eyes bore into hers. "I want
to help you. I'm the only one who can."

She realized it was true and sat quietly,
waiting for him to continue.

"Paul definitely accused you of deliberately
concealing Blansford material?"

Terra nodded.

"Did he say whether he was planning to make this accusation public?"

"He said that if I talked about the facsimile theory to anyone, he'd brand me a thief."

Grant shook his head, and again the wayward strand fell across his forehead. Impatiently he pushed it back. "I'm afraid you're in a dangerous spot. If you do anything to upset Paul further, I am certain he'll publicly accuse you of theft."

Terra's eyes opened wide. Although Paul had threatened to do that, she hadn't actually believed he would go through with it.

Grant's face was somber. "And on the surface his argument is very convincing."

Terra was appalled. "But I didn't even file any papers!"

"I know that, but all Paul would have to do is point out that you had the motive and the opportunity to misplace the papers. The rest would take care of itself. It wouldn't look very good, Terra."

"But how could he explain my motive without revealing doubts about the lost edition?"

"Come on, now. Think about it. He's in and you're out—a former employee!"

Terra winced, but Grant continued. "You know Paul can be very convincing when he wants to. He wouldn't have to be that specific in his accusations. The thing wouldn't have to go to court for your reputation to be ruined entirely. If you want to get another job in the rare-book field, you need to tread carefully at least for the next month or so. Once the bookfair is over and Paul has sold the pamphlets the danger won't be nearly so great.''

"Once the damage is done, you mean." The thought of Paul's passing off the facsimiles as genuine bothered her as much as the loss of her job.

"We're not going to go into that again."

"No," she said quietly, "I guess we're not." Without speaking further, she stared past Grant's shoulder in the direction of the foun-tain. In front of her unseeing eyes the bright spray of water disappeared and she saw the scene in Paul's office replayed. Grant was right. Paul would not hesitate to accuse her of theft if he had reason to believe she remained a threat to the lost edition. She felt Grant's hand, warm and persuasive, on her shoulder.

"I think you have to go away for a while, Terra. Take a vacation for a few weeks. When you get back all the dust will have settled and you can begin looking for a new job without worrying about Paul." He hesitated, as though he found it difficult to continue. "I know how much it hurts you to leave Paul. I realize how...how hard you've worked, how much you've wanted to help him be as successful as his father, but.... Well, things don't always work out the way we hope."

There was a sadness in his voice that Terra

could not quite understand. She felt he was going out of his way to be kind, and though she wanted more—much more—than simple kindness from him, she felt grateful, felt lucky to have him on her side, to have him beside her, if only for this brief time.

She cleared her throat and said, "It's a tempting idea, going away, but I don't see how I can afford it. As you pointed out, what I am now is a former employee—and they're not famous for having a lot of cash to throw around. Travel is expensive."

"Don't you have anyone you could stay with?" Grant asked. "Is there a good friend or a relative out of town?"

Terra reflected for a moment. "My Aunt Alice lives in La Jolla. She's invited me to come down for a vacation whenever I can."

"That sounds like the perfect solution," Grant said. "I'll take you home, and you can phone your aunt. Then we'll arrange for your ticket and I'll take you to the airport."

"Today?" Terra asked incredulously. "I'd rather take some time to adjust before rushing off to Southern California. Everything has happened so suddenly I need time to think."

"La Jolla will be perfect for that. Does your aunt live near the water?"

"I think her condominium is right by the beach on cliffs overlooking the ocean."

"Couldn't be better. You'll be able to think more clearly once you're away from all this."

"I don't know," Terra replied doubtfully. "It's all so sudden."

"If you stay here you're running a significant risk...."

She looked up at him. He was a hard man to understand. In Paul's office just an hour or so earlier he had been all business; now he was all gentleness. His manner was tender, solicitous, as though he really cared about her. He seemed to be almost frightened for her, and she couldn't imagine why. She would have felt more sure of everything if he had simply taken her in his strong arms, held her to his heart and told her everything was going to be all right. Of course, that could never happen. Grant might be acting very tenderly toward her at the moment, but he would never let himself forget that real problems needed real solutions. He wasn't offering comfort, however welcome the comfort of his closeness would be to her. He was offering escape. And Terra wondered whether that escape would be from him—or from a situation that seemed fraught with a danger she couldn't comprehend.

He seemed to sense her doubt, and leaning toward her, he placed his lips softly on her own. "Trust me," he whispered. And she did. He stood and, drawing her to her feet, put his arm across her shoulders and led her from the park.

Seated next to him in the Mercedes, Terra was very much aware of the powerful attraction of

Grant's presence. When his shoulder brushed her own, when their hands accidentally met, her nerves tingled and her breath came more quickly. Maybe it was a good idea to get away for more reasons than one.

Every touch seemed to hold false promise. She tried to fight off the desire that Grant sparked in her, but it was no use. Suddenly she realized why. She loved him. The moments in which he had offered comfort had been brief, but they had given her a glimpse of the man she had hoped he would become. It was easy to fight her feelings for him when she had thought he had become cold, calculating, unemotional. But when he was gentle and tender he seemed so much a natural extension of the Grant she had once known that her heart nearly burst.

She felt as though she were a child again, a child in the presence of an unattainable, wonderful, magical companion. Only now there was more than the companionship she had once vainly wished she could have with him forever. Now there was passion, a hurting, grinding, reaching desire that would know no quenching. She didn't want merely to make love with Grant. She wanted to be his love. And that was out of the question.

This morning he had been concerned about her and had helped her find a way out of a difficult situation, but she sensed his interest in her was not very different from what it had been. There was no question in her mind that getting her out of the way would ensure that no taint brushed the reputation of the precious lost edition. Once the bookfair was over he would again disappear from her life—this time for good. She might as well leave, she thought. She might as well make the break from him now, before it became any more painful than it already was.

IT TOOK A REMARKABLY SHORT TIME for the arrangements to be made. Terra's aunt could not contain her delight at the news that her niece was coming to visit, though she herself was about to leave for England. That meant they would share only a little time with each other and Terra would be alone for most of her trip. As much as she cared for her elderly relative, Terra was glad she'd have time to herself.

Grant saved her the trouble of finding someone to mind the house in her absence. He claimed he was familiar enough with it to care for it as well as she could herself, and she didn't argue with him.

As she headed for the stairs to her room, she heard him speaking to the airline office. She listened for a minute, half hoping there would be no space available, reluctant suddenly to leave Grant, despite her knowledge it was the best thing to do. In an agreeable but business-like voice he confirmed her booking.

Up in her room Terra pulled a large suitcase down from the top shelf of the closet and set it

across the arms of her bedroom chair. "Your
flight leaves at four-thirty," Grant said as he
entered the room. "That gives us a couple of
hours to get you ready." He walked over to the
bed and pulled Terra's pillows out from underneath the spread. After propping them up
against the headboard, he settled back against
them, looking comfortable and relaxed.

The sight of him lounging casually on her bed
was disconcerting to Terra. "I can move the
suitcase if you'd rather sit on the chair," she
offered.

"No, thanks. I'm quite comfortable here.
You do the work and I'll advise you," he
grinned.

Smiling, she said, "And what makes you
qualified to advise a woman on what to wear on
vacation?" As soon as the words were out she
regretted them. She could very well imagine
exactly what Grant's qualifications were in that
department.

"Experience, of course." His smile was wide
and infuriating. "Take your bathing suit, by all
means, and some shorts and sleeveless tops, but
don't forget something a little warmer for the
evenings. Better bring a sweater."

Although she had asked him, his answer nettled her. She was perfectly capable of choosing
her own clothes for a trip, even if he did consider himself an expert in women's attire. From
the way he was behaving she felt certain this
scene was not a new one for him. Only in the

previous scenarios he and the woman in question had undoubtedly planned to travel together. It was just like him to feel he had the right to select the clothes of his female companions, Terra fumed inwardly. She wished she had the nerve to ask him to wait downstairs while she packed, but that would be an admission that his presence in her bedroom bothered her. Better, she decided, to try to remain cool and distant.

She shuffled through several drawers before she located her new bikini. Before she had a chance to toss it into the suitcase Grant commented, "You have grown up, haven't you? That suit is considerably different from the kind you were wearing when I last knew you!"

Terra looked up at him, expecting to see his teasing grin. She was startled to find that his expression was seriously intent. He did not avert his gaze when she met it, and their eyes locked for several seconds. As she turned her head away, she was breathing rapidly.

"When you get back from La Jolla," Grant said softly, "things will have changed."

Terra busied herself with straightening the piles of clothes in her suitcase. Why did he feel it necessary to point that out? Why didn't he just take her to the airport and then disappear without a word? She guessed it was part of his code to make sure the rules of the game were clear. Well, he didn't have to bother. They had been clear to her from the start. She just wanted all

contact between them to end so she could start
to recover her equilibrium.

"Things always change," she said brightly.
"That's part of the fun of life. Something new
every day." She flounced into the bathroom,
ostensibly to pack her toiletries but really to
hide the fact she couldn't keep her mouth from
turning down at the corners, and she would
rather have died than have him see her cry at
that moment. As she put her cologne and talcum
powder into her cosmetic bag she tried to collect
her thoughts. Why did he feel he had to stay
there all afternoon? She was sure he had other
things to do, so it would probably be better for
both of them if she found her own way to the
airport.

The bathroom door was open, and she called
to him in the other room. "You don't need to
stay here waiting for me if you have other things
to do. I can take the bus to the airport."

"What did you say? I couldn't hear you."

She repeated her statement as she was packing
up the last of her cosmetics, and then, turning to
walk into the bedroom, she bumped into Grant.
She hadn't even heard him move to the door,
where he had stood, watching. He reached out
to steady her, and to her own surprise, the feel
of his powerful compelling hands on her frail
shoulders undid her. Without warning she burst
into tears. It was too much—things had been
too much for her to take for a long time.

"Oh, no," Grant said, "oh, Terra." Tenderly his arms enfolded her. She felt the muscled strength of his forearm across her waist and, more disturbing, the lean fingers of his other hand cupping her head. He drew her face tightly against his chest, and for a moment her tears stopped—and her breath. The only sound in the still room was the sound of his heart beating beneath her cheek. But when she heard the steady beat and realized what it was, a new wave of absolute misery swept over her and she couldn't hold back the gushing wetness that welled from her eyes and spilled over onto his shirtfront.

"Stop it, Terra. Sweetheart, please stop." Gently he smoothed her hair, stroking so softly she could barely feel the comforting motion of his hand. She didn't want his condolences; she wanted him. Fresh sobs racked her; she simply couldn't stop. Grant tightened his hold. So close was the embrace that his one arm held her entire back, his elbow at her waist, his fingertips grazing the sensitive skin at the nape of her neck. His other hand stroked her bent head as though she were the child he had once consoled after a fall or a scrape.

"Everything's going to be all right," he crooned, "you'll see."

But he was wrong, and she knew it. Everything was going to be all wrong from now on. Shaking her head, she attempted to pull away from him, to shrug off the arms that held her. He wouldn't let go. She was like a bird fluttering between his hands, a bird with no chance to resume flight.

"Come here, Terra," he said, leading her toward the bed. "Sit down." He lowered her, his arm remaining around her shoulders. For a moment she merely sat beside him at the bed's edge, her hands held still in her lap, her eyes cast down toward her own pale legs, which she self-consciously held stiff, as though to avoid touching his strong limbs.

"There, that's better." He smiled, seeing that she had become quiet.

But though her violent sobs had ceased, her tears had not. Slowly they rose at the corners of her downcast eyes and made their hopeless way down her soft pale cheeks. As though he could dam them, Grant reached up one tanned finger and slid it up her cheek against the direction of the flow.

At his touch she jumped, and the small motion seemed to move him. Again his arms reached across to her, surrounding her with his masculine strength. For a moment he held her as though he had no intention of ever letting her go. Wordlessly she responded, her own arms slowly lifting, circling his broad shoulders.

"Oh, my Terra," he whispered, drawing back so he could stare into her stricken face. Before she had a chance to think about what was happening his sensuously curved lips were inexorably descending toward her vulnerable mouth. It seemed to take an eternity for his soft mouth to reach her own, and in that space of time an image flashed across her inner vision—the image of Grant standing outlined against the window, a silhouette of undeniable virility. The desire she had felt when she had seen him then shot through her like a bolt of electricity, and when his lips finally met hers she felt charged, as if she had been struck by a burning current.

His lips were hungry, devouring her own. Both of his hands held her face, and her hands lay powerless on his wide shoulders, as though she had forgotten she could use them to resist the drive of his passionate kiss. Resistance was the furthest thing from her mind. She leaned toward him, eager to meet the demands of his searing mouth, his probing tongue.

His lips left hers to trail kisses along her tear-stained cheeks, to tease the soft line of her jaw, to nestle in the pulsating hollow at the base of her throat. Responding without thought, she buried her own lips in the springy blackness of his hair, and when she felt his fingers at the buttons of her blouse, she moved back slightly, instinctively, to give his hands the room they needed to loosen the fastenings.

In one smooth motion he opened the blouse and lowered her so that they lay across the bed. His fingers drew a trembling sensuous line from her shoulder to where her bra revealed the cleft between her breasts. She shuddered as his fingertips teased the dark hollows, then snapped open the front closure of the garment.

He drew lazy maddening circles on the white skin of her breasts, coming ever closer to her nipples without touching them. She arched to meet his touch—she couldn't help doing so—but her motion did not stop the tantalizing quality of his exploration. She wanted to cry out, "Touch me, oh please touch me. I want to feel you!" But she could say nothing, could only wait as his fingers continued to drive her into near madness.

She closed her eyes against the light of the room, for even the act of seeing seemed an interruption of the ecstasy of his caresses. She closed her eyes, so she was not aware he was about to lower his dark head and take her thrusting nipple between his warm moist lips. At the sensation of the hot flesh of his mouth against her breast her whole body reached up toward his, then, trembling, fell back against the bed. In response Grant shifted so that he lay atop her, supporting his weight with his hands at her side. He kissed her forehead, her cheeks, her shoulders. He drew his tongue down from the base of her neck toward her breast and again took it into his mouth. She grabbed at his bent head, making two hard small fists full of his sleek hair. She wanted to hold on to him, as hard as she could, as long as she could, but her hands were weak with passion, for he easily pulled away from her grasp.

"Kiss me, Terra." His voice was husky, his

lips so close to her own as he raised his head to stare into her clouded eyes. "Kiss me."

She kissed him teasingly, but the very touch of his skin, even on her closed lips, was so powerfully exciting to her she could not resist the urge to kiss him as a woman kisses a man, to kiss him again as she had kissed him in their first hunger. She parted her lips and thrust them toward the eager mouth that awaited them. And again she was lost to the ecstasy of Grant, her mouth probed by his, her hands, as if of their own accord, seeking and finding the buttons of his shirt. Her fingers did not fumble as they pulled the buttons from their holes, as they tore aside the creamy fabric and reached for what they wanted: the smooth muscled expanse, the hot skin.

It was his turn to shudder as he felt the small soft hand stroke his chest, tease his sensitive flank, circle up until it lay at his shoulder beneath the material of his shirt. In response his hand reached down to the edge of her skirt, which had ridden up nearly to her waist.

When she felt his fingers graze her bare thigh the motion of her own hand stopped. For an instant she lay perfectly still, but then the maddening circles began again, this time on the delicate skin of her inner leg, and she held in her quaking breath. With heart-stopping, teasing lightness his hands moved along the quivering curves of her. Everywhere he touched her sensitized flesh sent the same jolting message to her dazed brain: "Let him," her every nerve cried out, "let him do whatever he wants to do."

And desire rose in her more strongly, more irresistibly, than she had ever dreamed. Her whole being was filled with a longing so physical, so beyond rational thought, she did not even seem to remember who she was. She wanted this man as she had never wanted anything before, wanted his searing lips against her flesh, wanted his strong hands to stroke her willing, her eager skin.

"Grant," she moaned, her hoarse voice as unfamiliar as the voice of a wanton stranger. "Grant, I want you."

"Terra," he answered, his voice deep in his throat, "I want you, too. Thank God it's not too late."

Too late! The words stunned Terra out of her stupor. What did he mean? Was he really so hard as to have made sure she had plenty of time left before her flight to take care of this last little detail, this seduction he had begun the night of Maurice's dinner and was now about to finish off? He *had* changed; there was no denying it. He had spoken about passion the first day they had met as adults. She now knew passion was something he engaged in when he was sure he had enough time to fulfill his own desires.

She wanted to tell him exactly what she thought of his transparent maneuvering. And yet it was so hard to resist the dizzying effect of his nearness. Weakly she opened her mouth to speak her protest, to tell him she had changed her mind.

It was no use. To him her parted lips were just one more invitation. He thought she was asking for his mouth, and it came down upon her own with a power that was growing more familiar, more tempting, by the second.

"To kiss you is so different," he murmured, pulling away only far enough to be able to gaze into her passion-misted eyes. "You are so sweet," he whispered, "so unlike the others...."

And though he closed his eyes as he lowered his face toward hers, Terra's eyes were opened wide, staring at the ceiling. "The others," he had said. All the countless others. Why was it that every time he came near her she forgot who he was—Grant Ingraham, man about town—and who she was—just one more woman, no one in particular.

His hair brushed her cheek, but it could have been a wire brush. Realization robbed the moment of pleasure. There was no softness to his dark locks now and no softness in her voice as she said, "I can't," and rolled away from him so swiftly he didn't understand the situation had changed.

"Can't what, sweetheart?" he asked in a lazy sensuous drawl. His hand reached for her across the small space she had put between them, but when he touched her she rose to a sitting position, her back toward him as he lay on the bed, her legs dangling over the edge.

"I can't be number five hundred or so in a list of thousands."

"What are you talking about? What's the matter?"

His voice was edged with anger now—and something else. He was probably quite disappointed he hadn't been able to fit a little lovemaking into his busy schedule after all, Terra thought bitterly. "Nothing's the matter, Grant," she said. "Nothing is the matter exactly. There's nothing between us, and I can't make love just in order to have something to do until my plane is ready to board."

"You're ridiculous sometimes, you know that?" Grant nearly shouted. This time his anger was unmistakable. "I just can't figure you out. Either you're a child who'll never grow up, or else you're a very proud woman who's headed for a fall. I don't know who's feeding you statistics, but you're way off base. So cool all of a sudden, so collected, so sure about me. You think there's only one thing I'm after, don't you? You've got such a lot of theories, Terra. You think you know everything, but my guess is you've got a few things left to learn."

"Maybe I do," she replied, still keeping her back to him in order to hide her agony. But her voice was strong in defense, regardless of her feelings. "Maybe I do have something to learn, but you're not going to be the one to teach me."

"Love can't be taught, Terra," he said, and there was no anger in his voice now, only a lingering hint of that disappointment she had noticed earlier. "Your body knows all about love. I could tell that just by the way you respond when I touch you. But if you want to make love with your smart little head, that's your business. I'll wait for you downstairs." He stood, pulling closed his shirt, and headed for the door.

"I can get to the airport by myself, thank you," she called after him, her tone sarcastic.

"I'll wait for you downstairs," he repeated.

She got up, stood still for minutes after he had left. He had accused her of making love with her mind instead of her feelings, but he was wrong. Dead wrong. Her feelings had nearly overwhelmed her, and she was lucky to have escaped the way she had. *No,* an inner voice said, *you were not lucky, not lucky at all.*

She stayed upstairs as long as she dared, hesitant to face him. After the way she had melted in his arms he could have absolutely no doubt about her love for him. She felt like a total fool. Grant was right about one thing: she had a lot to learn.

Glancing at her watch, she realized she had better hurry if she was going to make her plane. Mechanically she finished her packing and descended the stairs. Head held high, she walked into the kitchen, where she found that Grant had made them coffee.

With businesslike formality they reviewed what had to be done at the house during the time she would be away. Then they rinsed and put away the coffee things, took her bags out to Grant's car and locked up the house.

The trip to the San Francisco airport was a silent one. Terra could not think of one word to say, though there were plenty of words going through her head. She had been stupid from the very beginning. She was glad she was going. She wanted to get as far away from Grant Ingraham as possible.

She expected him to let her out at the terminal, and she was surprised when he drove directly to the parking garage. Carrying her suitcase as though it were weightless, he led her through the maze of corridors to the check-in counter and then down to the gate. Throughout the silent ordeal Terra managed to keep a tight rein on her feelings, but when the time came for her to join the long line of passengers waiting to board, her composure started to slip. Fighting the almost irresistible impulse to throw her arms around Grant and hang on forever, she put out her hand instead.

For a minute she thought he was going to refuse her offer of a friendly farewell handshake. He merely stared at her hand as though he didn't know what she meant by extending it. But then he took her fingers in his own, and with a movement so swift it took Terra completely by surprise, he pulled her hand up against his chest and put his other arm at her back, holding her so tightly she couldn't speak. She had only a moment, when he released her, to see the expression on his face—an expression she couldn't read. She parted her lips to mutter goodbye, but he had turned his back. He moved so quickly he was soon lost in the crowd, leaving Terra to stare after him in open-mouthed astonishment.

CHAPTER TEN

"IT CERTAINLY TOOK YOU long enough to decide to come and visit me," Aunt Alice chided. "I could have gone to my grave without ever laying eyes on you again."

No, Aunt Alice hadn't changed at all, Terra chuckled to herself. The spritely woman must be approaching seventy, but she seemed to have lost none of her incredible energy. She was short and she was plump, but on her those qualities were virtues, for she was the most comfortable, the most perfect aunt a person could hope to have. Her white hair curled about her round face and she had two of the brightest bluest eyes that ever twinkled with love and delight.

She was an intrepid traveler, and the trip she was about to take to London was a simple jaunt compared to some of the journeys she had undertaken: boating up the coast to Alaska, range riding in Montana, tramping all over Europe. Someday, she always said, she would make it to China. It didn't matter to her that most people would have considered it difficult for a woman her age to attempt such a trip. Terra knew the day would come when Aunt

Alice would find herself trying to climb the Great Wall!

"Maybe after you've practiced on the easy stuff you'll be ready to tackle the grueling trip to Berkeley and come and see me," Terra teased.

"I'm so sorry I won't be home while you're here," her aunt said. "If I had known you wanted to come down I could have gone abroad at some other time."

"I didn't know I'd be free to come until this morning," Terra half explained. "I hope my last-minute arrival isn't too much of a bother for you."

"Nonsense," Aunt Alice exclaimed. "What's the bother? I get to have company for two days and someone to wave goodbye to me when I leave."

Once Aunt Alice had resided in a large rambling home, but eventually she had tired of the work of keeping up the garden and all the other details that went into being the owner of a house. Now she lived in a condominium that sat high on the cliffs of La Jolla, overlooking the Pacific. The entire west wall of the apartment was glass, providing a view of the ocean. Half of the huge main room was an open kitchen with a breakfast bar that faced the water. The rest of the room formed a living-room area, with several comfortable chairs strategically positioned to afford the best vista.

After they had finished the light supper Aunt

Alice had had waiting when she brought Terra in from the airport, the two sat quietly, chatting and watching the lowering sun graze the sparkling water.

"What happened that you were able to leave so suddenly and for so long?" Aunt Alice asked. "Don't misunderstand me," she added quickly, "I'm not trying to pry. I'm delighted to have you here with or without explanation...."

Although the directness of the question caught Terra off guard, she should have realized she couldn't fool Aunt Alice. And Terra was familiar enough with her relative's forthright personality to be certain the woman would continue to ask questions until she was satisfied with the answers.

"It was a problem at work," she began. "My boss and I have disagreed for quite a while about the way a particular project should be handled. The situation developed into a crisis today, and he fired me."

Her aunt looked at her intently. "You don't sound very angry. Were you expecting it to happen?"

"No...yes...no." Terra fished for words. "When I think about it it seems inevitable it should have happened," she said. She quickly summarized the problem of the lost edition, then shrugged. "Getting away from that job is probably all for the best, but I hate to leave a project undone."

"Isn't there anything you can do?" Aunt Alice asked.

"I thought at first I might be able to continue my research on my own, but a...a friend of dad's—" Terra paused and took a breath "—a friend of dad's who knows about these things convinced me otherwise." Involuntarily she let out a small, almost inaudible sigh, but the gesture did not escape the notice of her aunt.

The elderly woman looked as if she had been about to say something but had changed her mind. When she did speak it was to detail plans of her trip. And so lively was the conversation the hours passed swiftly.

Aunt Alice stood. "It's time for me to go to bed and read my guidebook," she announced. "Stay up as long as you like, and don't worry about getting up early tomorrow. Sounds to me as though you could do with a few mornings of sleeping in."

After her aunt left Terra stayed in the living room for a while. She turned out the lights and in the darkness watched the waves beyond the window roll in a thin white line to the shore. She hadn't mentioned Grant to Aunt Alice, at least not by name, but she had not stopped thinking about him for one minute from the time she had got on the plane. Through all the petty conversations necessitated by travel, and through all the pleasant chatter with her aunt, he had been there at the back of her mind.

Once more she saw his dark eyes, his tousled

hair. The scene in her bedroom was vivid as a movie unreeling in her brain. And the final parting at the airport—she could barely stand to think about it, it had so wrenched her heart. Grant had held on to her as though he didn't want her to fly out of his life. But that was what she had done, had had to do. The knowledge that everything was over between them was not softened by the fact there had really never been much in the first place. "Things will be changed." Was that what he had said? She felt she would never see him again, and the thought of it made her heart feel as heavy as the huge boulders that received the unceasing pounding of the ocean waves.

THE NEXT MORNING after breakfast Aunt Alice brought out her suitcases and started to pack. Terra could only watch in amazement as her aunt set to work. She was so organized she managed to pack a whole month's worth of clothes into two small bags. And when Terra lifted them she was astounded at how light they were.

"Travel teaches you how to travel," Aunt Alice remarked, laughing. "I never ever carry more than three things when I go. Two suitcases and my purse are all. If you're carrying three items, you know when you've left something behind. More than that and you can't be sure."

The afternoon slid pleasantly by as Terra went with Aunt Alice to have prescriptions filled, to buy film for her camera and to ask the travel agent a few last-minute questions. Then they went back home to pick up Agatha, Aunt Alice's cat, to deliver her to her sitter.

"I'd be happy to look after Agatha," Terra said as they coaxed the reluctant cat into the car.

"I won't hear of it," her aunt exclaimed. "I don't want you to feel tied down to this place. If anything comes up that convinces you to go back early, I want you to feel free to shut the door and leave."

"What could make me want to leave early?" Terra asked, but her aunt, busy with the cat, didn't answer.

Finally everything was done and Aunt Alice felt prepared to leave. They celebrated with a bon-voyage dinner at a tiny Mexican restaurant. After ordering margaritas for both of them, Terra proposed a toast. "To my aunt the world traveler. Long may she roam!"

They sipped the pale drink, and then Aunt Alice raised her glass. "To the successful conclusion of the problems that sent you fleeing down here."

A shadow passed over Terra's eyes at her aunt's words. "The door on those problems is already shut, Aunt Alice."

"Terra—" the older woman toyed with her drink for a moment, then looked up directly into her niece's eyes "—was there some other reason for this little visit—this escape?"

Terra turned away from the frank, questioning blue gaze. She struggled with her thoughts.

It would feel so good to unburden herself, to let just one other person know how her heart ached, now hopeless she felt. But she couldn't say anything about Grant. The whole thing didn't make any sense to her, so how could it make sense to anybody else?

"I have a feeling the problem you keep refer-ring to is more than a professional matter," her aunt persisted.

"It is," Terra replied, surprised she was able to get out even those two words.

"A problem of the heart, as they say?"

"Yes."

"Terra," her aunt began, gently taking her hand as it lay on the tablecloth, "you're a strong-willed girl—you always have been. But sometimes a person has to give in. It's not the same thing as giving up, you know."

Despite her unwillingness, her inability to dis-cuss what was really bothering her, Terra smiled down at her aunt, grateful she obviously cared.

"When you were a little tyke," the elderly woman continued, "you used to follow around that handsome young man—Grant—was that his name? I used to look at you then and think that someday you'd find someone of your own, someone who'd make you as happy as a woman as he made you happy as a girl. But in order to be happy you have to give, you have to take a risk. You would have followed that young Grant anywhere. Now I'm not saying you have to do everything a man wants you to do—not at all. What I'm saying is sometimes you have to let down your guard a little. You have to— Oh, my dear, what is it?'' Terra's aunt looked up to find an expression of tortured sadness on her niece's face. Never before had she seen the girl look so woebegone, so lost.

"What have I said? What is it?" Aunt Alice repeated.

"Grant." It was a whisper through barely opened lips.

"Oh. Oh, dear. I see." Aunt Alice's own lips were pursed into a shocked little O that perfectly matched the round orbs of her eyes. "Oh, my dear Terra, I understand."

Terra had told her nothing, but somehow she knew Aunt Alice did understand her misery. Aunts were sometimes magical, and Alice was no exception. If only she knew the magic that could mend Terra's spirit—and her heart.

THE NEXT MORNING Aunt Alice was in a dither. Even though she had allowed plenty of time to get to the airport, the trip turned into a last-minute rush. She kept remembering things that had to be done, and when they were finally driving down the freeway toward the airport they had scarcely more than an hour before the flight left.

Arriving at the terminal, Terra let her aunt out at the curb by the check-in counter and then parked the car. By the time she had rejoined the traveler, the other woman had checked her baggage and was waiting impatiently. Together they hurried down to the gate.

Aunt Alice threw her arms around Terra. "Give in," she said. "Give in to your heart. It will hurt less than you think."

Terra nodded mutely, unable to offer an argument. She kissed Aunt Alice and watched her until she disappeared down the jetbridge into the plane.

When she opened the door of Aunt Alice's condominium, the stillness of the empty rooms struck her immediately. Without her aunt bustling about the place seemed remote and lifeless. Terra moved through the rooms, tidying up and fixing lunch. Then she decided to take a walk along the cliffs by the beach. The day was cloudy but warm, and quite a few people were strolling along the promenade. She walked about a mile or so, then sat down on a bench facing the sea. The water was calm, the waves small, but her own thoughts were as turbulent as a storm.

It seemed to her her whole life had fallen about her in tattered shreds. She had lost her job; she had lost her companionship with Jeff; she had lost the sweet memory of the Grant of her youth, and she had lost the man himself. Leaning back, she extended her arm across the top of the bench and lay her head sideways upon it so that her eyes faced out over the stretches of water and sky. A gull swooped down, hovered over the waves for a moment, then winged

away. Terra watched until the bird was merely a
white speck against the gray sky. It was funny,
she thought, how painful freedom could be.

She spent the entire next day doing nothing.
She slept late, then went down to the beach,
then came back and slept again. She thought
about nothing. The troubles she had been
through were finally taking their toll. Her mind
and her body refused to suffer any longer, and
she let them have their way.

Friday morning she awoke with new alert-
ness, as though her rest had had an effect. She
felt strong enough to think once more about the
lost edition, and she remembered what Grant
and Paul had said about the Blansford exhibit
being open to the public, starting on Monday.

It occurred to her that the first day of the exhibit would be an ideal time to try to get a look
at the photocopies of the 1905 documents. It
was unlikely there would be a crowd in the very
first hours of the exhibition. It was also unlikely
that Grant, Paul or Nathaniel Blansford would
be present, since they would undoubtedly attend
the preview that very day. If she could just get a
glance at those copies she might be able to find
proof of her theory. Just one order, one sentence about the printing might be all she needed
to convince Blansford, for in a flash she realized
that if she had definite proof, undeniable irrefutable proof, Blansford was the one to go to.

She thought about the plan all morning, and
the more she thought about it the better it

seemed. She considered trying to get a flight out on Sunday, which would give her plenty of time to get to the Blansford first thing Monday morning, but when she phoned the airline she found that the only available seats were on a flight that evening and another late on Sunday evening. Not wanting to take a chance, she booked herself a seat on the flight that night.

It didn't take her long to pack—she had barely unpacked. But there was one detail she had to settle before she left for home. When she had started to think about the limited time she would have at the Blansford and the kind of material she would be seeking, she remembered she had taken notes early in her investigation that might help speed things now. The only problem was they were in her desk drawer at Fosters'. How to get them? Terra considered the question, then decided to take a risk and call Margaret. After a brief explanation of where Terra was and what she wanted, Margaret agreed to try to get the notes. "Paul has kept the door to the third floor locked, but I still haven't brought your plants out yet, so I'm sure he'll give me the key for that."

Terra explained where the folders were and agreed to meet Margaret at her house late in the evening to pick up the notes. "My plane doesn't get in until nine, so I won't be able to get to your house before eleven. Will that be too late?"

"Are you kidding? The evening is just beginning at eleven. Come on over when you can."

Feeling pleased she had made the decision to go back to the Blansford and had been able to carry out the preliminaries of her plan so easily, Terra sat back to relax for a while before it would be time to call a cab for the airport. La Jolla was a beautiful place for a vacation, she thought, but it would still be there when the difficulties with the lost edition were settled.

And as for the other little matter that had driven her to Southern California—the matter of Grant Ingraham—it was never going to be settled, so sticking around wouldn't have helped. Unbidden, Aunt Alice's words floated into Terra's mind. "You have to give," the elderly woman had said. Terra would have been glad to have given Grant anything—if there had been the tiniest chance he would have given anything in return.

"THE CAPTAIN HAS TURNED ON the no-smoking sign in preparation for our landing in San Francisco. At this time please...."

As she followed the cabin attendant's directions Terra could see the lights below becoming larger and more distinct. In a few minutes the wheels hit the runway and the plane braked to a stop. It was a little after nine, and she hoped she wouldn't be late in getting to Margaret's. Anxious to start the trip home, she jumped up as soon as the seat-belt sign went off and joined the line of people waiting in the aisle.

Finally the door slid open, but there was yet

another holdup while an airport employee handed a message to the cabin attendant. They consulted briefly, and then the cabin attendant announced over the intercom, "Will passenger Terra Scott please identify herself...."

The line of people, restless with the delay, surged forward before Terra had a chance to speak out, so she stepped aside quickly and let the rest of the passengers stream by. While she was waiting to speak to the attendant, anxious thoughts filled her mind. Had her luggage been damaged? Surely they wouldn't send a special message to the airplane just for that. Had something happened to Aunt Alice! Her aunt's friend, the cat sitter, knew the flight Terra had planned to take to San Francisco; Terra had called to ask her to keep an eye on Alice's apartment. Fearful the message must concern her aunt, Terra suddenly remembered that Margaret also knew she would be on this plane. Letting out a relieved sigh, Terra concluded it was far more likely that Margaret's plans had suddenly changed and she had chosen this slightly unusual but effective way of getting in touch with her.

She introduced herself to the attendant, expecting to be handed a piece of paper, and was startled when she was directed to the uniformed airport employee who had delivered the message.

"Miss Scott?" he inquired politely. When she nodded he continued, "Will you follow me, please?'' Without waiting for a reply, he began walking.

Terra hurried after him, her uneasiness returning. ''Can you tell me what the problem is?'' she asked anxiously.

He turned an impersonal glance toward her. ''There is an urgent message for you at the airline office. I'm afraid that's all I know.''

Tagging along behind him in silence, Terra began to worry again. Even Margaret wouldn't intercept someone at the airport just to say she wouldn't be at home that evening. The problem had to concern Aunt Alice after all. She had seemed to be in good health, but she was almost seventy. The excitement and strain of preparing for yet another long trip may have taken its toll before the elderly woman had barely begun her vacation.

They reached the airline counter, and Terra's escort held the gate for her, motioning her to go on into the office. There she was introduced to the shift supervisor, who apologized profusely for the inconvenience.

''Can you tell me what's the matter?'' Terra asked again, her voice trembling slightly.

''We understand that an urgent message is on its way to the airport for you. The front office has asked that you wait here for a few minutes until the messenger contacts you.''

''I don't understand.'' Terra was totally bewildered. ''Do you know where the message is from?''

The supervisor shook his head. "I've told you all I know. Our instructions came from the head office. Other than that, you know as much as I do." He gestured toward a chair. "If you'll have a seat I'll send someone for your luggage, and then you'll be ready to go as soon as the message arrives."

He detached Terra's luggage claim stubs from her ticket and left the office. When he returned he was carrying her suitcase.

"How long do you think it will be?" she asked. "I've made arrangements to meet someone, and it's getting quite late."

"I shouldn't think it would be very long, miss. But I really don't know. All I know is that the front office says it's vital for you to wait for the message." He looked at her curiously. "This kind of thing doesn't happen very often, so I'd say the message must be important. But I really don't know," he repeated, sitting down at his desk and picking up some papers.

Terra moved restlessly in her chair. She hated just sitting there, waiting, but there was no alternative. The man at the desk didn't seem willing or able to do any more. She looked at her watch and, three minutes later, looked at it again. After another five minutes she had about decided she had to do something, anything, when the telephone rang. Terra leaped forward eagerly, but she could learn nothing from the supervisor's short responses.

When he hung up he picked up her bag. "If you'll follow me, miss."

She gathered her things and stood up.

"What's happened? Where are we going?" she asked, but the supervisor was already half out of the door and didn't seem to hear her. He walked through the terminal at a brisk pace, and Terra hurried along behind him, her anxiety increasing steadily.

They walked toward the terminal exit. Through the automatic doors she could see a sleek black limousine with a uniformed driver hovering by its side. As soon as he saw them approaching he advanced toward them. Terra's heart almost stopped beating. Was this an embassy car? Aunt Alice!

"Miss Scott," the driver said without a hint of a question in his voice. He had no doubt about her identity.

"Yes, yes," she replied impatiently. "What's the matter? What's happened to my aunt?"

Moving toward the limousine, the driver answered by holding the door open. Terra stepped forward quickly, then caution asserted itself. "Where are we going?" she demanded of the driver. "Will someone please tell me what this is all about?"

"Get in, Terra," the low voice from the back seat of the limousine commanded quietly.

CHAPTER ELEVEN

HER FIRST IMPULSE was to turn and run, and she took one small step back. But the driver was standing directly behind her—so close she bumped into him. At the same moment Grant's large hand reached out to grab her wrist. "Come on," he said, and there was a tone to his voice that made Terra reluctantly hand her suitcase to the driver before climbing into the car.

"What's this all about?" she demanded, suddenly no longer fearing for Aunt Alice but for herself. "What sort of a dirty trick are you playing?" Suspicion and anger combined to make her voice almost shrill.

"It's a little inappropriate, isn't it, for you to accuse me of trickery." Grant's voice was hard and thin, and Terra could almost see the displeasure on his face, though it was too dark to read his expression. "Correct me if I'm wrong, but it was my distinct understanding you had agreed to stay in La Jolla for at least three weeks. Sneaking back after three days doesn't seem entirely aboveboard, does it?"

"What do you mean, 'sneaking back'?" Terra's anger was increasing by the moment, and she didn't even notice that the driver had come around to the front of the car after having deposited her suitcase in the trunk. He slid behind the wheel, waiting for Grant to give instructions.

"I am not sneaking back. I am not a child you can send to her room. I intended to stay longer when I left, but I've changed my mind. I don't see how that's any concern of yours...."

"Why didn't you call me, Terra?" A note of concern had crept into his voice, but it was lost on her.

"I don't have to report all my actions to you," she responded tartly. Why didn't he just leave her alone? She would never be able to get over wanting him, losing him, if he kept popping up every time she turned around. She scowled at him, then whirled her head around and stared out the window.

"I'll tell you why you didn't phone me." Grant's angry tone compelled her to turn back toward him. "You knew I would tell you on the telephone what I'm telling you now. Coming back was a damn stupid thing to do." His words exploded from him with increasing force.

"I don't understand why you're so upset," Terra began after a short silence. "You don't have to worry that I'll get in your way...."

"At least we agree on something," Grant said sarcastically. "I don't intend to *let* you get in my way, but if you cooperate for a change," he added significantly, "then things will be a lot easier for everyone."

"If by 'everyone' you mean Stephanie Duke," Terra retorted hotly, "you can set your mind at ease. And you can just let me out of here...." She made a lunge for the door, but Grant's hand covered hers before it reached the handle. His skin was warm as his long fingers surrounded her own, and she felt the unwelcome fire of his touch shoot through her.

"Take me home to Berkeley. You won't have to see me again. I don't know how I can cooperate any more than that." Tears started to form in her eyes. Under the veil of darkness she blinked hard to keep them back. Grant's anger and his obvious resentment of her hurt more than she was prepared for, and his open admission that he didn't want to see her again stung like salt in a wound.

Before she could say another word she felt his arms around her. "No tears, Terra," he said softly. She struggled to get out of his grasp, but though he did not tighten his embrace, she found herself unable to get free. The feel of him so close, the memory of the other times those strong arms had enfolded her, weakened her, and she sank back against the strength of his broad shoulder.

"How did you know I'd be on this plane?" she asked.

"Margaret."

"I can't trust anyone anymore," was all she could respond.

"Yes, you can," Grant said, his voice holding none of its former anger. "You can trust me.

You've got to get away, and since you don't seem to be able to do it alone, I'm going to help. Head for the plane, Charlie," he said to the driver.

"The plane?" Terra asked in astonishment. Whatever did he mean? "What plane? Where are you taking me? What is this?"

"Relax, honey," Grant said, a hint of amusement in his voice. Again Terra began to struggle to release herself from his arms, but he drew her closer, and relaxing against the smooth leather of the car's upholstery, he pulled her back, so that both of them reclined in a posture that was almost casual. Somehow Terra's head had come to rest against the hard wall of his chest, and somehow she didn't have the energy to raise it.

Grant's fingers stroked her cheek, as though to calm her, and the touch of his skin against her own was hypnotic. She could not think of one more thing to say. The powerful engine of the limousine started almost silently, and the long car pulled into the darkness. It seemed only minutes before it stopped again on a brightly lit section of tarmac. They had not left the airport, and Terra could see a small private plane ahead of them. She turned to Grant, a question in her eyes.

"Remember that bachelor hideaway you've heard so much about?" There was a teasing laughter in his voice. "Well, tonight you're going to see it for yourself."

"I can't!" she cried. "I can't go there!"

"Terra, you need a break and I'm going to make sure you get it. Where else do you have to go?"

There was no answer to that question and she knew it. She didn't bother to wonder how Grant's plane was going to take off at night amid the traffic of larger planes. He had made some sort of arrangement. He always did. There was absolutely no way she could escape the ridiculous situation in which she found herself. To run would be useless—and dangerous. Wordlessly she gave him her hand, and he led her out of the car and into the cockpit of the small plane. Glancing out the window, she could see the limousine disappearing out of the lit area. She turned toward Grant, who introduced her to the man at the controls.

"This is Luke Savage," Grant said, and the handsome, rugged-looking young pilot extended his hand. Terra shook it and murmured a polite greeting. "Luke's an ace. Trained as a bush pilot up in the Canadian north. He can fly under any conditions. But you don't have to worry. This flight's going to be a piece of cake. The weather is clear, and we won't be up for all that long."

Luke smiled and nodded in agreement, then focused his attention on his instruments.

Grant made sure Terra's seat belt was fastened. Then he knelt beside her seat and took both her hands in his. "I know what I'm doing, Terra," he said, his low voice melodious to her ear. "We'll just relax for a few days. You have nothing to worry about. I'm going to sit up front and talk business with Luke. I suggest you just lean back and doze if you feel like it. We shouldn't be up longer than a couple of hours."

He moved toward the seat beside the pilot but hesitated and turned back. For a moment he looked at her without speaking. Then his tanned fingers cupped her chin, and he lifted her face slightly so he could stare directly into her eyes. "I won't. . .you don't have to worry about my intentions," he said. "If you like you can consider this a business trip. There *is* unfinished business between us, but I don't need to abduct you to conclude it. Do you know what I mean?"

She nodded without speaking and pulled her face from his hand. Turning back toward the window, she could feel him beside her for a moment longer. But he said nothing, and neither did she.

She did not know how long the flight was. She didn't know where they were going—or why. She didn't know why Grant had to point out to her in any way he could think of that he didn't want her. She tried to sort things out in her mind, but it did no good. The more she tried to understand Grant, the more confused she became. He wanted her out of San Francisco so badly he was escorting her himself. And yet he didn't want her. He had made that abundantly clear. She was a fool to acquiesce to him, a fool to be taking this trip into what could only prove to be unknown territory in every sense of the word. She was a fool to....

When she felt his hand on her arm she awoke with a start, not able to figure out where she was.

"We're landing at the camp now," Grant said. "Up and at 'em."

Terra shook herself fully awake. It was pitch-black outside the windows of the plane, and a jolt of fear shot through her. She caught a glimpse of Luke Savage's face in the light of the instrument panel. There was a calm relaxed look about him, as though he were just about to pull his car into some suburban driveway rather than land a plane. Terra let out a sigh. If she was in danger it wasn't from any mistake on the part of the pilot. It was obvious he knew what he was doing.

A few moments later she could see flares and lights on the ground, and moments after that the small plane glided smoothly to earth. Two tall men, both wearing checked flannel shirts, ran up to meet Grant and Luke as they stepped from the plane. Grant turned to help Terra climb down.

"The car's ready, boss," one of the men said to Grant, who nodded and took Terra by the elbow.

"Thanks, Luke," Grant said to the pilot. "I'll be up at the schoolhouse for a few days. Drive up if you need me."

The car was a Jeep, but Grant handled it with

the same smooth efficiency with which he handled his Mercedes, though Terra could tell the road they were driving on was no public highway. Against a sky bright with more stars than she could ever remember seeing, the tall silhouettes of trees were outlined.

"Oregon," Grant said, finally answering her unspoken question. "Thirty-third state of the Union. Timber country."

Again Terra's eyes turned to the black shapes of the trees against the lighter sky.

"This was my grandfather's country, and he inherited his love for it, as well as his land, from his own father. Now the Ingraham Corporation deals mostly in communication technology, microchips, computers. In my own father's day it was books, paper. But in the days of my great-grandfather our operations were more basic—trees. It's not really a natural step from trees to microchips, but you can see the connection."

"This land belonged to your family?" Terra asked.

"Still does," Grant replied—which meant, she knew, that it now belonged to him.

"I'm aware it doesn't fit the usual stereotype of a lustful bachelor's retreat," he continued with a note of mockery in his tone, "but mine is a sort of working retreat." His laughter filled the car and lifted Terra's spirits in spite of herself. "What we have here is a full-scale lumbering operation. The airstrip is about a mile from the lumber camp. Ten miles beyond that, in the direction in which we're headed now, is an old schoolhouse that used to serve the lumbering community in my great-grandfather's day. I've had it redone for my own use—new kitchen and washroom—but I've kept as much of the flavor of the old building as I could. It was built in the 1880s. The exterior is brick—and still as good as new. You won't be able to see much in the dark, but tomorrow you'll be able to have a good look.''

"What will we do up here?" Terra asked, not really wanting to guess the answer.

"I think we'll teach the city girl a little bit about the country," Grant said, and she could feel the wicked smile in his voice without even having to see his face.

Before long they turned the only corner they had come to in the long road, and ahead Terra could make out a light burning. As they neared she caught the outline of a medium-sized rectangular building with a cupola that housed a bell.

"Here we are," said Grant, pulling off the road and entering through a metal gate. He stopped the Jeep at the side of the building, but before he had come around to help Terra out she was standing beside the car. All around her the vivid sounds of a country night joined as though in a symphony. Crickets chirped; leaves rustled in the gentle breeze. It was magical, and for a moment Terra forgot she had been forced to go there.

The light she had seen shone beside the wide wooden door Grant now unlocked. He ushered her into a vestibule, then flicked a switch. Instantly soft light filled the interior of the building, which was one huge room, the beauty of which was totally unexpected. It still looked like the school it had once been, for at the far end a chalkboard covered the expanse of the wall. However, it was filled not with desks but with an array of antique furniture whose oiled wood gleamed faintly in the light.

A long table of smooth pine with matching pine chairs glowed in one corner, its surface partially covered by a cotton tablecloth embroidered in large red poppies. There was a comfortable-looking couch over which was flung a crocheted afghan in bright country colors. There were stuffed chairs; end tables; a beautiful oak bookcase that was so large it served as a breakfront, dividing off one section of the room. Moving a little, Terra caught a glimpse of what was behind the bookcase: a bed with a tall brass head that sparkled above a hand-sewn quilt in a pattern Terra knew was called Log Cabin. In the center of the room stood a black cast-iron heating stove, and beside it a neat pile of split logs waited in readiness for the hand that would spark them into fire.

She didn't try to keep the delight out of her voice as she swung around to Grant, who stood behind her. "It's beautiful! Oh, Grant, it's so beautiful!" She surprised a look in his eyes that

startled her. His expression, soft in the low
light, was full of love—full of a tenderness so
evident Terra caught her breath. She cleared her
throat and took a small step back. No doubt the
look, though it had seemed to be directed at her,
had really been meant for that beautiful room.

Grant, too, cleared his throat. "Lest you
worry about conveniences," he said, smiling,
"let me show you this." He directed her to a
door behind him, and when he opened it Terra
saw a completely modern kitchen not unlike the
one in his San Francisco home. There was a
modern bathroom, as well, and he offered Terra
the opportunity to freshen up. When she again
stepped into the main room she saw he had
brought in the suitcases and was starting a fire
in the wood stove.

"I'll make us some coffee," he said, motioning her toward a chair near the fire, which began
to leap up and dispel the slight chill in the air.

For the few moments it took him in the kitch-
en Terra simply sat and stared at her surroundings. This, it was true, was not the sort of place
anyone would consider the love nest of a foot-
loose rake. There was a warm comfort to the old
schoolhouse, as though its walls had absorbed
the laughter of children, the hope of young
people just starting out in life. The thought
made Terra both happy and sad at the same
time: happy for those who had eventually found
love, had had children of their own; sad for
herself.

She scanned the arrangement of furniture, which was like that of a whole house without walls. When her eyes fell on the bed she shivered.

She didn't hear Grant come up behind her, but he had not missed the direction of her glance. "You'll find that bed very comfortable," he said. "For me, that couch over there will do just fine."

Much to her surprise the emotion that shot through Terra at his words was not relief. It was regret.

Standing before her, Grant bent down and handed her a mug of coffee. She noted absently that the cup must have been handmade by a potter, so unusual was its design. She circled her hands around the warmth it offered and raised her eyes to meet Grant's.

"Grant," she began, her voice low and almost pleading, "you've got to tell me what we're doing here. Does it have to do with Paul?"

"No." He said it so brusquely Terra was frightened for a moment. But she did not take her eyes from his face, and after a few seconds his expression softened. He lowered himself so that his face was directly opposite hers. "Terra," he whispered, "whatever we do has to do with us, not with anyone else."

Unable to withstand the new intensity in his gaze she turned her head, but one lean finger reached up and slowly pivoted her face until her eyes stared into the dark depths of his own.

Before she could read what those eyes said his lips took hers. The hot eagerness of the unexpected kiss, the warm mouth that seemed intent on devouring her own, did not unnerve her. As though her lips had longed for, had prepared for his, she responded with a hunger that was beyond thought. Her arms flew up to hold him in as tight an embrace as her slim arms could make. And his arms, so much stronger yet gentle in their power, surrounded her, engulfed her, took away the breath she had almost forgotten to draw.

"Grant," she breathed, "oh, Grant! What are you doing to me?"

"No more than what you're doing to me," he replied, his voice broken and throaty. "Oh, my Terra, if only I could tell you. . . ."

"Tell me what?" she asked. And though her own voice was as impassioned as his, the question fell into the silence like a meteorite crashing on the desert sand.

He drew back, holding her at arm's length. Emotion struggled with reason, and the contest was evident in the expression on his face. "Terra," he uttered softly, "I didn't bring you here to—to compromise the ideals of the chairman of the Love Is Glue committee. I. . . ."

Briefly passion again lit his face. But it was quickly damped, and mockery filled his eyes. "I think it's time for you to hit the sack—solo. This is the country, and people bed down early. Time you learned that city ways aren't the only ones. Anyway, it's past midnight. Not so very early after all.''

She stared up at him in bewilderment. What was he trying to do? She was beyond questioning him, except on technicalities. "Do I use the bathroom first?" was the only inquiry she could manage.

DESPITE THE LENGTH OF TIME it had taken her to fall asleep; despite the fact it had seemed hours that she had lain beneath the Log Cabin quilt, unable even to keep her eyes closed, so strong was the presence of Grant lying with her but apart in the darkness of the schoolhouse; despite the fact it was very late when she finally did drift off into troubled dreams—despite all that, she awoke as refreshed as if she had been sleeping for a week.

A sparkling clarity infused the air. She breathed deeply and felt the clean country morning fill her whole body. Moving quietly, she dressed behind the breakfront, then gingerly stepped out to see whether Grant was awake. It was silly, but it was true; her heart beat faster just in anticipation of the sight of him.

It was the sound of him, though, that captured her attention. He was singing—a soft but full and lusty voice came to her from the kitchen. It seemed totally impossible that the president and chairman of the board of the Ingraham Corporation could be singing in the kitchen, but that was the case, and the knowledge of it filled Terra's heart with new tenderness.

"Up and at 'em," he called out, and she made her way toward the sound of his voice. He was dressed as she had never seen him dressed before, but the new look did him credit. A red-and-black flannel lumberjack's shirt set off the black of his hair, which was not carefully styled now but fell casually across his broad forehead. Dark dungarees encased his masculine thighs, and despite herself Terra stared at his well-shaped derriere.

"Come on, come on," he said, laughing. "Time for breakfast. We've got a lot of countrifying to do today, no time to waste."

"What time *is* it?" Terra asked. Her watch had stopped, and she couldn't tell by the sun, which streamed through the eight tall windows of the schoolhouse, filling it with light.

"It's 7:00 A.M.," he responded cheerfully. "No farmer—or lumberman, either—who had even an ounce of self-respect would be in bed at this time of the morning. Unless, of course, he was on his honeymoon."

He winked wickedly at her, and to her dismay she blushed. Pulling back one of the polished maple kitchen chairs, she sat down to the breakfast Grant had cooked. She was amazed at the spread of dishes on the table: crisp strips of bacon, eggs, pancakes, fruit cut up and doused with cream, little bowls of honey and jelly and a mound of pearly yellow butter that was not squared off as though it had been made in a machine.

"Cream and butter from a dairy farm down

the way,'' Grant said, pointing, ''honey from a
neighboring farm, jelly made by the farmer's
wife. Come on, now. Eat up. You need lots of
fuel out here.''

Even his speech seemed to have changed with
the environment. He was so relaxed, so smiling-
ly cheerful, that she rapidly began to forget she
was isolated with him in the middle of nowhere
for a reason she couldn't begin to understand.

They ate rather quickly and in silence, for
Grant seemed eager to get going, to show her
the country. He was acting as though the whole
state were a personal possession he was dying
for her to have a look at, eager for her to ap-
preciate. And since his happiness was infec-
tious, she was willing to look—to love whatever
it was he loved.

When they had cleared away and washed the
breakfast things and Terra had had a chance to
perform a quick morning ritual that did not include the application of makeup, Grant led her
toward the bed in which she had slept. When she
saw where they were headed she stopped in her
tracks, but laughingly he propelled her forward.
''Don't be afraid, little Terra,'' he said. ''I'm
merely about to show you the fire escape. Take
off your shoes.''

''What?''

''Your shoes. Off with 'em. You can't climb
out of this fire escape with shoes on unless you
want to ruin Mrs. Fine's Log Cabin quilt.'' He
bent down and removed his own shoes. Before

Terra could figure out what he was up to he was standing on the bed near the window, lifting the sash. "Get on up here."

Though it seemed crazy, she followed, and was soon standing beside him. "This is the fire escape," he said, and he took her hand and helped her out the raised window. Just outside the window ledge was a small platform from which steps descended to the ground. They stopped for a moment to slip their shoes back on.

"These old schools weren't built to be slept in," Grant explained, helping her down the steps. "They didn't feel it necessary to have a second exit, but when I redid this building I didn't want to take any chances. To cut a back door into the place was a possibility, but I thought it would wreck the exterior, so...."

Without waiting for comment, he grabbed Terra's hand and led her to a hedge that marked off the schoolyard at the rear. Cutting through, she had to keep her head low, and when they reached the other side and she raised her eyes, she thought she must be seeing things. Before her stretched a narrow street lined with buildings that formed a perfectly preserved small-town Main Street—the main street of a century ago.

There was a general store with a wide veranda and wooden awning, a blacksmith's shop and forgery, the inevitable saloon, a dry-goods store with a dressmaker's shop beside it and, set off at the end of the street, a white clapboard church that gleamed in the morning sun. Everything looked as though it had just been built, and Terra felt she must have stepped back a hundred years.

"Oh, Grant! What is this? Where are we?"

He smiled with delight at the childlike wonder in her fresh face.

"This is Millersville," he said simply, as if that would answer her question.

"But what . . . how . . . ?"

"When my great-grandfather was in charge the lumber camp was near here. As the trees were felled, it moved to follow the forest. Eventually the town that had sprung up to serve the camp became a ghost town. For years I've been restoring it. I've had work done mostly on the exteriors, so it's not nearly as perfect as it appears. There's still a lot to be done, but when it's finished the streetscape will be a complete replica of what it once was, though the interiors will be modern."

"Do you mean it will be a tourist attraction?" Terra asked, appalled at the idea Grant would want to bring tourists to an area as unspoiled as this one was.

"Oh, no, of course not," he answered. "This is a pet project of mine. It's going to be used as a retreat for writers and artists who need to get away from the city for a while. When the buildings are finished the interiors will be studios and offices—not business offices, though. I want it to be a haven for writers. That's why it's called Millersville.''

"Oh? I don't understand.''

"George Miller was a local poet in these parts. A damn good one, too.''

"But I've never heard of him.''

"He traveled all over North America, reading poems in his booming voice. But he didn't believe in publishing his work, so his fame was strictly confined to those who heard him in person. His work has been preserved, though. I have a collection of manuscripts that I'll let you see. . . .''

He took her hand in his once again, and together they walked down the narrow street, exploring the buildings, laughing and talking as if no misunderstanding had ever come between them, as if no danger had ever threatened their safety—or their hearts.

After wandering through the town and the surrounding countryside they went back to the schoolhouse, where Terra prepared a fine lunch that had Grant conceding the "burnt-brownie girl'' had indeed turned into an excellent cook.

"What are we going to do now?'' Terra asked when lunch was over. Grant was rummaging in a closet, kneeling and tossing various items over his shoulder onto the floor behind him. She had lost all the self-consciousness she had previously felt in his presence. It was as though she were a child again, happy in the adventure of having Grant with her and so intent on the pleasure of being with him she had forgotten that good times end, that her playful good times with him had ended years ago.

"Fishin'," he said in the clipped country accents that revealed his state of relaxation. "We're going fishing."

"I CAN'T. I just can't do it!" Terra whined. For the second time Grant was attempting to untangle her fishing line, which had got caught in a bush behind her when she tried to cast. He pulled his knife from his pocket, cut off the knotted line, reattached and baited the hook.

"If that line gets any shorter," she commented, "I'll only be able to catch any fish that happen to swim between my feet."

She looked down at the tall rubber wading boots that were much too large for her. She had stood in one place for some time, unwilling to lift the heavy boots in order to take a step. The clear water of the river eddied about her in its shallows. Beyond the far shore the tall lean pines reached down to the water's edge, and three times they had seen deer come down to the little lapping waves to drink.

"No," Grant said, his deep voice ringing in the country silence, "you'll be all right. Look, let me show you one more time."

He lifted the rod, and with a motion as smooth as that of a dancer he swung his muscled arm. The line sang as it spun out from the reel, and in the middle of the small river the hook with its sinker made a precise, gentle, clearly audible plop.

"Here," he said, handing her the rod, "keep at it. You'll catch something." In the large pail beside him the three fish he had caught waited to be turned into supper. "One more should do it. We don't want to catch more than we can eat."

She didn't catch any fish. The tall grasses of the fields they walked through in order to get back from the river scared her as they whipped against her face. She thought she had heard that tall grass hid ticks that could burrow into one's skin and make an unwelcome home there. Grant laughed in genuine amusement at her fears. He said that in all his years of coming to the camp he had never had a tick. They walked along, and suddenly Terra heard a sound that sent her flying into his arms in fright.

"What's that?"

"What?"

"That sound."

"What sound?" Grant asked, straightening the tanned column of his neck as though to extend the range of his hearing. "I can't hear a thing."

"It's a sort of—oh! What's that?" She moved closer into the circle of his arms, but she could feel his chest shaking with laughter.

"Oh, Terra, dear little Terra. That's a cow! That's the sound they make when they eat their way through a field of grass! Don't tell me you've never seen a cow!"

"Only from the window of a car," she answered, piqued that she was out of her element, embarrassed to have acted so ignorantly.

But Grant seemed to find her ignorance charming. He kissed her on the tip of her nose, and with his strong arm around her slender shoulders they walked on. Through the fields they went, over a narrow bridge that spanned a gurgling stream, past places where the light through the leaves made a pattern that danced with sun and shadow on the moist forest floor. Birds sang strange and wonderful songs in the trees, and here and there a small animal skittered out of their path.

A peace filled Terra, a peace she had never felt previously. She had thought that Grant's world was the glittering social whirl of New York, the high-powered boardrooms, the sleek apartments where a night's love was as transient as the tenants who moved in, set up, moved out.

But this was a different world and a different Grant. Here in the country he was not commanding, not imperious, not unemotional or disappointing at all. If she had thought he had been warm and appealing the night they had visited Maurice, she now thought he was simply the most wonderful man she had ever known.

No matter what he did he never lacked surety. His every movement here in the forest was as certain, as without doubt, as his movements had been in their business encounters. But in business he was formal, reserved, seemingly without feeling. Here he was casual, natural. He laughed with delight, and more than once she had again caught him in song. It was as though he had truly opened himself to her and was holding back nothing.

It should have filled her with sorrow to realize that when this idyll in the country was over, when they were back in the real world of San Francisco, this Grant would disappear. And indeed, every once in a while sadness threatened. But for the most part she lost herself in the magic of his presence. She forgot everything in her attempt to keep up with the lilting step of the tall man beside her. She felt she would be content to walk forever with the man whose large hand had not let her own drop from its grasp all afternoon.

The day passed with a slow and delicious idleness. They did not see one other person, did not hear any other human voices but their own, laughing and talking in concert with the rustle of leaves and the low drone of summer insects. When it came time for dinner Grant cooked the fish, but it was Terra who picked and prepared fresh vegetables from the small garden at the side of the schoolhouse.

"How can you keep such a lovely garden when you're only here once in a while?" she asked.

"Luke comes by once a week," Grant replied, then paused. "I've been here quite often this year. I'm winding things down in New York. I—"

But he was interrupted by two short rings on the phone. It didn't sound like the phones in the city, and Grant didn't respond, though he had tensed expectantly at the sound.

"Aren't you going to answer?" Terra asked.

"It's not my ring. Out here we have a party line and everyone has his own combination of long and short rings. Mine is three long rings." The conversation turned to other matters, and Terra forgot what Grant had said about his New York office.

With crickets crooning to the accompaniment of the swish of night breeze coming in through the open door they sat by the light of low lamps, Grant working on some business papers and Terra trying to read. But her eyes kept straying from the page, now stealing a quick look at the man across from her, now staring into space.

Grant caught her errant glance. "Are you thinking about Paul again?" he asked, a note almost of warning in his tone.

"I'm thinking about my presently nonexistent career," she replied sadly.

Touched by her sorrowful expression, Grant put aside his papers and moved to sit on the couch beside her. He put his arm around her shoulder, and his hand rested lightly at the top of her arm, sending little shivery darts down its length.

"Terra," he said quietly, "it's all going to work out for the best. When this whole thing blows over you can start looking for another job. But I have a feeling you won't have to look long. You're a professional—and a valuable one at that."

She wasn't listening. She had been in the sun all day. Perhaps that accounted for the heat that seemed to have seeped under her skin, for beneath Grant's fingers her flesh flamed. She could feel the rough flannel of his shirt against her bare shoulders, the brief tube top she wore providing little protection against the sensations that coursed through her merely at the touch of his arm across her back.

All day he had touched her, taking her slim fingers in his own, placing his strong hand at the small of her back to guide her along, once even lifting her by the waist when she had tried to step down from a steep incline. Those touches had seemed to mean nothing, but now it was as though her body had been storing them like money in the bank. And the sum was infinitely more than Terra had realized, for a hot wave of desire engulfed her and shivers shook her slender frame.

In response Grant tightened his hold. "What is it?" he asked, but when she turned her open lips toward his he needed no further answer.

Gently, almost without contact, he took her mouth with his wide sensuous lips, but in her hunger Terra pressed closer, until his kiss was a devouring pressure, a demand for a response she was eager to give. His lips seared her, burning now at the corners of her mouth, now at her

cheeks, her chin, her eyelids and back again to
her own open lips. She felt the thrust of his
tongue and answered with hers.

His hands seemed large enough to cover her
whole body, and she could feel one hand clasp-
ing her head, her hair twined in its hold, while
the other brushed feathery flaming touches back
and forth across the top of her breasts. Instinctively she arched toward him, as though starving
for even the slightest pressure of his fingertips
on her breast. But his teasing touch eluded her,
and the more she strained toward it, the more
elusive it became, until she feared he would
tease her forever, forever denying the full pressure of his hand on the sensitive places it now
merely grazed.

"Touch me, Grant," she moaned, unable to
stop herself. "Please touch me!" And in response one swift movement of his hand pulled
down the tube top and took full possession of
her exposed breasts, holding both of them in its
grasp.

Her breath caught in her throat, but she was
unable to utter even a sigh. The hand that had
held her head now played at the soft recesses between her ear and her shoulder, then traced a
fiery trail down to join his other hand, until her
curves completely filled his hold. Her nipples
were tender against the hardness of his palms,
and without realizing it, she shifted ever so
slightly back and forth so that she would feel his
calloused skin against the sensitized points. The

sensation was so electrifying she could stand only a few moments of it before she reached up, threw her arms around Grant's neck and pressed her naked breasts against his chest to stop the throbbing pleasure that threatened to break her in two.

But it did no good, for now it was the coarse flannel of his shirt that met her tender skin, enflaming it even further. And worse, as she lifted herself up against him his hands cupped her buttocks. Through the soft faded denim of her jeans she felt the strong fingers mold her, knead her flesh, send sparks forward and upward into her, igniting her entire body.

She clung to him, but her arms seemed to have lost their power, and when Grant lowered her so that she lay along the couch she uttered no protest. Instead she found his lips with her own, and did not relinquish them as he lay atop her, the heavy weight of him painlessly pressing against her breasts, her abdomen, her hungry thighs. For a moment they simply rested in each other's arms, lost in a world of passion that knew no time but the present, no motion but that of their eager lips, no sound but the rapid beating of two hearts that pounded out the primal rhythm of their mutual longing.

And then he undressed her. With maddening slowness his fingers pulled away each garment until she lay before him, slim, lovely, waiting.

But though he gazed at her, he did not touch her, and she watched in desirous anticipation as he stood and began to remove his flannel shirt. His shoulders rippled with muscle, his broad chest gleamed in the soft light of the lamps. When he slid out of his jeans and whatever he had worn beneath them, he was standing slightly at an angle, so that Terra could see the dark hollow where the slim strong flanks of his hips met the rounded power of his masculine buttocks. And when he turned toward her, her eyes opened wide to capture the full virility of him.

He was as beautiful as a sculpture, as solid and perfect as stone. But he was flesh, and her own flesh yearned for contact with his. He stood before her, silent and still, and there again flashed into her mind the dark silhouette of him she had seen etched against the light of the office window. He was not a dark silhouette now; he was alive with light; he was coming toward her, the passion in his eyes an irresistible invitation, an enticement she did not want to resist.

He sat beside her on the couch, his thigh touching her own as she reclined. The place where his skin met hers burned, and she tried hard to fight back the urge to touch him, to rush the moment. With her hands curled into small tight fists she lay immobile, waiting for him to do what he so clearly intended to do.

He lifted his tanned hand and drew a long sensuous line from the base of her throat, between her upthrust breasts, down over her gently rounded abdomen and beyond, until his hand rested on the soft smooth flesh of her inner thigh.

The pressure of his fingers increased, and Terra could no longer bear the shooting fire that radiated from his hand. With a groan she pulled herself up and threw her hungry body into his arms.

He kissed her then as though they might kiss forever yet never put out the raging fire that consumed them both. Without releasing her lips or the quivering form that clung to him, he lowered her until his body touched, covered every inch of her own. "Terra," he breathed. "Oh, my Terra, my love."

"Grant—" She tried to reply, but his lips had captured hers again and she was powerless to respond, to tell him how her love for him had grown to fill every corner of her heart. But it was not a time for speaking. His arms held her; his muscled length pinned her beneath him. Yet the burden of his body on hers was a sweetness that nothing could make her relinquish.

"There are consequences," he whispered, his breath a warm moistness on her flushed cheek. "There are consequences to making love...."

"What?" she asked. "Do you mean precautions—because if you do, it's not necessary. I mean...I take care of that."

"Oh?" he said a little teasingly. "So you do this often?"

She could tell by the sound of his voice that that was not what he believed.

"No," she answered very quietly, "not often, not ever. But I'm a woman now—I knew the time would come...."

Wordlessly he stroked the soft curves of her cheek. "How could I ever have accused you of teasing me?" he asked, as though speaking to himself.

"Teasing you?" she repeated, not understanding.

"That day I took you to the airport. I thought you were teasing. I thought you were trying to prove how sophisticated you'd become. But now I see such innocence. Terra, sweet Terra, there are consequences. This can change everything. This is important...."

"I know."

"Do you? Do you really, sweetheart?" His voice seemed to catch in his throat, as though he were trying hard to hold back the passion that glazed his eyes, that communicated itself to her.

For a moment she closed her own eyes in response to the wave of feeling that washed over her. Every time he made the slightest move her body tingled with new excitement. His skin against her own was fire.

"I want you," he breathed. "I want you so much. But I don't want to take you. I want you to give—I want to give to you...."

"Grant," she sighed, and her soft utterance of his name was a pledge and a plea. She accepted the responsibility of loving him, of letting him make love to her. It was a gift she had never given before: the gift of herself. Love made her unafraid. "Please," she whispered, "Grant, please...."

At the sound of his name on her asking lips desire claimed him utterly. Even the gentleness with which he treated her did not seem to diminish the racking pleasure that shook his strong frame—a pleasure into which he led her, coaxing, coaching, until lost in each other they became one desire and one fulfillment of desire.

After, she lay in his arms in perfect silence. Words were so unnecessary she thought she might never have to speak again. Tenderly he dropped random kisses on the top of her head where it lay nestled in the crook of his arm. It was so quiet. Even the crickets seemed to have stopped. She could hear Grant's breathing and his heartbeat, and it was all she needed to hear. No other sound would have been welcome—especially the sound of three long rings. . . .

At the summons of the phone the pliant mellow softness of his body beside hers disappeared. He stiffened.

"No," she whispered, "don't. Let it be. . . ."

But her words did no good. He was up in a flash, and the instant she lost the contact of his skin she felt a wave of cold air brush over her, extinguishing the last embers of passion, blowing away the precious togetherness.

He grabbed his jeans and put them on as he held the phone between his shoulder and his ear. There was nothing for Terra to do but put on her own clothes. She could hear snatches of Grant's conversation, though he was keeping his voice very low. Twice he mentioned Stephanie, though he did not seem to be speaking to her. But there was an urgency to his tone that made Terra realize the matter he was discussing was of the utmost importance.

Trying to fight down her disappointment, she sat fully clothed while he finished the call. She knew from the way in which he was speaking that this was not an interruption of their love-making—it was an end to it.

He replaced the receiver and came to her. His face bore a distracted look, as though there were things on his mind more important than the pleasure he had just shared with her.

"I've got to drive over to see Luke," he said, not really looking at Terra but beginning to gather the papers he had been working on and shoving them into his briefcase. His voice was the dead businesslike voice he had used so often in her presence.

But then it softened for the briefest of moments as his hand reached out and gently stroked her upturned face. "I'm sorry," he began. "I didn't...I wish...." He didn't finish. He shook his head as though to settle his thoughts, then cleared his throat.

"I'll be back later tonight. I don't want you to worry. There's wine in the fridge and the TV works, though there's only one channel. I've got to run."

And he was gone.

It was well past midnight when she finally went to bed, and though she dozed now and then, she was fully aware of the passage of time, fully aware it was after three when Grant returned. She would have gone to him then, but she didn't. He had turned off so completely, so quickly, that she feared he would reject her. And she knew it had all been a mistake anyway—a mistake to be so willing to give herself, when, with just a single phone call, Grant could forget the fire that had blazed between them.

Somehow, though, just knowing he had returned, knowing that he slept not far from her, eased her mind, and she fell into a deep sleep.

WHEN SHE AWOKE the full light of morning was streaming in through the eight windows of the schoolhouse, and Terra sensed it was rather late. She rose quickly and dressed, then ran toward the couch Grant had slept on. There was no sign that he had rested there except for a neatly folded blanket laid across the back of the couch.

Thinking he might be fixing breakfast, she headed for the kitchen. The moment she opened the door she saw it, and she knew what it meant. Propped against the salt and pepper shakers on the red-checked cloth of the kitchen table was a folded piece of paper that stared up at her starkly white and forbidding. She held it in her trembling fingers for a minute before she opened it to read Grant's message: "Stay put. I'll be back for you in a few days. The fridge is stocked."

She pulled out one of the kitchen chairs and

sank into it. Whatever Grant's game, she was still his pawn. This lovely time, this idyll in the country, was just one more attempt to manipulate her, to get her out of the way and keep her away. She should have known better, but once more she had let her emotions cloud her better judgment.

There was no denying it now; things had become crystal clear to her. There was only one person with whom Grant could be involved that would necessitate keeping Terra at bay up in the country. And that person, she somehow knew, was not Stephanie Duke. That person was Paul Foster. He was intending, intending fully, to defraud his customers, and in order to do so he was counting on the assistance of a well-respected accomplice: Grant Ingraham.

She didn't take the time to reflect on her own crushing disappointment. She didn't bother to consider the danger she might be in. She found a knapsack she had seen in the closet when Grant had been rummaging there, and she packed only a few of her belongings. Then, locking the door behind her, she took off.

It took Terra five hours to walk the eleven miles to the lumber camp, and the first hour was spent traipsing in what she finally had figured out must be the wrong direction. At first her anger, her determination to get back to San Francisco to see Blansford and convince him of the fraud had been the only things that had filled her mind. Her step had been fast and unfettered. But then the images had started to come: Grant singing in the kitchen; Grant asleep under a tree, the summer breeze softly stirring his dark hair; Grant laughing at her fear of cows; Grant naked in the light of the evening lamps, his skin bronze and perfect before her longing eyes....

The tears had made it hard to see the road, and twice she'd fallen. After she had walked for about three hours she'd come upon a farm. It had taken some convincing before the farmer had agreed to drive her to the camp, and then he discovered that the battery of his truck was dead.

In the middle of the afternoon, having eaten nothing since the previous night, hot and dusty and thoroughly distraught, she finally stumbled onto the gravel drive that led directly to Luke Savage's office.

He was sitting at a large pine desk, drinking coffee, smoking a pipe, reading the Sunday paper as though he were in some cozy living room instead of amid the towering trees of the wilderness.

"You've got to fly me out," was all she said in greeting.

"No way," Luke answered succinctly. "I've got orders and the boss's got the plane."

After an hour of pleading, three cups of strong coffee and a quick wash and change, she succeeded in persuading him to drive her into Salem.

"This just might cost me my job," he commented as he dropped her off in front of the bus station.

Buying her ticket, she reflected that it was lucky she had taken plenty of money with her when she had gone down to see Aunt Alice. With a start she realized that that had been only days earlier. It seemed like years.

She waited for the bus, the smell of stale cigarette smoke assaulting her nostrils. Other passengers ate sandwiches while they waited, and the crumple of countless cellophane packages set her on edge. The grind of the information officer's voice over the intercom made her feel more depressed each time he announced another arrival or departure.

She waited for the plane in Portland, was fortunate to have got a flight. *I'm so lucky,* she thought with bitterness, *so very lucky indeed*.

It was 2:00 A.M. when she reached her house. She ate ravenously, even though the food was tasteless in her mouth. She showered away the dust of the country, the grime of her travels and the touch of Grant Ingraham's imperious manipulative fingers. She went over her plan for the morning. And then she sobbed herself into a restless, dreamracked sleep.

CHAPTER TWELVE

SHE WAS NERVOUS. She had gone over the whole plan several times and it seemed simple enough. All she had to do was glance at the photocopies of the missing documents. She didn't need to remove them; just knowing what they contained would be enough to allow her to approach Nathaniel Blansford. It didn't even occur to her that she might be grasping at straws, that the documents might contain nothing that had anything to do with the lost edition. She was nervous because she knew she was right.

As she approached the entrance she began to worry she would have to sign a register in order to be admitted to the exhibit. She knew that those scholars who came to work in the library during the exhibit were required to apply for a user's pass, but she hoped that anyone who just wanted to look would be allowed in without formality.

When she rounded the bend Terra could see quite a few cars parked in the courtyard. A uniformed guard was standing on duty, and he motioned her to a parking space. She hadn't really expected so many people would be there so soon after eight o'clock. She hoped the cars belonged to scholars who were using particular sections of the library and not to casual visitors who might be viewing the exhibit in the room in which the photocopies were displayed. The success of her plan lay in having an opportunity to read the copies without being disturbed.

As she walked past the guards standing at either side of the entrance to the mansion, she recognized them from the day of her previous visit. She drew her breath in sharply when she realized that one of the guards had followed her into the marbled hall, and then she relaxed as he veered away from her into an anteroom. Admonishing herself not to be so jumpy, she walked over to a map that showed which rooms were open to the public.

It took a little time, but she managed to locate the nineteenth-century rooms at the far end of the building. The diagram was complex, and looking at it, she couldn't tell precisely which room would contain what she wanted, so she made a mental note of the numbers and locations of all the possibilities and began to stroll down the hall. She forced herself not to go too quickly, not to do anything that might arouse suspicion.

After seeing so many cars in the parking lot, she was surprised at how few people were looking at the exhibits, and she concluded that most of the early-morning visitors were indeed scholars. She breathed a small sigh of relief.

As she walked down the black-and-white checkerboard hallway, she caught glimpses into the rooms of the Blansford mansion. In addition to the furniture and paintings that she had seen before, the rooms were filled with special displays of china, drawings and books.

Ahead of her she noted a central fountain underneath a high glass dome, and she recognized it from the map as the crossroads of the building. If her memory was correct, she should turn right there.

As she approached the fountain, its splashing filled her ears with sound. Above the noise of the water she thought she heard footsteps. Convinced that someone was running toward her and would be rounding the corner momentarily, she stepped back quickly into one of the alcoves that surrounded the fountain.

From behind the decorative marble work that hid her Terra watched anxiously. The sound of footsteps became louder, and Paul burst into view, followed only seconds later by Grant. Both men were running as fast as they could. Terra's hand flew to her mouth in astonishment. She had feared they might be here. It would make matters infinitely more difficult for her knowing they could burst in on her while she was checking the copies, and if they discovered her, her plan was next to useless. She would never be able to prove anything then; they would make sure of that.

But why were they running? Her heart sank.

Seeing the two men together like that could only mean she had been right in assuming Grant and Paul were in this thing together. There was no denying it. Were they running from the guards?

Before she had time to figure out the implications of what she had just seen, more footsteps sounded in her ears and two policemen skidded around the corner, slipping on the slick marble floor. Terra screamed as she caught sight of the guns in their hands, but they did not notice her outcry. Several of the Blansford's guards appeared in the doorways along the hall. They reacted quickly, as though trained for an emergency. Some followed the police, while others remained behind to guard the rooms in their charge.

Horrified, Terra watched Grant and Paul disappear around a corner, and then, shaking off the astonishment that had held her immobile, she ran after them. Rounding the corner, she could see no trace of anyone. Then a gunshot split the air. Cries and the sounds of a scuffle ensued. Terra, headed in the direction of the commotion, burst through two tall doors into an elegantly furnished room.

The first, the only thing she could see was Grant sprawled facedown on the floor. One of the policemen hovered over him, while the other, she soon noted, held Paul, pinning his arms behind his back. She barely noticed as a door on the other side of the room sprang open, admitting Nathaniel Blansford, followed by

Stephanie Duke, Dan Forbush and several more guards.

Oblivious to everyone else, full only of concern for the man she loved, Terra flung herself across the room, pushing aside the officer who was standing over Grant. Tears rushed to her eyes, and tenderness filled her. Kneeling down beside him and whispering caressing phrases, she took his dark head in her soft hands and cradled it. With gentle fingers she stroked his forehead. She could see no sign of a wound, but he seemed dazed and only barely conscious.

Then he drew back from her soothing hands and shook his head as though to clear it. He struggled to sit up, but in low tones she urged him to lie still until help could come. Shaking his head again, this time indicating his unwillingness to do as she asked, he put one hand behind him and hoisted himnself to his feet. He seemed to sway for a moment, and rubbed his shoulder gingerly.

Between the lean fingers, Terra saw a little trickle of blood. She lunged for him, but the policeman, not to be put off this time, restrained her. One of the guards rushed toward Grant, but he pushed the man aside. The room grew quiet as, with barely faltering steps, Grant approached Paul.

"It's all over," he said quietly. "I'm sorry, Paul."

Paul's head was lowered. "I never intended

to have to fire at you...." His expression was more agonized than Terra had ever seen.

"Hand over the photocopies, Paul."

Paul reached under his sweater and removed a few sheets of paper that had been tucked beneath his belt. "How long have you known?" he asked in the tones of a defeated man.

"I've suspected since you were in England. And I know this isn't the first time. So do Blansford and Forbush. You were always clever, but this time you overstepped yourself."

"This exhibit was a trap, wasn't it?"

"No," Grant answered, "not exactly. But we did have a tip-off. Naturally we had to wait until we could catch you in the act...."

"Damn you!" Paul shouted suddenly. Yet it was not at Grant that he directed his anger. It was at Stephanie.

"Whatever do you mean?" she asked coolly, but from where she stood Terra could see the woman was shaking.

"You tipped him off, didn't you? You just couldn't resist the charms of good old Grant."

Grant began to shake his head in a silent no at this exchange, but Paul had not finished.

"What's he going to think when he finds out you're as much a part of this as I am?"

All eyes turned toward Stephanie, waiting for her to confirm or deny Paul's accusation. Stephanie's eyes darted from Paul's to Grant's to those of her grandfather, who watched in quiet sadness. "Granddaddy," she began, her voice losing its sophisticated evenness. "Granddaddy, I'm sorry!"

She seemed to crumple as she moved slowly toward Nathaniel Blansford. The old man opened his arms, and Stephanie hesitantly stepped into his embrace. "I didn't think it would matter if I helped Paul. I didn't really do anything except take a few papers, and I'll give them back. Paul believed in me. He's the only one who ever has.... I thought—I thought that to help him was only a small favor, a small thing...." She began to sob, and Nathaniel Blansford enfolded her in his arms.

Paul stared at the display with disgust, but Grant seemed more sympathetic. "Tell us why you took those documents, Stephanie," he said quietly.

"Why bother asking?" Paul spat out, his lip curled in defiance. "You've got it all figured out, haven't you?" he hurled at Grant. "All right," he nearly shouted, "all right. The pamphlets are facsimiles. Waltham printed them in 1905. They were identical in every way to the first edition, except they had an extra wraparound title page describing them as copies. I found them in Miss Waltham's library, and although she wouldn't sell them to me, she promised I could have them when she died."

Dan Forbush was listening to this with an expression on his face that revealed no surprise. Terra sensed he had known about this for some

time. "What did you do with the title pages?"
he asked.

"What difference does it make?" Paul answered contemptuously. "It was a perfect
plan—and it would have worked except for little
Miss Goody Two-shoes." His angry eyes sought
Terra, and she cringed at the ugliness there. "If
it hadn't been for you," he threw at her, "I
would have been able to do it. But you wouldn't
let go, would you? No wonder dad liked you so
much. You're just like him. Honest as the day is
long—and just as stupid. You wouldn't stop until you knew everything, would you? You just
wouldn't lay off."

"Oh, Paul." Terra sighed. She was so embarrassed for him, so ashamed. It was hard for her
to take in the fact that he was a criminal, that he
had brought this sorrow and shame upon himself.

"Don't blame her," Grant cut in. "A lot of
other people had real doubts about those pamphlets. Dan Forbush came to me to ask me to
look into them on behalf of the Bookman's
Club, but I've known for longer than that,
Paul. All I needed was proof. True, I wouldn't
have known where to find it without Terra's discovery, but it was only a matter of time...."

Terra stared at Grant, and she felt a great
weight lift from her. She had been right—and he
had known it all along. It would take her some
time to fit all these pieces together, but now it
was certain that Grant was innocent of any com-

plicity in the fraud. And more than that, she now knew he respected her as a professional. That thought would be cold comfort when this matter was concluded, for obviously Grant had been quite honest when he had said that their trip up north was a business trip. Yet even if her heart would never quite recover from her encounter with Grant, at least she knew he had no doubts about her competence. Perhaps that knowledge would enable her to search for a new job with confidence. She didn't know where she'd find the confidence, though, to search for a new love.

"I couldn't understand why all the tests came out positive," Grant continued. "And then Terra discovered that Robert Waltham had hit on the idea of printing facsimiles of famous earlier editions that his father had printed. I understood immediately what you must have done, Paul."

"Why did you try to dissuade me?" Terra asked Grant. "Why did you say that I didn't have enough proof?"

"I didn't dare let you realize what you'd stumbled on," Grant explained. Then a wry smile lit his eyes. "I didn't really know how determined you can be. I thought you'd be easy to persuade. When I saw you were not going to be put off, I realized you'd have to be sent off. I just didn't want you involved in a shoot-out, and I knew from the start there might be one."

At that moment two white-uniformed men

came into the room, followed by one of the guards. "The ambulance is here, sir," the man said to Nathaniel Blansford. Reluctantly Grant allowed himself to be led away, insisting his wound was too minor to warrant such attention.

"Let me go with you," Terra pleaded, unable to hide the tears that again sprang to her eyes.

"We'll talk later," he said softly, as though it were a promise. She watched as he walked away between the two men. It was strange; he was bigger and much more vital-looking than the men who were escorting him to the hospital.

The policemen took Paul away without protest; they did not even approach Stephanie, who sobbed quietly as her grandfather led her from the room.

Dan Forbush stepped over to Terra, and in a low voice he thanked her for her part in unmasking the truth about the edition.

"When you're ready to go back to work, come and see me," he suggested. "The rare-book business needs researchers like you. I'm sure we'll be able to find an excellent position for you."

Right then Terra felt too disorganized to take Forbush up on his offer or even to consider it seriously, but she was grateful for his kindness. She thanked him and promised to give him a call. He patted her shoulder fondly and then walked to the door. The few remaining guards spoke softly to one another as they left to return to their posts, and Terra found herself alone in the large room.

A hushed quiet had descended on the mansion once more, and she wondered briefly whether all this could have been a dream. She didn't want to believe Paul had deliberately tried to swindle the rare-book world, and yet she realized it was true. If only he had been content with selling the pamphlets as facsimiles, she thought sadly.

But that, apparently, was not Paul's way. She remembered that Grant had said that this was not the first time, and she considered what that might mean. She wondered whether his father had suspected his son was less than honest. He must have worried about what would happen when he was no longer able to keep his eyes on Paul. Now that worry had proved agonizingly justified. What would happen to the business—and to Paul?

Terra's heart was heavy with regret. But it was not only regret for Paul. It was regret for herself. Grant had not even had time to take note of the fact she had escaped from his hideaway. He hadn't even seemed surprised to see her there, hundreds of miles from the place in which he had left her. He had promised they would talk. But what was there left to say? The case was closed. All that remained was to say goodbye.

The picture of him lying sprawled on the floor returned to her with such force that she felt dizzy. For one wild moment she had thought that he was dead, that she would have to live the rest of her life with just the memory of him. And yet, though she could only rejoice in the fact that he was not seriously hurt, she knew she still faced life without him. Soon he would return to New York or to Oregon or to his home in San Francisco. It didn't really matter whether he was five minutes or three thousand miles away. He would be gone—that was what mattered. That mattered more than anything else that could result from the crazy events that had shattered Terra's life.

CHAPTER THIRTEEN

THE NEWSCASTER'S FACE was a sickly shade of purple, but Terra didn't bother to adjust the set. She let the six-o'clock news flicker across her weary eyes. The clip was exactly the same on this program as it had been on the news at noon: a shot of the Blansford mansion, brief interviews with two of the guards, a statement by the police and the announcement that both Nathaniel Blansford and Grant Ingraham were unavailable for comment.

Blansford had called in the middle of the afternoon to thank her, waking her from a nap. He had sounded subdued but not upset, and he had assured her that as far as he was concerned she could write her own ticket when it came to working for him. Suddenly she seemed to have more job offers than she knew what to do with. Blansford had also assured her that Grant was all right, that his wound had been superficial, that he was there right then, in consultation with the police and with the Blansford attorneys. But when Terra had asked to speak to Grant, Nathaniel had said, "He told me to tell you he would contact you later." Unavailable for comment.

When she had called Margaret the woman had been frantic. She, too, had seen the news at noon.

"This is it!" Margaret commented. "As far as I can see, we're all about to join you in the unemployment line. I'm sorry for Paul, but I'm not really surprised. There's been something rotten going on around here for some time, if you ask me. I can just see applying for another job with the fine record of having been sales manager for a crook!"

Despite the dramatic intensity of Margaret's complaint Terra had to smile to herself. In a way she had been luckier than the others. As unprepared as she felt to deal with them at the moment, she *did* have job prospects. It might not be so easy for the other members of the staff. Yet she had no real worries for Margaret. A woman of her verve would not be at a loss for long.

Terra had passed the day as though in a daze, but now that it was early evening she was beginning to get things into perspective. Paul was the misguided son of a good man. He wasn't the first to take advantage of the good reputation built up by a conscientious father, and unfortunately he would not be the last. He had lost the book firm—that much was clear. No doubt Blansford and Forbush would absorb some of the stock, but the store itself would undoubtedly be liquidated. With such a smear on the Foster name no one would want to buy the business as it stood.

Despite the unfair, even cruel treatment she had received at his hands Terra's heart went out to Paul. Of one thing she was certain: if Grant had anything to do with it, Paul would be given every advantage—including the best lawyers. Terra now felt she knew Grant well enough to be sure he was a fair man, not a man to give in to vindictiveness or vengeance. And after all, he was an outsider in all this, an impartial observer. He had his own business interests to look out for; he didn't have to worry about taking revenge in the name of the late William Foster.

Grant. For what must have been the millionth time she tried to push thoughts of him away. But it did no good. As though her future were written in a script, she saw the scenario clearly before her: Grant calls to say everything has been settled; Grant thanks her for her "cooperation"; Grant closes up his San Francisco apartment until the next time he happens to wander into town; Grant, relieved to have all this behind him, hops on a plane to New York and picks up where he left off. Mission accomplished.

Terra wiped the tears from her cheek with the back of her hand. She really should start supper. She really should fold and put away the clothes she had brought up from the basement laundry room. She had washed the grimy things she had worn on her trek back to Berkeley, but she had left quite a few things up at the schoolhouse, including the heavy sweater Grant had recommended she take when she had set out to visit Aunt Alice. It seemed too incredible to believe that so much had happened to her in so short a time. Without really wanting to, she remembered Grant as he had lounged on her bed, advising her to take something warm to wear. Now, with the wisdom of hindsight, it occurred to her that he must have planned even then to take her up north if things didn't work out in La Jolla. Well, things hadn't worked out up north, either....

Mechanically she folded the clothes and put them away. She was standing by the fridge, leaning on the open door, when she heard the knock. It was just a single rap, and it was at the back door. It was either Jeff or the paperboy. No one else ever came around the back. She didn't really want to answer any of Jeff's questions just at the moment. He would want to know all about what had happened on her trip, not to mention the news story about the Blansford. But she couldn't ignore the knock. He would be able to see her through the kitchen window, and she didn't want to be blatantly unfriendly. Slowly she moved toward the door.

The instant she undid the lock, the door flew open and she was crushed tightly in the grasp of one strong arm. The other arm held what appeared to be a bag of groceries, but it was soon deposited on the floor at her feet, and then both arms came around her in an embrace that took away every possibility of drawing a breath.

His lips sought hers, not in hunger but in relief, almost in celebration—in the way in which lovers kiss when they have been through a terrible ordeal that is now clearly over. She gave herself to the pressure of his lips, arcing her body against him as though she were afraid he would disappear. When he finally released her she stepped back, knocking the bag of groceries over without even noticing.

"I thought... I thought you were wounded," she said stupidly, wondering how he could have held her so tightly when he had obviously been injured earlier in the day.

"I am—but only superficially. It looked pretty dramatic, didn't it? But it was nothing. However—" he took a step toward her and closed the small distance between them "—I thought you were in Oregon...."

"I—"

"You escaped." His eyes frowned down into hers, but she knew they held mockery. "It's all right, Terra, no excuses, no apologies. I knew you would."

"You knew I would escape? Then why bother leaving me in the wilderness?" Her own light tone matched his, but his answer was serious.

"I was stalling for time. That phone call, as you now know, was a tip-off. It was Blansford. He had found the missing originals of the 1905 documents in Stephanie's handbag. Quite accidentally, by the way—he doesn't make a habit of inspecting the belongings of his family. However, though we hadn't known—and were disappointed to find out—that Stephanie was involved, finding the papers in her possession made it quite clear what had to happen next. We knew Paul was about to make some sort of a move—we have been watching him for months. The only logical move he could make was to go for the photocopies on Monday morning, when the exhibit would be relatively uncrowded. He had to make his move on Monday, and I knew it would take you at least until then to get back here.''

Terra opened her lips to utter a protest at his presumption that he could predict her every move, but before she could make a sound, his tanned finger lay across her mouth. She trembled at his touch, and in response Grant's voice became low and tempting. ''It won't be quite so easy to get away from my bachelor retreat the next time, though soon I'm going to have to stop referring to it as a *bachelor* retreat.''

What was he talking about? Why did he always have to be such a tease? Flustered, Terra pulled away from him. ''What's in the bag?'' she asked, trying to sound nonchalant.

''That, sweetheart, is dinner.'' They both bent to pick up the sack at the same time, and as Terra reached to retrieve a stray potato that had rolled a little distance across the floor, Grant's hand came down on top of hers. A spark shot through her at his touch, and she stared at the strong brown fingers that covered her own. She remembered the night his whole body had covered hers, and unbidden tears sprung to her eyes. His hand left hers to cup her chin as he raised her eyes to meet his own. "The day's going to come," he said slowly, "when I teach you not to do that," and he put his lips to her wet cheeks, then to her own lips, where she tasted the saltiness before the tenderness of his kiss erased all sadness.

Pulling away, he cleared his throat. "Come on," he said, "let's get supper on. You haven't eaten, have you?"

She shook her head wordlessly, still stunned by his kiss. He stared at the mistiness of her eyes, and then he smiled—such a sweet winning smile that Terra simply had to smile in return.

"What's this?" she asked, drawing a large, paper-wrapped parcel from the sack.

"It's a roast," Grant replied.

"A roast?" Terra queried. "But it will take hours to cook!"

"Right," Grant said as though that were the idea.

Despite herself she giggled. Together they moved toward the kitchen counter, laughing and teasing each other as they spiced the meat and put it into the oven. There were vegetables and a bottle of wine among the things Grant had brought, and when the roast was in he poured glasses for them both and led Terra into the living room. He sat on the couch and pulled her down close beside him.

"We've got some very serious talking to do, Ms. Scott," he said. "I hardly know where to begin."

"Begin with Stephanie," Terra replied. Grant stared at her for a moment as if trying to figure out why Terra should mention her first, but from the look on Terra's face he could see she was no longer jealous of the other woman. She probably realized that Stephanie's part in all this would be the easiest to explain. Once again it occurred to Grant that Terra was a very intelligent woman. The thought filled him with pride.

"Stephanie has never been in real trouble in her life," he began, "and she's not in trouble now. She did steal the documents. Paul took advantage of her, but it wasn't difficult. Her main problem is that nobody ever takes her seriously. When Paul decided to make her an accomplice she felt important, so she agreed. I doubt that the implications of what she was doing ever really sank in. However, granddaddy to the rescue. Naturally Blansford wouldn't lay charges, and since he's the victim of her so-called crime—well, you get the picture."

Terra nodded. "I feel sorry for her," she said.

"I do, too," Grant answered sadly. "I've been trying to help her for years, but until she finds something valuable to do with her life there's not much hope. Some people are ruined by being rich, just as some people are ruined by being poor."

They sat in silence for a few minutes before Terra could ask the big question. "What will happen to Paul?" she finally got out.

Grant turned to her so that he could look her fully in the face. "Terra," he said, "I'm so sorry, I really am."

She stared at him blankly, not quite understanding his tone. "It is a shame," she said, not sure that was the right comment to make, but Grant spoke as though he hadn't heard her.

"You'll get over him. I know what a disappointment it must be to you, but every now and then we just happen to fall in love with the wrong person. It takes time, but eventually you'll realize that it could never have worked out between you...."

"Grant, what are you talking about?" Terra asked, totally confused.

"Why, I'm talking about you and Paul, of course. Perhaps you expected to marry him, though I suppose his engagement to Stephanie would have dampened your hopes...."

"Marry Paul?" Terra gasped, clearly incredulous.

Grant stared at her, the expression on his face changing from one of condolence to one almost of triumph. "But you've always been so considerate of him, so concerned for him, even when he treated you so badly...."

"I once dated Paul, it's true. But I soon realized there could never be anything between us. I cared for him—care for him—mostly because of William Foster. I never loved Paul. I don't now.''

"That makes things easier for both of us,'' Grant said. There was relief in his voice, and a kind of resolve—as though he had been planning something and was now determined to go through with it.

"What things?'' Terra questioned.

"It makes it easier to tell you Paul is probably in for quite a rough time of it. He's been implicated in several attempted swindles. Fortunately it's been possible for the board of trustees at Fosters' to bail him out until now, but the game is up. He can be charged with shooting at me. He can't be charged in connection with the pamphlets, since he's done nothing definite in trying to unload them. But he's got to change his ways. Whether that's possible, only time will tell. . . .''

"What will happen with the firm?'' Terra asked, afraid to hear the answer.

"Ah,'' Grant said, relaxing back against the couch, his arm around Terra's shoulder. "That brings us to the real topic of this conversation. . . .''

She stared at him, waiting for him to speak.

"I've heard you received a couple of job offers today.''

"Yes, but—''

"And that you didn't take up either of them.''

"Well, they were pretty vague, but, yes, I did receive them, and, no, I didn't take up—''

"Good," he interrupted, "because I'm about to make you an offer I don't think you'll want to refuse."

"You?" Terra couldn't see where all this was leading.

"I want you to take over at Fosters'. I want you to run it."

"Me? Run Fosters'? How can you...how can I?"

"Terra, I own the business. I've owned it for the past eight months. That's the real reason I've had my eye on Paul. It was a private deal between me and his father's estate. The news never leaked out, but of course it will now. And I'd like the press releases to include the information that Ms. Terra—uh—Scott will be the new head of the firm."

She sat in absolute silence, but Grant did not seem to expect an answer just yet.

"I know that being a researcher and running the company are two different things, but you're so intelligent, so sharp, that you'll catch on in no time. You'll have Margaret's help. She might appear to be a flighty woman, but when it comes to business she knows what she's doing. And then, of course, you'll have my help...."

"Your help? But you'll be in New York most of the time...."

"No, Terra, I won't be in New York. I've been winding things down there for a while. I've already moved the most important divisions out here. The publishing concern stays in the East, but I've got an excellent bunch out there taking care of things. I'm here to stay, little Terra." He ran a lazy finger along her cheek, as though he had forgotten about business, but it was not like him to forget for long.

"You see, we'll be part of a team. I won't interfere unless you ask, but if you run into a snag I'll be on hand to see you through."

Just what I need, Terra thought, *to be on Grant's "team"!* She could just picture it. She'd be working for him, answerable to him, his perfect little business associate. It was the last thing she wanted: to work side by side with the one man in the world with whom she wanted only to sleep side by side. It would never work. It was too much. It was too little.

"Grant, I . . . ."

"I said this was an offer I didn't think you'd refuse. I'm not finished. There's one more part to the deal." He sat forward, drawing Terra up and placing his hands on her shoulders so that he held her directly opposite him, so that he could see every slight motion of her face as he spoke.

"One of the reasons it made sense to me for you to want to marry Paul was that it seemed natural that the head researcher should want a closer relationship with the boss. . . ."

"You're teasing again." Terra sighed helplessly.

"No," Grant said, though there was a hint of lightness to his voice. "I think it's only right you should have the chance to marry the boss of Fosters'. I want you to marry *me*, Terra. I love you and I want you to be my wife...."

The words made her head spin. She must have heard wrong. This was the offer she wouldn't be able to refuse? He was right. Right again.

"I..." she began, but the sobs stopped her, welling up in her throat and choking off her voice.

"Oh, my Lord, not again!" Grant cried in mock exasperation. He pulled her toward him with rough impatient tenderness and cradled her head against his chest, smoothing her hair with his long gentle fingers.

"Are you crying because you don't want to marry me?"

He could feel the slight motion of her head against him. She was shaking her head no.

"Okay," he said, "let me guess again. You're crying because you can't make up your mind?"

Again the silken head held against him gestured no.

"Then," he said with slow emphasis, like a lawyer making his final point, "you're crying because you *do* want to marry me."

And this time she merely dipped her chin once, but it was the answer he wanted.

"Oh, my Terra," he breathed, and he raised her lips to meet his.

Their kiss was a declaration, a seal. It was not their first kiss, but it was their first promise that neither would have to be alone again as long as

God granted them breath. For long moments they lingered in each other's arms, their little touches, their eager kisses like so many clauses in the contract they were making of their love. When at long last they drew apart, it was only inches apart.

"From the moment I saw you in the book shop I knew I wanted more than the memories I've treasured of you all these years," Grant said. "Somehow it just never had occurred to me you must have grown up. I had thought of you often, but always as a bright, happy and somewhat pesky little girl. It just didn't come into my mind that you had to have grown into a woman. And when I saw that woman my heart just leapt. Sitting up there in that little alcove, surrounded by plants, with the light falling across the space you had made for yourself, you were a picture of such loveliness I had to know you again. You knocked me for a loop."

"You didn't show it, did you?" Terra asked languidly, toying with the button of his open shirt.

"If you had known me the way you're going to know me, you would have realized I was flustered."

"Flustered? You?"

"Yes." And another deep kiss stalled the conversation.

"I'm the one who was flustered," Terra finally replied.

"We'll make a perfect team," Grant laughed,

"cool, collected, unflappable—until we get home, that is."

"Speaking of home..." Terra began, but she had to stop. The thought of making a home with Grant sent quivers of joy shooting through her.

"I can't understand this," she said, sighing. "What happened to the man who was so dead set against commitment? Correct me if I'm wrong, but aren't you the one who said he didn't believe in love, that it was an unnecessary impediment to—uh—adult freedom?"

"Seems to me I said that if the day ever came that I ran across someone who could change my mind about love, I'd change it. True, I doubted it would ever happen. In a way I was hoping it never would. But in another way I guess I was waiting. I guess I've waited for a long time. It takes someone very special to change the mind of an old bachelor. But seeing is believing, and now...."

"Now?"

"Now," he said softly, staring deeply into her eyes, "now, I believe." Again he clasped her to him for a few silent minutes.

"Speaking of home," she finally reminded him.

Grant raised his head to look around the cozy room in which they sat. "We've each spent so many happy hours in this house it seems a shame to let it go...."

"But your house is the family home. Grant," she said, hardly daring to continue, "I—I want our children to grow up in their father's house. I know it's old-fashioned, but—"

Her explanation was cut off by the pressure of his lips on hers, by his embrace, which seemed to hold her to him with all the care that one lavishes on that which is most precious to one.

"I won't argue," he said after a few moments. "We can rent this place if we decide not to sell it. I want to keep it for just a little while— for sentimental reasons."

"I've heard of keepsakes, but a whole house?" Terra was joking, but her comment brought a new seriousness to Grant's tone.

"Terra," he said thoughtfully, "I hope that my...our money will never become a problem. I know you were raised in a way far different from the way in which I was raised, but I think you understand that to me love is the important thing, not money. I love business—the risk, the excitement—but that comes to nothing if the other love, the greater love, is absent."

"I know, Grant," she said softly.

"What I want, what I really want, is a family," he said, "a bunch of people who can share and laugh and not care whether you and I are being reasonable impeccable career people. I have no doubt we can get Fosters' back on its feet, but the important thing is that there's no reason for us to do it for ourselves alone."

"Oh, I know, Grant. I know."

And she slid closer into the circle of his

powerful arms. The tousled softness of his deep black hair brushed her cheek as he lowered his mouth toward her eager lips. Her arms flew up to surround him, to hold him to her as though she would never let him go. He had come back to her—it was a miracle, but it was true. And the truth of it would color all their days with joy.

ROBERTA LEIGH

Collector's Edition

A specially designed collection of six exciting love stories by one of the world's favorite romance writers—Roberta Leigh, author of more than 60 bestselling novels!

1 **Love in Store**	4 **The Savage Aristocrat**
2 **Night of Love**	5 **The Facts of Love**
3 **Flower of the Desert**	6 **Too Young to Love**

Available in August wherever paperback books are sold, or available through Harlequin Reader Service. Simply complete and mail the coupon below.